❖ VOLUME ONE ❖

THE WORLD OF
ELDATERRA
THE DRAGON
CONSPIRACY

P. R. MOREDUN

An Imprint of HarperCollins*Publishers*

Eos is an imprint of HarperCollins Publishers.

The World of Eldaterra, Volume I: The Dragon Conspiracy
Copyright © 2005 by Allistair Ewen Mitchell
A hardcover edition of this book was first published in the United
Kingdom in 2004 by Rookstone Publishing.
Printed in the United States of America. For information address
HarperCollins Children's Books, a division of HarperCollins
Publishers, 1350 Avenue of the Americas, New York, NY 10019.
www.harpereos.com

Library of Congress Cataloging-in-Publication Data
Moredun, P. R.
    The dragon conspiracy / P.R. Moredun.— 1st U.S. ed.
        p.   cm. — (The world of Eldaterra ; v. 1)
    Summary: The fates of a police inspector in 1895 and a fourteen-
year-old boy in 1910 are entwined as they both strive to stop an evil
plot that has originated in a world of magic, and threatens that
world and their own.
    ISBN-10: 0-06-076663-8 — ISBN-10: 0-06-076664-6 (lib. bdg.)
    ISBN-13: 978-0-06-076663-4 — ISBN-13: 978-0-06-076664-1
(lib. bdg.)
    [1. Magic—Fiction. 2. Space and time—Fiction. 3. Dragons—
Fiction. 4. Heroes—Fiction. 5. Fate and fatalism—Fiction.
6. England—Fiction.] I. Title.
PZ7.M789453Dra 2005   2004030084
[Fic]—dc22   CIP
                                                        AC

Typography by Christopher Stengel
1 2 3 4 5 6 7 8 9 10
❖
First U.S. Edition

For Duncan and Edward, who prompted the stories, and for Amanda, who is brilliant.

For Eda and Tim, who never wavered in their support. For Stuart, who read the roughest draft and still believed.

For everyone who helped, and everyone who reads it. Thank you.

∽ Contents ∽

✌ PRINCIPAL CHARACTERS ✌

THE KINGHORN FAMILY

James A boy who holds the fate of two worlds in his hands

Sir Philip James's father and a minister for Military Intelligence

Lady Jennifer James's mother and a skilled crossword puzzle solver

THE INVESTIGATORS – 1895

Chief Inspector Corrick A dogged and determined policeman

Harrington An elusive civil servant working in the British Foreign Office

Inspector La Forge A Belgian policeman who assists Corrick

OTHERS – 1910

Frau Colbetz An enigmatic woman with a strange power over men, reportedly descended from Attila the Hun

Herr Dorpmuller A "fixer" for his employer, Frau Colbetz, whom he worships

Frau Feder Companion and second-in-command to Frau Colbetz

Sibelius Principal Wizard of the Western Tower, Keeper of the Sword of Lind, and Master of the Shadows

Solomon and Bartholomew Bandamire Warrior dwarves employed by Sibelius

Tempus and Baranor Parlanimals and good friends to James

Rawlings A spy for Sir Philip

Otto Freislung A messenger for dangerous persons

⌁ HISTORICAL NOTE ⌁

At the turn of the twentieth century, Europe was a place of fierce economic, military, and political rivalry among the three great powers: Britain, France, and Germany.

This story is set against that backdrop, a time when nations were threatening war and politicians on all sides were taking enormous risks to protect their national interests.

Events, places, and incidents mentioned are fictitious, and any resemblance to any persons (living or dead) is purely coincidental for the purposes of this story.

The rise to power of other nations was still in the future in 1910.

⤳ Prologue ⟨

EVIL BEGINNINGS, 1895

February in the Fens. A thin moon had risen early, and now the pale crescent slid back toward the horizon, yellowing in the mist that rose in eerie swirls from the dark wetlands. It was as if the ground were exhaling. Somewhere in the emptiness an owl hooted. A little later a fox barked in reply.

In the distance a forlorn rank of winter trees marched nowhere, their barren branches thrust upward as if praying to an unseen deity high up in the ink-night sky. Beyond the trees a large stone building reared up. Hollow black windows were set evenly into the walls of an old country mansion. A faint glow stole from a shuttered first-floor window, the only sign of life in the otherwise abandoned dwelling.

Inside a figure lay huddled beneath a pile of coarse blankets upon an old four-poster bed pushed against the far wall of the cavernous room. Feverish and frightened, she groaned in pain and rolled on her side, flinging the blankets from her body. The feeble lamplight set shadows dancing on the walls. She cried out, alone, afraid, knowing her child would be born soon, very soon.

∾ 1 ∽

THE SEA ARCH, MAY 1910

James Kinghorn had escaped!

He had escaped, if only for half term, from the school where last September he had arrived for the first time, a reluctant fourteen-year-old sent to honor a family tradition. Every generation of Kinghorns since Waterloo had dispatched a son to Drinkett College (the "Eton of the North"), and James was not about to let down the family name.

He stood amid the sand dunes that lined the barren coast of Northumberland in northern England. Wisps of cloud traced across the brilliant blue sky. A crab scuttled into the surf, its claws raised in defiance of marauding seagulls. James spied a small, wretched boat left stranded above the high-water line— its hull planking staved in, a casualty of a winter gale—and he trudged through the sand to investigate. Inspecting the broken vessel, he imagined himself shipwrecked and alone, on some great adventure.

His father, Sir Philip Kinghorn, worked in the War Office— in what capacity James was not quite sure, but he was pretty certain it was an important job. Sir Philip had arranged for James to spend the weekend with him and his mother, Lady Jennifer, while Sir Philip attended a naval gunnery demonstration held off the Farne Islands, just up the coast. Today was the day of the demonstration and James, let loose to explore the desolate coastline, was intent on having an adventure of one sort or another.

The distant rumble of gunfire was carried on the sea breeze, and James turned in the direction of the sound, half expecting to see giant dreadnoughts and battleships on the horizon, sheathed in flames and smoke. Instead he was amazed to see an enormous stone arch only a dozen yards from where he stood. As he looked at the arch, it appeared to shimmer and become translucent, like a mirage, before finally solidifying into stone. The arch was colossal, towering over him like a leviathan. Set into the archway was a pair of enormous iron gates, chained and padlocked. The lock was so large James's fist could easily fit into the keyhole. He couldn't understand how he had failed to notice the arch earlier—it was so grand and imposing—and he could see from his footprints that he had already passed close by. There was something very peculiar about it.

James walked around the arch and studied it more closely. It was made of great blocks of white marble, smooth to the touch. Across the top, just visible from below, he could make out the words "Sea Arch" carved faintly into the stone.

What on earth is it here to commemorate? he wondered. The distant boom of gunfire had faded away now and, except for the gentle rolling of the sea, all was quiet and still.

Suddenly, with a machine-gun stutter, the chain snaked off

the gates and fell with a thump to the sand. James jumped in surprise. At the foot of the gates, the big, lumpy padlock lay sprung. The chain links, each one as big as a man's fist, had cascaded into a haphazard pile that sank into the sand under its own weight. Only seconds before when he had looked at the padlock, it was secured, the chain tightly wrapped about the central rails of the gates. Now the gates stood ajar. James shivered as he looked down at the chain and padlock and saw how clean and rust-free they were. He took a step closer, feeling the temptation of the open gates. Then he slipped between them and was gone!

· *1895* ·

The gamekeeper broke open his double-barreled shotgun, checked the cartridges and, hanging the fowling piece in the crook of his arm, waited patiently for the approaching figures. Constable Tauning, the only officer of the law for ten miles in any direction, marched up the drive. Next to the constable, the parish vicar kept pace. Behind them, wheeling his cycle, was young Finnigan, the lad who had raised the alarm.

"Good day to you," called the vicar. The gamekeeper nodded solemnly in reply.

"I understand there's a body," said the constable as he removed his helmet and mopped his brow.

"It were me and the lad who found it. This here be the estate." The gamekeeper swung his arm in a gesture that took in the full sweep of surrounding countryside. "And that"—he jerked a gnarled and weathered hand over his shoulder—"that be what's left of Purbeck Hall." He paused before adding, "I've hunted and fished most things, but in all my life I've never seen anything like what's in there."

Leaving the gamekeeper and the boy standing on the gravel drive, Constable Tauning and the vicar climbed the stone steps leading to the once-grand front entrance. The constable shouldered open the double doors. Light flooded into the cavernous hallway, and dust swirled at the men's feet like marsh mist. Ahead a broad staircase climbed up and around in a grand sweep, the dark mahogany banister like a snake coiling the stone steps. A grimy stained-glass window filled the wall above the stairs, framed with heavy, worn, crimson drapes. Neither man took any notice of the surroundings. They stood in shock, gazing at the strange bloodied object that lay in the center of the hall.

The vicar fell trembling to his knees, his hands clasped white as he quavered through the Lord's Prayer. The constable stepped up and gripped the man's shoulder, shaking him to his senses.

"Reverend, please go at once and send the lad to the nearest railway halt. We must get word to headquarters in Cambridge. Tell him to say—" But there was no point in continuing. The vicar had scrambled to his feet and ran from the building as if Satan were at his heels.

· *1910* ·

James had no idea where he was. At one moment he had been standing on the shoreline in broad daylight; the next he found himself in a clearing surrounded by dense conifers, with only a hint of a path threading into the distance. A fresh breeze blew through the trees, carrying the familiar scent of pine. On the horizon the sinking sun, now bloodred, set the treeline into relief. James turned to retrace his steps back through the arch, but found his way blocked. The gates stood padlocked and chained!

Beyond the gates he could see the waters breaking on the shoreline and the bright sunlit sky. His hands grabbed at the chain, but it was solid and unyielding. Panic welled up in his chest.

"This is not happening," he said aloud, and then, to reassure himself added, "walk around the arch and let's go home." He rounded the arch, but he did not find the beach. Instead the forest crowded in on all sides, forming an unbroken wall around the increasingly gloomy glade. James looked at the arch again, trying to rationalize what had happened. The Sea Arch had somehow taken him from the seaside to the middle of a forest, but how? He studied the structure more closely, searching for a clue. His eyes alighted on a dull brass plaque, set into the stonework, with an inscription on it:

> *The roaring seas are silent now*
> *And secrets are themselves once more*
> *Complete the earth and fill the void*
> *To mark the time when earth was whole*
> *Locked are these gates to keep the vow*
> *To end a world on barren shore*
> *Protect a place to be destroyed*
> *By man's belief, a lack of soul*

Yet stand a vigil and wait a time
When stranger from the stranger land
Before the gates, behind the sun
Gives passage to the unsouled son
To pass to wild and pass to grime
The places split by sea and sand
Where one is slaved beneath the gun
The other stalked, evil begun

James couldn't make any sense of the words. He kept looking for other clues, ones he might understand. On the far side of the arch, he could now see inscribed, "Where Westerly," but that made no sense either.

He would have to find another way back to the beach. He had been alone among the sand dunes earlier, so it was unlikely he'd be rescued by someone from the other side, or that his cries for help would be heard. The increasing gloom reminded him that the sun was sinking fast, and James spotted friendly Polaris, the North Star, drawing comfort from its presence. He would have to find shelter for the night and hope to return to the hotel and his parents tomorrow. His parents! The thought of them made James feel both guilty and embarrassed that he had got himself lost. He set off at a run, following the path that led from the Sea Arch into the cooling forest, hoping to find safety before night fell.

As if a curtain had been drawn, the path plunged into darkness. The treetops creaked and swished in their strange language. James stumbled over an exposed root and fell, pine needles puncturing his palms. He smelled his own blood. The panic that he had held in check rose to the surface. His nerves were about to crack.

"There's nothing to be afraid of. This path must lead somewhere, and somebody will be able to explain where I am and contact my parents, and then I'll get home." His words spilled out and were unconvincing. He got to his feet and hurried on.

A smear of daylight lingered in the highest clouds, but there was not enough to penetrate the forest. James could no longer make out the path. The wind grew stronger, whipping the treetops into a roof of noise. Fear of the unknown and the unseen crept through the dark pines and began to stalk him. James stumbled on, his hands groping in the darkness. He focused his thoughts on the invisible path, imagining that it would lead him onward to someplace safe.

All I need is some light, he pleaded. As if in answer to his wish, James found that he could see just enough detail to pick out the lighter-colored path from the dark forest floor. Looking up, he discovered a cloud of fireflies silently swarming above him, the iridescent glow of their bodies bathing him in a greenish light. They moved farther down the path, lighting the way. He followed, and they led him into a clearing, the trees falling back beyond the pool of light. A low stone wall materialized from the gloom. Back in the valley a creature howled, and it sounded to James like a call of anger and frustration, as if the quarry had evaded the hunter.

The wall ended at a courtyard, and he found himself standing before a wooden door with a heavy knocker set into it. He was about to lift the knocker when the door swung open, revealing a stout figure silhouetted by a fire burning in the hearth.

"Come in, come in! We've been expecting you."

2

THE BROTHERS BANDAMIRE

James staggered over the threshold, eager to escape the forest and its dark secrets, and found himself in a long, low-beamed room, an open fireplace in the far wall providing the only light. Thick logs of wood crackled in the grate, sending swirls of sparks up the chimney.

Nervously James watched his host shoulder the door shut and set a crossbar in place. He caught sight of a second figure seated by the hearth, almost lost in the flickering shadows. A big animal skin lay stretched across the floor in front of the fire. The man by the door motioned James toward an inviting wing-backed chair, the sort that is all too easy to fall asleep in.

"Sit yourself down." His voice was gruff but friendly. James sank into the seat and felt the warmth of the fire lulling his eyes closed.

"There'll be time for that later," his host said, jolting James awake. "We've got a pressing schedule and some things to discuss first. Your arrival is of interest to many."

"Please, where am I?" James asked.

"Well, that's a good question," the man said, warming his hands by the fire.

James waited for an answer.

The seated figure spoke instead: "We're not far from where you were—but many miles from where you've just been." James caught sight of his hands. They were large, weather-beaten, and powerful looking, the gnarled hands of someone used to heavy manual labor. His eyes growing used to the fire-light, James saw the same characteristics in the man's features. Riven with creases, the bearded face was worn and determined, yet compassionate. But the eyes were what grabbed James's attention. They were cobalt blue, piercing and alive. It struck him that both of the figures looked like dwarves. And they seemed familiar . . .

"Excuse me, but that doesn't exactly help. I was on the beach between Beadnell and—"

"Dunstanburh Castle. Yes, we know. We've been waiting for you."

"You took your time getting here," added the second dwarf as he rose and busied himself in the corner. Presently a lamp shone, revealing more of the room. The dwarf came forward and extended his hand to James.

"My name is Solomon Brunel Bandamire." Solomon's gray-streaked mane stood in all directions and merged with his eye-brows and beard. "And that is my twin brother, Bartholomew Shakespeare Bandamire." He too had amazing eyes, pearlescent gray and set beneath big bushy brows and above a crooked nose that seemed to burst from his face. A mass of dark hair flecked with streaks of gray gave him an equally wild look.

"The *elder* twin brother," Bartholomew pointed out. "Though only a matter of six months separated us which, in dwarfish midwifery, is quite a short period of time. Sometimes twins can be born a decade apart, much to the mother's discomfort."

"And while you got all the haste, I got all the stealth," his brother said with a grin.

"Fast brains over slow brawn, that's always been the difference between us." Bartholomew winked at James.

"Say whatever you want, but blessed be our mother!" Solomon declared.

"And may our mother who bore us never forget the joyful pain of our birth!" the dwarves recited together as James's confusion grew.

"That's an ancient dwarven saying," Bartholomew told him. "We're proud of our roots and our pain. It makes life worth living, so to speak."

Solomon smiled at the sudden look of recognition on James's face. "I reckon this young man has seen us before, Bartholomew."

"It was one of you at the fair!" James watched as Solomon's smile widened. Danart, the Dwarfen King, had been a popular sideshow attraction touring the north of England Gypsy fairs during the spring.

"Indeed. And as well as that bit of theater, we had occasion to deliver coal to your school, tend to the gardens at your home, and sweep your chimneys! Bartholomew even worked for the local smithy to keep an eye on your family's comings and goings," Solomon said triumphantly.

James's troubled look hastened him to continue. "Don't worry, we weren't spying on you. We were there to look after you. We were there under orders."

"Secret orders," added Bartholomew as he laid the table for supper.

"Could you explain a few things to me?" James asked as the dwarves ushered him to the table. "Where am I and why am I here?" he spoke between mouthfuls of stew and dumplings. As confused and nervous as he was, James had discovered he was also surprisingly hungry.

"You've made a remarkable journey. You are in Lauderley Forest, and you came here through the portal," Bartholomew said.

"What kind of portal?" James's hand suddenly shook, and his spoon fell onto the table with a clatter.

"It's a gateway of sorts, that allows one to travel between the two worlds."

"Two worlds? I don't understand. There aren't two—" His voice rose in panic.

"Aye," interrupted Bartholomew calmly. "Your world and this one, Eldaterra."

"It means 'Old World,'" Solomon explained.

"The fact that you've come through the Sea Arch means that you're important . . . very important," Bartholomew said in a serious voice. "Neither my brother nor I know why; that's a question the Guild will answer. And that is where we're heading."

"Please, Mr. Bandamire, what is the Guild?" James tried to focus on his questions and push aside his growing fears.

"The Guild are the wisest and most learned in the land. It was the Guild who ordered us to watch over you and, when the time was right, deliver you to them."

"And sure enough, that's what will happen," declared Solomon.

"So how long have you been keeping an eye on me?" James asked cautiously.

The dwarves exchanged glances. "Twenty-two months," replied Bartholomew.

"Twenty-two months! But that's impossible."

Bartholomew laughed. "Yes, imagine how hard it was for two not-so-inconspicuous dwarves to shadow you to northern Italy on your summer holidays. We had to pretend to be traveling monks on a pilgrimage. We've never given so many blessings to so many strangers!

"Your religion is astonishing," he went on. "Who'd have believed it could be so powerful, influence so many people, and yet possess no magic whatsoever?"

"But getting back to our story," Solomon said, "in keeping you under surveillance, we traveled through the portal many times. And for that to be possible, something unprecedented is occurring between the two worlds."

Bartholomew began, "The Guild acts for the Good, but there are many who tread the paths of wickedness—"

Solomon cut him off, rising from the table. "We'll learn soon enough what the Guild has in store for you, my boy, after a good night's sleep."

This brought back thoughts of home. "But my parents will be wondering what has happened to me. Mother will be worried," James said.

"Your father will comfort her," Solomon reassured him. "And there's a good deal more about your father than either of us know."

Another look passed between the two dwarves.

James said nothing. He had given up on his meal as his stomach was in knots. Now his attention was caught by movement on the fireside rug. What he had thought was a rug slowly shook itself and stood up, padding silently toward him.

"Don't mind Tempus." Solomon chuckled. It was a giant dog, as big as an Irish wolfhound.

"He's as gentle as a pussycat," Bartholomew added merrily.

James woke in a narrow bunk, a blanket thrown over him. He had fallen asleep in his clothes. Light streamed through small windows. A few feet away Tempus sat patiently watching him.

"Good morning, James," Bartholomew called. "We'll have you fed and watered in two ticks, and then we'll be off."

James sat and ate a breakfast of bread and honey washed down with a cup of water, and then stepped outside.

"Good morning, James," Solomon said. "I'm just packing the last of our equipment." He pointed toward his brother. "And he's preparing the traps."

James watched as Bartholomew dragged the jagged metal jaws apart and set the trigger plate. The traps were crude devices that nonetheless looked deadly.

"That's the last of them out here," Bartholomew said as he placed the trap carefully in the middle of the path leading directly to the front door. The next second the trap vanished. "I'll just set the ones inside and then we're done." He picked up a big, clanking sack and disappeared inside.

"I've packed a bag of provisions for you." Solomon indicated a knapsack which stood next to two mountainous rucksacks. "Those are for my brother and I, as we're more experienced at hiking in these parts." In comparison, James's knapsack looked embarrassingly small.

"And we would like you to accept this gift. It may come in handy." He held up a leather scabbard and drew out a long, sleek, double-edged knife, the polished blade catching the sunlight. "It's just a dagger, I'm afraid. But we'd feel a lot happier knowing you are in a position to defend yourself should the need arise." Solomon passed it to James, who thanked him, although his hand shook as he took the knife. *What kind of need?* he wondered.

Still, stuck in a forest in a strange land with only two burly dwarves and a giant hound for company, James was glad to be carrying a weapon. The dagger was fashioned with a stout hilt of bone, a blade at least a foot in length, and a scabbard to protect it. Engraved patterns wove a long, looping design down each side of the blade.

James fastened the dagger to his belt and picked up the knapsack as Bartholomew joined them. Then with a whistle from Solomon to Tempus, they set off to meet the Guild.

· *1895* ·

Chief Inspector Corrick rubbed his stubbly chin, deep in thought. He stood in the second-floor room where the body had been found. Apart from the enormous four-poster bed, the room was empty, bare floorboards and cracked plaster echoing footsteps as they searched for evidence. Various officers and technicians came and went, recording the grisly scene. Out on the landing, Corrick's deputy was taking statements from witnesses while a photographer and his assistant set up their equipment.

"I want a photograph showing the details of the wounds," Corrick called to them.

The bed held the remains of a female body. On first inspection it appeared as if the corpse had been eaten by scavenging animals, but closer examination suggested that this was the state in which the murderer had left his victim. Both hands bore abrasions, as if she had tried to ward off her attacker. Corrick sighed. There was something inhuman, diabolical, about the way she had died. He made a brief entry in his notebook. So far no one had come forward to report a missing person, and the "thing" downstairs in the entrance hall could not be explained.

The deputy came into the room. "Sir, I've got their statements. The reverend kept declaring that evil was abroad and it was all the Devil's work. Not very helpful, I'm afraid. Didn't recognize the victim."

"Well, we can't expect him to know every soul in the parish. Have a final word before you let them go. Tell them if they gossip, we'll arrest them, even Officer Tauning."

"Very good, sir."

A new figure stepped forward.

"My name is Harrington. I'm with the Foreign Office." The man was of fair complexion, with a slimmer build than the policeman. The academic type: glasses, a rather limp handshake, but a keen pair of eyes, bright and impishly alert.

Corrick nodded. "Yes, I've been expecting you, though I can't see why your office is interested in this incident." He noted how Harrington's gaze expertly took in the scene. Then the two of them stood, sizing each other up.

"I'm to help you in any way possible," said Corrick, "but maybe you can help me as well."

"Yes, perhaps I can. I'm from a small department, trying to keep tabs on illegal aliens in the country. Refugees, diplomats on the run for fleecing their embassy, that sort of thing. You wouldn't believe the stranger aspects of the job." Harrington's eyes flicked back to the murder scene, and Corrick caught a glint of hardness in his gaze, clearly untroubled by the horrific surroundings.

"As I understand it," Harrington continued, "the investigation centers on the death of a young woman."

Corrick wondered if this man was fishing for information or suggesting the direction the investigation should take. He took Harrington by the elbow and led him from the room. "Let me tell you what we know so far, and see what you make of it," he said, watching the man's every move.

· *1910* ·

Bartholomew guided them through the seemingly endless forest. Ahead Tempus loped through the trees, snuffling the ground and scenting the wind. Though the brothers had to take three or four steps for every stride of James's, they happily bowled along at a considerable pace.

"It'll be a push to reach our destination by nightfall," said Solomon, "but we should arrive before the moon is up.

Provided we don't meet any trouble on the way."

"Trouble?" James asked, trying to keep his voice steady.

"This is a strange land, nothing like the world you come from. And there are forces that may seek to stop us. We're not alone out here in these woods."

"But we have no intention of allowing it," Bartholomew added hastily.

James knew they had not explained the situation fully. He let the matter drop, but kept a wary eye. The two brothers were indeed prepared for trouble. Bartholomew carried a long broadsword across his back, partially obscured by his rucksack. Hidden in the folds of his green travel cloak, the tip of a scabbard jutted out, similar to the one James wore. Looking behind him, James could see the flat profile of an axhead strapped to Solomon's back, in easy reach.

"So where are we heading?" James asked.

Bartholomew pointed down the trail. "We'll descend this valley, cross the Crashing River. Then it's on up to the Col." Ranks of pines and firs flanked the valley walls. On the far side the pine trees soared up a hundred feet or more, mere matchsticks set against the vast mountains which hemmed them in.

At length they reached the valley floor, where the Crashing River blocked their route. Stone and broken rock lay piled along the banks. The river rumbled a deep, angry growl and the ground shook. Great boulders rolled along the riverbed while smaller stones simply flowed like water in the current. A fine spray filled the air and fed the green moss that clung to everything. They turned northward, following the river upstream. After a while they reached a fallen tree, its lower trunk caught between two mighty stones, much of its length suspended over the racing waters.

"We'll cross here," called Bartholomew. They all shrugged off their packs and the dwarves began unpacking coils of rope. Tempus leaped nimbly onto the tree, ran along its length, and sprang into the air, sailing over the last stretch of open water to land on the far bank.

"Pity it isn't so simple for us," Solomon said. "There is a bridge downstream but no time." He heaved his rucksack onto the tree trunk. "Now then, James, pay attention." He took a length of rope and tied it securely to the straps of his rucksack. The other end he handed to James. "I'll carry my pack over. If for any reason I have to let go of it, you'll be able to retrieve it. If you slip, the important thing is to save yourself—let go of your pack. We can pull your pack from the water in one piece, but not you. Nothing, neither fish nor fiend, can survive in this river."

Solomon heaved himself up onto the trunk and walked its length as if it were nothing more than a garden path. At the end he crouched and sprang forward like a giant frog. Even with the rucksack in his arms, he landed well beyond the water's edge.

"Now you, James!" Solomon shouted, and James felt Bartholomew give him an encouraging nudge. He tied the rope to the straps of his knapsack just as Solomon had done, handed the other end to the dwarf, and pulled himself up onto the fallen tree. He set off taking slow, deliberate steps. In his whole life he had never attempted anything so dangerous. Shadowy boulders, as big as shire horses, rolled along the riverbed, and the blood surging in his ears drowned the crashing sound. He shuffled forward, clutching his knapsack to his chest as if it were a life jacket.

He was midway along the trunk when something punched him in the shoulder and he lost his balance. Just as he started to topple, something jerked him upright again. Despite Solomon's instructions, James instinctively clung to the knapsack. And then . . . he was falling!

He threw an arm out and caught hold of a branch. Somehow his grip held, leaving his legs dangling over the plume of raging waters.

"A dragonspider!" Bartholomew shouted. "He's attached his thread to you! You must cut it before you're pulled off that branch."

James nodded his understanding, but everything was happening too quickly. Letting go of the knapsack, he managed to pull himself up between the branch stump and the trunk, his legs still swinging free. He reached down and scrambled nervously as he unsheathed the dagger, fortunately without dropping it, and tentatively slashed at the thick strand around his middle. Over on the far bank, Solomon and Tempus ran off into the forest to hunt down the unseen attacker.

Desperation took hold of James. A few strands broke, but the thread still gripped him across his back, pulling on his coat, tightening it like a tourniquet. His left shoulder strained at the socket, and it felt as though his whole arm would be ripped off. Blindly he hacked and hacked, with Bartholomew yelling for him to hurry. Suddenly the spider strand gave way with the crack of a whip. He hung on the trunk, exhausted and on the verge of tears, but still holding on to the dagger. His pack was nowhere to be seen.

By the time Solomon and Tempus returned, Bartholomew had carried James the rest of the way and was examining his bruised body on the riverbank.

"No broken bones," he said. "Well done."

James rose unsteadily to his feet and glanced at his torn coat.

"Not much use as a traveling cloak anyway. This'll serve you better." Bartholomew handed him a spare from his pack.

James struggled into it. He picked up his dagger and sheathed it, now truly grateful for the gift.

After James had rested a moment, they continued on their way.

"Did you catch it?" James asked.

"No," Solomon replied.

"It was one of the dragonspiders that live under these mountains. A fair-sized one; you can tell by the thickness of the thread," Bartholomew explained. "They're a mongrel breed of two species that were never meant to be joined, part spider and part dragonfly. It's said they arose when the last of the dragons departed the land eons ago, as if they are a crude replacement. But then, there are many strange new creatures that have crawled into the light of day since the ancient times."

"Dragons?"

"We can talk about that later. . . ." Solomon said.

"But the spider must be enormous to spin a thread like rope," James said.

"Aye, it is," Bartholomew replied. "But the one that attacked you wasn't as big as it might have been. They come a great deal bigger."

"And that's why we are here to lead you." Solomon punctuated this with a cautious glance about them and a wave of his ax. "Hard to believe the forest was once a safe haven for travelers."

"Listen, James," Bartholomew said. "Can you hear birdsong? Can you hear anything of nature in this place?"

Only the trees moving and the sound of their own breathing disturbed the eerie silence.

"The forest has been invaded." Bartholomew's voice was tinged with anger.

"But now there may be some real hope," said Solomon.

"What makes you say that?" James asked. The dwarves stopped mid-stride and turned to him.

"Why, you, of course!" they answered in unison.

"We haven't been keeping an eye on you for nothing," said Bartholomew.

"On the express orders of the Guild," added Solomon gruffly. "Now let's press on."

Hidden deep within a stand of trees, a pair of yellow eyes observed the passing of the small party. For an instant the trees moved and afternoon sunlight spilled through the branches, revealing the creature. It flinched in the warmth of the sun. The head was hooded, revealing only a cruel beak, yellowed and riven with tiny fissures like those on a skull. It stood on enormous clawed feet with long talons biting into the solid ground beneath. The *Drezghul*, "dark resurrection" in the language of the enemy, stood motionless long after the trio had vanished. Its reincarnation, after millennia as nothing more than dust, had left it weak. Exhumed from beneath the cold mountains at the behest of its masters, the Drezghul was conserving its strength and would act only if others failed. . . .

All afternoon James and the dwarves toiled across the valley. The path petered out, and Solomon had to use his ax to force a way through the thorn bushes and dense scrub. He complained repeatedly about having to dull the blade on such a chore.

"The path we used not a month ago has disappeared so quickly," Bartholomew noted in a low voice.

Long, cruel thorns stabbed and tore at their cloaks. Tempus followed behind, picking his way carefully.

"Why did the dragonspider attack?" James asked. "Was it hunting for food?"

"No," Solomon answered as he swung the ax.

"He can sometimes be a dwarf of few words," Bartholomew said before explaining, "there are too many of us for the creature to dare attack if it was simply hunting for food."

"If you are as important as the Guild believes you to be, then the enemy will call upon all manner of evil and base creatures to kill or capture you," said Solomon.

"Don't let that gruff brother of mine scare you. They've lost the element of surprise. But they'll be more determined next time. Especially as we draw nearer to safety. We can only hope that they have few allies in these parts." Bartholomew motioned at the thick thorn scrub still ahead of them.

"But if it slows us, it slows the enemy," suggested James. "And as long as we're in this stuff, we're hidden from view."

"True . . . as long as there's nothing that can fly or burrow."

James gulped and fell silent.

Once they got clear of the thorny forest, they made better time. Suddenly Tempus gave a warning bark. To their left a large tangle of ropes hung amidst the pines, bending the trees under the tension of the web.

"More dragonspiders?" asked James.

"Judging by that trap, it's Morbidren," Bartholomew said. "Her name means 'deadly in the dark.' She's bigger than a horse, they say, and the only dragonspider that would dare to venture so far aboveground. We've never set eyes on her." He let out his breath in a whistle. "She's too big to fly. When she catches a meal, she drags it into the branches to dine in peace. Sometimes we find piles of bleached bones at the bottom of a tree, and we reckon it's the remains of her feast."

"What does it . . . I mean, she . . . eat?" James stuttered.

"Well, we've found the remains of bear and deer, wolves and forest-phant—a small, hairy relative of your elephant. I suppose she eats anything," Bartholomew said.

"Anything she can haul up to her lair," added Solomon.

"We're lucky we avoided her trap," James said.

"I'm afraid it's a bit more serious than that. Morbidren never comes this far down the valley. She's setting her webs to herd us, toward an ambush probably. There can be only one reason."

"Me? I've never hurt anyone. What have I done wrong?"

"Nothing yet, James." Bartholomew placed a steadying hand on his good shoulder. "Know this, Bartholomew and Solomon Bandamire are not about to fail. Keep a keen eye, and we may yet avoid the enemy."

The party picked its way over the broken ground and slowly snaked up the mountainside. Above them the Col towered, a good thousand feet up. Finally they arrived at the summit, just as the shadows of the mountains stretched across the pass. Solomon gave a nod to his brother and turned to James. "In the distance you can make out the Western Tower." He pointed. "But between here and the tower lie enemies that are as frightening as the creature behind us. And in the dark of night they'll have the advantage."

James stared at the dwarves.

"Are you saying now that we haven't got a hope?"

They instantly broke into belly laughs and knee slapping. Bartholomew spoke first. "My brother, Solomon Brunel Bandamire, and I, Bartholomew Shakespeare Bandamire, are sons of the dwarfish clan of Bandamire, fabled for noble deeds and heroic failures. Our grandfather, Borrowmason Goldenbeard Bandamire, fell in the titanic but hopeless struggle that became legend as the Battle of Highfall Heights. Our father, Splayfoot Teutonica Bandamire, languishes in the dungeons of the enemy, captured at the cataclysmic fall of Palalia."

His chest visibly swelled with pride as he continued. "We are ennobled to the challenge of a forlorn hope, a hopeless situation, a doomed venture, a catastrophe waiting to happen. We draw upon our great heritage to ensure that, should no future await our bloodline, our blood shall be spilled in glorious great pools." His voice boomed across the valley, reverberating back in a ghostly echo.

Solomon took up the battle cry. "In glorious great pools! With wounds that carve our bodies, and gore to fill a barrel!" Together they chanted:

Make a stand, heed the horn,
Swing the ax, cleave the bone,
Unsheathe the sword, knock the bow,
Now we pray to fight a foe.

Followed by,

Killing is a pleasure,
When fighting over treasure.

Then,

Fighting dwarves, rally round,
Let not the enemy steal this ground.

And,

Dwwwwaaarrrvvvessss,
Dwwwwaaarrrvvvessss,
Makers-of-warrrrrrrrrrrrrrrrs.

And finally,

Take our lives, take our arms,
But leave us with our family charms!

The dwarves were apparently looking forward to a bloody battle with the enemy. And they weren't afraid if anyone heard them. A wave of dizziness hit James and he slumped to the ground.

The dwarves quit their chanting and fell into an embarrassed, shuffling-feet silence. Bartholomew gave a polite cough and mumbled, "Of course our mission is to save you, James. That is the most important part. Before we find ourselves in a pickle the sort of which"—he coughed again—"we were singing about a few moments ago, we would ensure your personal safety."

James looked up at the dwarves, both wringing their hands at having upset him. Trying to sound confident, he said, "I may not understand the ways of dwarves, but I do appreciate your helping me." This seemed to cheer them up.

"If you don't mind a suggestion," James ventured, "I'd like to keep going. Whatever lies in front can't be any more frightening than what's behind us. I'm sure Tempus would agree." The big dog came over and nuzzled his hand. "I don't think turning back will do us any good."

"We'll light the torches and be off then," declared Bartholomew, and dug into his rucksack for the tinderbox.

In the gathering darkness they made their way down, guided by the flickering torchlight. Each of them held a stout wicker torch bound with rags and soaked in tar. The flames guttered off into the star-encrusted sky. James was comforted by the sight of Taurus and the Centaur, but he had few moments to star watch. The ground slid away beneath their feet in fields of shale and flint. Tempus padded noiselessly ahead, senses alert. Only the scrabble of their boots on the rock and the whistle of the wind filled the air.

High above, the yellow eyes followed their progress into the night.

∽ 3 ∽

A Wicked and Cruel Night Out

Despite his thick cloak, the evening air cut into James like a frozen blade. Shepherded by Tempus, the companions descended the Col quickly, their legs aching with fatigue. First James, then Solomon stumbled.

"Careful now," Bartholomew warned.

"It'll be even more dangerous once we're in the trees," said Solomon. It was only moments later that the first stunted trunks materialized out of the darkness. Solomon unstrapped the ax from his back and led them in a zigzag through the smattering of trees and laurel bushes that clung to the slope, avoiding potential ambush sites.

The dwarves used all their skill and instinct, but eventually they ran into trouble.

Tempus gave the first warning with a single bark and bounded over beside them. James was so tired he barely stopped himself stumbling into Solomon's back. The dwarf spoke to the hound in a hushed voice, and then whispered in James's ear, "He's scented something, but he's not sure what. Draw your dagger and be ready." James stared intently into the darkness but heard nothing.

"Nerves are a good sign; blood is a bad one," Bartholomew told him reassuringly.

The words were barely spoken when, out of the dark, a great rushing noise descended.

"James!" Bartholomew crashed into him, sending James tumbling to the ground. With his sword drawn, the dwarf stood over the boy. "Solomon," he called in a low, restrained voice. There was no answer. "Tempus?" Again no answer. The chill of the night felt a lot colder.

Bartholomew crouched and whispered to James, "They are hoping to split us up. We must find the others quickly." James scrambled to his feet and followed as the dwarf retrieved the discarded torches and scoured the hillside. When they came across Solomon, he lay unconscious, a deep and ugly wound in his shoulder. Beyond—a pale, inert mass stretched out into the darkness, Solomon's ax embedded deep within it.

"It's the great slitherer, Alabaster," hissed Bartholomew. At a distance the creature looked dead, but as they drew closer the serpent's head swung around toward them, hitting James like a steam hammer. He collapsed to the ground. Even in the final moments of death, the creature sought out its intended victim.

Bartholomew stepped over the fallen boy and rammed his sword into the slitherer's luminescent eye. The point of the blade exploded out the back of its skull.

"Grab your sword and this torch and stand guard over Solomon." James rose shakily to his feet and did as he was told, his hand scrambling over the rocky ground to retrieve his dagger. Bartholomew swept up a torch and raced into the night. When he returned, he was carrying the broken body of Tempus, which he lay down next to his unconscious brother. Tempus licked Bartholomew's hand in gratitude.

"We must make a stand here. There is nowhere else for it. We can't move these two and defend ourselves at the same time." He looked down at Solomon. Then he sighed and sank down next to James. "Not quite the way I envisioned it," he said absently. James thought he saw a tear roll down the dwarf's worn features. Bartholomew turned away and scanned the perimeter of torchlight. "Sit with your back to me that we may guard every direction," he said, and they prepared for the long night ahead.

The hours crawled slowly. They talked to keep each other awake as Solomon and Tempus lay in fitful sleep.

"Morbidren may decide not to attack after seeing Alabaster killed, but I doubt it. She cannot refuse her masters any more than we could abandon you, James. No, she'll make her move, before sunrise."

Higher up the slope the Drezghul landed, folded its wings, and awaited the final assault. It still held as a "soul slave" one of the wild creatures—the dragonspider—compelled to do the Drezghul's will. The night breeze brought the scent of blood. Only the human and one companion remained to be dealt with. The masters would be pleased.

· *1895* ·

"I've seen a case like this before," Harrington informed Chief Inspector Corrick and, for the first time, Harrington's calm exterior showed a hint of concern. "The other victims were also left in a hideous fashion."

"I suspected as much," replied Corrick. "And the Foreign Office would never have sent you unless they were fairly certain this was a similar attack. So what can you tell me about the others? How many have there been?"

"This is the fourth."

"Four! Can you tell me the similarities between the cases?"

Harrington paused for a moment before answering.

"The victims were all female and appeared to be in their early twenties. They were all murdered in remote locations, and they died in a similarly distressing condition. Other than that, I cannot tell you."

Corrick considered whether the last sentence was an admission or a refusal.

The long day was almost spent. He had ordered the house secured and the forensic evidence sent to Cambridge for examination. The body needed identifying, and there was that other thing. *What was it?* He could not quite remember; it kept slipping away from him.

He signaled to a police sergeant. "Get the shutters closed. We can do without the publicity."

"Very good, sir."

· *1910* ·

James's torch spluttered before finally going out. They had only one remaining torch, and sunrise was at least an hour away.

"She'll have to attack soon," said Bartholomew. "Dragon-spiders hate daylight even more than they hate fire." He peered into the dark, but the torchlight revealed nothing except stony ground. James noticed Venus cresting the horizon to the east, a faint herald of dawn, but it did little to lessen the terror and confusion gripping his chest.

"Over here," a voice called from down the hill. James looked around in surprise. The voice sounded familiar. He turned to Bartholomew.

"A useful trick, being able to throw one's voice." The whisper came from up the hill now. "The enemy might think there are more of us." James smiled weakly but was too tired to talk more. His questions, and fears, would just have to wait.

The remaining torch burned low and died. Darkness closed in. Slowly their eyes grew accustomed to the night until the whole valley was infused with the powdery light from Venus and the stars.

"A maiden of the night to ease our plight," Bartholomew recited. "A line of dwarfish poetry and, in our case, I hope it's true. With this canopy of stars, it should be difficult for an attacker to surprise us."

James caught a flash of movement and whispered, "I see something. Over there, to your left by that clump of bushes." Now they both saw the enemy looming out of the night. Even across a distance of thirty yards or more, the sheer size of the creature confirmed that it was Morbidren. She looked immense, easily bigger than a grand piano.

The dragonspider sat low on her eight legs as if sagging under the weight of her immensely bloated body. She edged closer until she was only ten yards away. Bartholomew and James crouched side by side, shielding their wounded companions. A filament of web shot out and arced over the huddled group. Bartholomew used the ax to ward off the falling line. The ax stuck fast, and he had to let go of the weapon as it was dragged off into the dark.

"Go for her legs or eyes, James. Forget the abdomen. It'll be too tough to inflict much damage. But, above all, avoid her jaws! One bite and you're done for." Bartholomew raised his sword, and James held the dagger in his trembling hand.

The dragonspider covered the distance faster than a galloping horse. She sprang at them, attempting to isolate James like she was catching a fly. James slashed at a leg with no effect. Something wet ran down his neck, and he looked up at the gaping jaws scissoring open and closed. Above the jagged, claw-like mouth, eight gleaming black-button eyes stared soullessly down at him. Time slowed. James could see every tiny hair that sprouted over the horrible face. The mouth pulled back and a slime-coated, needle-thin proboscis slid down between her jaws, ready to stab and inject her poison.

Bartholomew bellowed as his sword crashed into the creature's legs, and he was rewarded as two of them sliced clean at the joint. Morbidren lost her balance and retreated a few paces, her useless stumps leaking trails of blackness. James's cloak ripped free from her pincers, and he rolled away. Angry at the loss of her prey, Morbidren struggled on her remaining legs as she sought an opportunity to strike. Her ineffective wings buzzed furiously as her spinner shot out a thick streak of webbing across the ground like a fire hose spraying water. But this spray was a deadly trap, and the ground glistened with filaments. Dwarf and boy edged backward as the trail of material threatened to snare them.

"Wait a moment for it to dry, then use your sword to cut it to pieces. I'll keep her off us!" Bartholomew advanced a pace, placing his foot firmly in the mesh, and roared a battle cry. Now there could be no retreat. He stabbed his sword at the spider's face. James slashed at the webbing, but it was hopeless. Web glued Bartholomew to where he stood, and then James. Morbidren grew bolder and shot a jet straight at the dwarf, the filament hitting him in the chest and arms and seizing him in a mess of stickiness. Another jet caught him in the face and abruptly ceased his battle chant. James looked up, and the cold, empty gaze of Morbidren was upon him. In that moment he fell under the hunter's spell, mesmerized, the prey that knows there is no escape. His sword slipped from his hand.

But then Morbidren froze and, with a sound like thunder, the monstrous dragonspider collapsed in slow motion, her remaining legs splaying in all directions. Something equally large and dreadful reared up over her back. Teeth and claws flashed, black liquid spilled into a wide pool, and Morbidren was dead.

James and Bartholomew watched in amazement. An enormous mound of shaggy black hair growled from on top of the dragonspider's body. The big black bear looked at them and said, "That's an old score settled."

The band of travelers huddled together on the bleak hillside. James watched the sky lighten and darkness fade to the west. Tempus lay stretched out next to him, too injured to sleep. Solomon had woken a short while earlier with a groan of pain, and his brother tended to his wounds before lighting a fire.

James looked at Solomon's exposed shoulder but quickly turned away, sickened by the sight of white bones sticking out from the mangled flesh. He sat up and gazed over at the lifeless form of the spider, listing on the ground like a boat left by the receding tide. The bear was nowhere to be seen. James laid his head back and shut his eyes. Daylight would bring safety and maybe some answers to all the questions pounding in his head.

His gaze took in the sweep of hillside all around; it was empty, but it did not feel safe. Something was out there.

"Get up!" Bartholomew commanded. "We're not finished yet." James saw that a fire had been lit. He must have dozed off. Slowly he rose to his feet as dawn beckoned. He had slept only a few moments. He groaned.

"We have to sleep some—" But the words froze on his lips. In that fraction of time, the hillside was plunged once more into inky night, the sun's first light blotted out completely. James let out a cry of fear as the fire was snuffed. Then there was a thump of heavy leather wings.

The Drezghul crashed down from a great height, its outline invisible against the darkness. Tempus howled in fear. Clawed feet knocked Bartholomew over and raked the ground, just missing him, tearing at the rocky hillside. The hideous creature reared on its hind legs, leather wings pinned behind its body. Then the Drezghul's attention locked on to James. The savage, ragged beak stretched out toward him, but he did not see it. He was transfixed by the yellow slits of its eyes. Its black mouth gaped and the reek of vile filth, of pestilence and disease escaped it.

James felt his consciousness slipping away, his body and soul separating. . . .

But in that instant doubt flickered in the yellow slits. The Drezghul stumbled, clawing the air between them. A small shard of intense light appeared, then exploded into a ball of incandescence, blasting the creature back. A shrill screech tore the sky and ripped the false night away.

Metal streaked across James's vision. A broad ax blade sliced into the Drezghul's upper leg, severing it in a cloud of smoke. Wings thrashing wildly, it flew off into the retreating darkness. Bartholomew crouched next to James, ax in hand. They searched above them, but the bitter cry of the Drezghul was already far away.

In the Western Tower a cloaked figure sank slowly into a chair. He had only just managed to intervene in time. He had felt the overwhelming threat of evil, but the enemy's strength had surprised him. It proved the boy was the key!

"Luck again, by Odin! Twice in a night!" exclaimed Bartholomew. James lay on his back, wanting to sleep, but the mixture of exhaustion and exhilaration made it impossible. The dwarf had restarted the fire and was brewing coffee, glancing at the boy from time to time. "I would never have believed it. Not for all the gold in the City of Oloris would I willingly stand up to one of those demons. That was the bravest thing I've ever witnessed. Truly you're the stuff of legend. And sorcery!"

"But it wasn't bravery, or magic," James said. "It scared me senseless. I couldn't move. It felt as if I was dying."

"What I saw was: the Drezghul's spell was upon you and its powers failed. Something in you countered the black sorcery.

When I swung the ax, it was already defeated."

Solomon spoke quietly to his brother as they drank coffee over the campfire. A spoon clanked around in a tin mug. The aroma of coffee overcame the repugnant smell of death that lingered on the hillside. James reached over and gently wrapped an arm around the injured dog, burying his face in Tempus's fur as he fell into a dreamless sleep.

~ 4 ~

CLUES, NOW AND THEN

· *1895* ·

In Cambridge Inspector Corrick sat at his desk lost in thought. He was trying to picture the scene he had witnessed at Purbeck Hall. He recalled images of the dead woman. And with them he felt the pull of long-buried emotions, but he pushed those away. That part of his life was in the past.

It was a week since he had made the trip to Purbeck. His superiors expected him to solve the case quickly, but he had no answers. The scene had provided no clues. A violent crime such as this with no obvious motive would require detailed science to solve it.

Scotland Yard was being difficult. For some reason they had sent Harrington from the Foreign Office to assist, and Corrick had also discovered the forensic evidence had been sent to London for examination behind his back. His investigation was losing momentum. He was supposed to finish writing the report. Something at the back of his mind was telling him not to bother. . . .

Corrick stood abruptly.

What had he been thinking? This was his job, all that he had left, the one thing which defined and motivated him. He would not allow this case to stagnate and be forgotten.

Searching through the Purbeck file he found there was no autopsy report on the victim. Methodically he reread the witness statements and the coroner's report. They were both inconclusive. They recorded a dead body being found on the second floor, a female vagrant who had entered the unoccupied house. She hadn't been identified by name but . . .

"Nothing says that she was a murder victim!" Corrick exclaimed. Had it been deliberately left out . . . ?

Just then a short, sharp pain stabbed behind his eyes and he winced, rubbing his temples with his fingertips. The pain eased.

Where was I? He had taken some notes when he first arrived on the scene and sat back down to scan through his notebook.

BODY—2nd floor
2nd *body?*—Hall, ground floor. Victim/culprit?
Foreign Office—Harrington to call

Corrick looked at the words he had written, but he had no recollection now of a second body. And it was not mentioned in the witness statement or in the police reports. For a moment he doubted his own notes. Had there been a second body?

The pain in his head returned, and for a moment he was racked in agony. When it had passed, a thought struck him, born of instinct, connecting two apparently unrelated events. The last entry he had written concerned Harrington. The headache returned stronger than ever, but Corrick gritted his teeth and ignored it.

If his notes were correct and there was a second body, somehow it had been overlooked, as if someone wanted the second body to be forgotten. He wondered if Harrington had anything to do with it. Now the pain grew intense, but he concentrated on holding his thoughts in focus, talking aloud as he went. "Whatever this is goes further and deeper than Scotland Yard, or Harrington." Abruptly the pain left him, and he slowly slumped back in his chair.

The telephone rang. He reached over and lifted the handset. The exchange operator put through a call.

"Hello. Hello. Can you hear me? Is that Chief Inspector Corrick of Cambridge?"

"Yes, it is." Corrick raised his voice over the crackle of interference.

"This is Harrington. Foreign Office, Illegal Aliens Department. You remember?"

"Yes." It was as if Harrington had been reading his mind. Corrick dismissed the idea, but his instinct now said the man was directly connected with these mysterious events.

"Listen, Chief Inspector, I don't suppose you've had much luck with your investigations. I have a proposition for you." Harrington cleared this throat. "It appears that the Belgians have a similar case to your Purbeck affair. Suffice to say, they are not really up to the task. Now, I need to get over there, but I don't have any official capacity that would allow me to review their evidence."

"So you would like me to get us both invited."

"Well put. I am sure we will benefit from a trip to the continent. Will you meet me tomorrow morning, ten sharp, at St. Katherine's Dock?"

"By Tower Bridge? Yes, I'll be there, but I'd like to know—"

He heard a click. Harrington had rung off.

St. Katherine's Dock was a hive of industry; lighters and small riverboats crowding the wharves, cranes and gantries swinging overhead in a feverish race to unload and stow the cargoes from a dozen merchantmen moored in the main channel. Porters and stevedores scurried like ants over the dock and boats. Boatmen's calls, the chugging of steam winches, and the cry of gulls added to the cacophony of the scene.

The riverside of London, the mightiest port in the world, was a microcosm of the largest empire ever known. Men slaved to keep its industrial engine turning. Men from the Niger Delta rubbed shoulders with those from the Empire's East Africa territories, who in turn toiled alongside Egyptians, Arabs, Chinese, Hindus, Muslims, and men from every city and town throughout the length and breadth of the kingdom. The stench of humanity was almost overpowering, yet the air also carried the smell of exotic spices, lumber, burning coal, and wet rope.

Corrick strode down a rocking gangway. The waters beneath were oily and turgid, floating scum and rubbish slopping against stone walls. A dead rat bobbed upside down. He continued along the wharf past a line of small sailing craft. A docker dodged out of his way, his back bent beneath a heavy sack of grain.

Harrington stood talking to another man, and waved as Corrick approached. The other man stepped briskly away; Corrick noted he was heavyset and had on a morning coat and a top hat pulled forward as if not wanting to be recognized.

"An early start, I'm afraid, but it will be worth it," Harrington said.

"We'll have to wait and see."

A small launch was arrowing toward them, and beyond lay a naval gunboat with the name on the bow, HMS *Obedience*.

"Our little venture has the blessing of some important people," Harrington responded to the curious look on Corrick's face.

They clambered down a short iron ladder and sat in the waist of the launch as it retreated across the River Thames to the gunboat.

Once they were in the captain's cabin, Harrington found a decanter of sherry and poured two glasses.

"It's going to be a long day," he said, handing one to Corrick. "The captain has kindly lent us the use of his cabin for the duration of the journey." He took a sip and went on, settling in the captain's chair. "The Belgians mustn't know my official status, since it may complicate diplomatic relations. So I would be grateful if you would refer to me as your assistant."

"Then I ask the questions," Corrick said, his eyes firmly on Harrington.

"Very well." The man smiled. Corrick wondered if he ever played by the rules.

Harrington continued, "We've already sent word to the

police in Zeebrugge that you've a similar case in hand." Above them a donkey winch began its mechanical braying as it hauled up the anchor. "They've agreed to let us examine the crime scene. Apparently nothing has been touched. It was discovered yesterday afternoon. A bridge arch near the docks. Woman's body, horrible mutilations. They'll try to pump us for information. Of course, we'll say we have no leads as of yet." His eyes glinted with meaning.

Corrick perched on the corner of the desk and leaned forward. "And what information, *precisely*, don't we have?"

· *1910* ·

"James! James!" The words were lost in the rising wind. Up and down the coast, dozens of police and locals were conducting a search.

When Sir Philip and Lady Jennifer Kinghorn returned from their day trip, they were not initially concerned by their son's absence. It was only when James failed to return by nightfall that his father alerted the police. At ten o'clock that evening, a policeman interviewed Sir Philip and his wife and took statements from hotel staff. The police arranged a search at first light. James's parents did not sleep that night.

Before dawn Sir Philip was on the telephone to his staff in the War Office. Soon a detachment from the local army garrison at Alnwick in Northumberland was en route to join the search. In addition, a warship at Tynemouth would cruise along the coast for the next forty-eight hours.

Lady Jennifer was desperate to join the search, but Philip requested that she remain at the hotel in case James made his own way back. Then he motored down the coast to join the search among the sand dunes.

Sir Philip stood looking out over the line of soldiers and civilians that necklaced the countryside. They were conducting a sweep south behind Embleton Bay, toward the castle on the headland. The young officer standing next to him raised his binoculars and scanned the grassy hillocks, watching as a policeman tripped and fell in the long grass. Away to the west the bank of dark clouds over the moors heralded a turn in the weather. Standing solemn and majestic, no more than twenty paces from the two men, the Sea Arch loomed above them.

Leaving the distracted officer behind, Philip clambered down the dune, his black leather shoes filling with sand. He stopped before the padlocked gates.

It was not the first time he had seen the Arch, but the last had been many years ago. And somehow, since then, he had forgotten it existed. The memories were coming back now, and with them the knowledge that the Sea Arch was, in every way, an enigma.

Sir Philip walked around the arch until he came to the brass plaque on the seaward side. He read the inscription:

A son you gave this world has gone
And journeyed from this crossing place
Seek not what's lost when lost it's not
But mind the comings of this way
For his return will be anon
A gun to start a desperate race

His motive ancestry forgot
To still the killing of a day

Steady now your hand must act
And recall silence in your past
Your father's eyes you too may see
That which empire may not spy
Seek out the other in this pact
Who sifts for one in numbers vast
And chase the wates in ministry
Or heralds forth a time to die

Digging into his coat pocket he drew out a small black note-book and pencil stub and carefully wrote down the words.

James picked up one end of the makeshift stretcher on which Tempus lay. Bartholomew carried the other end, together with their weapons. The three of them refused to abandon Tempus. Solomon was on his feet, a sling cradling his right arm and a mound of bandages swathing his shoulder. Groggy with pain, he limped along behind the stretcher. His backpack was hidden among the rocks, to be retrieved later.

They made slow progress, stopping frequently, but at last they passed through the valley and out of the pine forests into more open, wooded country. Here oak and ash softened the landscape. It was warmer, and the meadows hummed with bees while birdsong filled the air. It felt as if the earlier events had been a dream. Or maybe this was the dream?

Ahead, in the distance, James could see the Western Tower the dwarves had spoken of, what felt like a long time ago.

They eventually arrived after nightfall.

James was confined to bed with his injuries once the bedraggled, weary companions had finally reached the tower. On the morning of the second day, Bartholomew visited him with news. The wound Solomon received had not poisoned him, and he was making a rapid recovery. News of Tempus was less encouraging. Bartholomew struggled to keep the tears from his eyes as he reported, "Tempus is in that place between Here and There. They don't know if he'll pull through. I said you'd grown attached to him and you'd be sorely hurt were he to die. I thought it might encourage their help, knowing you to be an important visitor of the Guilds."

James leaned forward and grabbed the dwarf's hand. "Tempus is a great hound. The best I've ever known."

Bartholomew was soon ushered out by a nurse, who said, "Now sleep, young man, for it is rest you need." And James was asleep in an instant.

· 1895 ·

The gunboat bumped against the fenders on the quayside. While Harrington went up to the bridge to have a talk with the captain, Corrick stood thinking of what he'd learned on the trip over to Belgium. He was also worried about his headaches and memory loss, something he became acutely aware of when relying on Harrington to recount the recent scene at Purbeck Hall.

According to Harrington, the first of the four similar crimes was originally thought to be the work of a madman, although inquiries around Burnham, where the murder took place, revealed no likely culprits. The next victim was found in the Thames and thought to have been attacked by a large predatory fish, but on finding a third victim with similar wounds in a barn, this theory was also discounted. All had died by extreme violence, as if a series of murders was taking place, possibly by the same culprit.

This last point was the most troubling to Corrick. He'd even wondered if it could be the work of Jack the Ripper, still unknown and at large. But he could feel there was more that linked these cases than just the murders of four women. What it was, only time could tell.

Harrington also revealed that the Purbeck victim had been transferred to the London Natural History Museum for investigation. Corrick didn't understand why, but there was little he could do about it now. He made a note to visit there on his return. He sensed he was deliberately being kept from the evidence. Something sparked in his memory, but he could not put his finger on it.

Corrick sorted the clues in his head. Four reports: the first from Burnham; the second, and the first that Harrington attended, was in London, where the body had been in water for some time; the third report from Southend; fourth, Purbeck. And now possibly a fifth? The only common factors so far linking all the murders were age and gender of the victims and the horrible manner of their deaths.

Where is the motive? Something plucked again at the edges of Corrick's memory. . . .

A Belgian policeman greeted the Englishmen and led them along the muddy canal path. Above them the sky was slate gray and it was steadily raining. They ducked and passed beneath a low railway bridge. Other policemen waited in the bridge's shadow. Portable arc lights focused attention on a crumpled figure on the ground.

A senior officer saluted the newcomers. He held out his hand. "I am Inspector La Forge. I am to assist you with your inquiries."

"I hope we may work together to solve both investigations," Corrick said. La Forge nodded in agreement and stepped aside to let them examine the body.

It was a terrible sight. The lower portion had been torn to shreds and bones lay smashed, protruding white against the red pulp. There was hardly any blood. Inspector La Forge clicked his fingers. A policeman opened a pocket notebook and read aloud in good English: "Victim unknown female. Aged approximately twenty-three years. Occupation . . . uncertain."

He looked up to his superior, who added, "She was probably a 'lady of the night.'"

The policeman continued. "Of no fixed abode."

"*Merci, monsieur,*" said Corrick. He squatted on his haunches to study the corpse. "This attack looks like Purbeck," he said to Harrington. "There is a link, something we are missing. Perhaps the perpetrators are religious maniacs, anarchists, possibly a secret society?"

"Is there nothing more, Inspector La Forge? No, then thank you once again." Harrington extended his hand to the confused

Belgian and signaled Corrick to follow.

Corrick ran a few steps to catch up. "What was that?" he demanded.

"We saw everything there was to see. A corpse mutilated like Purbeck and Burnham and the others, nothing more."

Corrick grabbed his arm and spun him around.

"Yes?" Harrington said testily.

"We didn't come here for a cursory visit." Corrick kept his voice low.

Harrington met his anger with a calm but challenging silence.

Still Corrick saw a hint of something behind the other man's gaze. What was it? Knowledge? Sympathy? Harrington turned away and splashed off down the path. Corrick followed.

· 1910 ·

Sir Philip sat next to his wife, cradling her hands. Lady Jennifer had put on a brave show for the police, but now, in private, she gave in to her despair. His notebook lay open on the coffee table in front of them. He told her all he knew about the Sea Arch and the inscription.

As a boy, he had often visited the Northumberland coast with his family. He and his brother would go hiking with their father, Sir Neville. Their favorite destination was the Sea Arch.

They imagined the arch was a monument to some forgotten battle or triumphant victory. But the most perplexing thing about the Sea Arch was that, while Philip and his father could see it as plain as the sun, no amount of pointing or teasing could make his brother see it. When Philip was older, Sir Neville explained to him that he had sometimes visited the Sea Arch, but Philip was the only other person he knew of who had ever been able to see it. His father would say no more on the matter and eventually it left Philip's thoughts. And then this morning he had seen the arch again.

His wife sat back to ponder this. She had walked the beach many times, but she had never seen an arch. For a fleeting instant she considered her husband's sanity, driven as they both were by thoughts of James. But she knew him and accepted his story.

She studied the text that he had copied from the inscription.

"It would appear to be both a message and a riddle," she said after a while, "and I think it is telling us that James is alive." She pointed to one line. "Look here."

Seek not what's lost when lost it's not

"Maybe this can help get him back." She turned to Philip with a small smile. "At least it will take my mind off worrying for a while." She scrutinized his notes. "And I am good with puzzles. You don't know this, but I've been completing the crossword in the paper every day for the past three years."

"How extraordinary you are," he said softly, and squeezed her hand.

"Now let's look at this verse and see if we can unravel its meaning." She read the first two lines.

A son you gave this world has gone
And journeyed from this crossing place

"Well, it seems the inscription is meant for you."

"But the gates were locked."

"Perhaps they closed after James passed through." She saw his look. "Now, Philip. *You* asked me to believe in an arch I cannot see. If this archway is visible to some but not others, then it must be magical." Sir Philip raised his eyebrows but she continued, "Either you accept this or you must seriously consider that you're losing your senses."

He reluctantly nodded. "I never allowed myself to consider the possibilities. Let's see where they take us."

Seek not what's lost when lost it's not

But mind the comings of this way

"This line's telling me—*us*," he corrected, "that James isn't lost: he knows where he's going, somewhere beyond the arch."

"And that we must keep an eye on the arch in case there are more comings and goings," she added.

For his return will be anon

A gun to start a desperate race

"This gives the clearest sign he'll be coming back," Sir Philip concluded.

"If 'he' means James. And what about the word 'gun'!"

"Maybe a starter's gun . . ." His voice trailed off. "It could be metaphorical, do you think? James might be some sort of catalyst for events?"

"Anyone disappearing through a magical archway could surely provoke some sort of event," Lady Jennifer said. They looked at each other, hardly able to believe any of this was happening, but praying the event would be James's return.

She read the next two lines aloud:

His motive ancestry forgot

To still the killing of a day

After a few moments of silence she said, "Let's leave those lines for now. I always find that's the best way to approach a tricky clue."

Sir Philip couldn't help but laugh. "Perhaps one day you'll even have a letter published in *The Times*."

"But I have, dear," Lady Jennifer replied calmly. "*The Times* knows me as the Very Reverend Maurice Todpole." He was speechless.

James's parents worked late before finally going to bed. By then they were both convinced that cracking the clues would somehow help him.

The next morning they reviewed their plans over breakfast. Philip was to return to London while Jennifer would stay on, renting a farmhouse near the Sea Arch where she would keep watch, as the inscription advised. Though the arch remained invisible to her, Sir Philip showed Jennifer its exact location after breakfast, pointing out landmarks to help identify the precise spot. He also arranged for the War Office to install a telephone line to the house so they could be in direct contact. They agreed it was best if the Sea Arch and its inscription continued to remain a secret, but they would invite their niece Amanda to come north and keep her aunt company while she kept her vigil over the coming days.

Back in London, Sir Philip made arrangements for a car to be at his wife's disposal and he ordered the telephone line, which caused a stir since in the entire War Office, with over twelve hundred people, there were only thirty-seven lines. He also sent a maid to keep house for her.

Then Sir Philip went to visit a man called Rawlings in Fleet Street.

Over the years Sir Philip had dealt with a number of rather delicate matters. Some concerned affairs of state, while others were of a more private nature. In both he had come to regard Rawlings as exceptionally talented with a rare combination of skills and discretion. He was a spy, and he came with a colorful past.

Sir Philip had first learned of him many years ago. Two drunken army officers were discussing a fellow officer who had recently been dishonorably discharged. "Quite brilliant" was how one described the man in question. "Brilliant, but maverick. Didn't fit in," said the other.

Curious, Philip tracked down the individual. Needless to say, the young man was feeling bitter toward the army after recent events. Sir Philip approached him and, despite Rawlings's initial wariness, he was soon in Philip's employ and quickly set about making himself indispensable.

"This is an unusual matter," Sir Philip began, but Rawlings interrupted him.

"Aren't they all, Phil?"

"Indeed, but this time it's much more."

Philip looked at the man sitting opposite him. Ten years of sleuthing and skulduggery had taken their toll on Rawlings. He was prematurely balding and overweight. Philip knew Rawlings had an energy and resourcefulness that had pulled him through many a tight spot, and Rawlings had always come through for him. He could only pray that this time would be the same.

The Natural History Museum in South Kensington was one of the most magnificent recent buildings in London. Opened just fourteen years previously, it was an architectural gem, but a complicated place to find your way around in. As Corrick walked through the building, he marveled at the intricate Romanesque interior, enormous fossil creatures on display, and endless ranks of glass cabinets housing stuffed creatures.

After requesting to see someone regarding a specimen delivery, he had been directed through the maze of corridors to what turned out to be the head secretary's office. Here he repeated his request and was led back through the building to the west wing, where the head secretary knocked at another door. A muffled voice answered, and his guide slipped through, leaving Corrick standing in the corridor.

Moments later the door swung open, and he was invited to enter.

The short man behind the desk rose and signaled him to take a seat.

"My name is Sir Roland Crozier. I am the Museum's chief curator. How may I help you?" Corrick noted the man's over-egged attitude and reluctantly repeated his purpose yet again.

"The specimen was found at a crime scene I am handling," Corrick added, choosing his words carefully.

Sir Roland sat back, his elbows resting on the leather armrests and his hands forming a delicate arch, fingertips to fingertips. "How odd to send a crime specimen to the Natural History Museum. I can't imagine any reason for it."

"I agree. That's why I'm here, to retrieve it and have it examined."

"Yeees," said the curator.

Corrick waited, but the man seemed reluctant to elaborate. "If you would be so kind to have someone furnish me with the specimen, I'll be on my way."

"Yeees" was all Sir Roland said, and another stretch of silence passed between them.

"Is there a problem?"

"Weeell." Sir Roland contemplated the chandelier above his head. "There is a slight complication."

Corrick leaned forward to give the man the full glare of his attention.

"You see," the curator began in a reedy voice, "with such a new and large institution, and so many wonderful exhibits to catalogue—we have recently brought five separate museums under one roof, you do realize—well . . ." He tried a worldly sigh on Corrick. "We are unable to say precisely what we have in storage at this time."

The chief inspector continued to glare.

"Of course," Sir Roland blurted, "the likelihood is that we haven't got it. Even under present circumstances, I am fairly confident we would have returned any inappropriate material."

Corrick stood. "You have been of great assistance," he said, his voice hardened with anger. Sir Roland's prominent Adam's apple bobbed like a duck in a storm.

"You might wish to check with the Natural History Museum in Oxford. They do get our mail from time to time," the curator called as the door swung shut behind the departing policeman.

Outside, Corrick let his anger settle. This visit only reinforced his feeling that the evidence was deliberately being kept from him. If necessary, he would obtain a search warrant and forcibly drag the evidence out of the museum. *If it was there . . .* But Sir Roland had mentioned Oxford. Corrick could not afford to ignore any possibility, no matter how remote. He checked his battered pocket watch, a memento of the past he preferred to forget, then hailed a hansom cab.

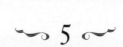

THE WESTERN TOWER

When James woke he vaguely recalled being carried into the room and a visit by one of the dwarves, but little else. He sat up in bed and glanced around. The room looked like a hospital ward, with immaculately made beds and whitewashed walls. His heart leaped! He was back . . . ? The sudden burst of joy faded as swiftly as it had arrived. He knew he was still far from home and that the events of that night on the hillside were not a dream. It felt like his first day at boarding school, alone and cut off from the ones he loved.

His clothes had been folded and placed on a chair by the bed. His belt and dagger hung there as well. He studied his surroundings in an effort to stop thinking of home. Narrow, slitlike windows cut through a thick stone wall that ran in a graceful curve. He realized he must be in the tower.

His thoughts were interrupted by the nurse at the door.

"Good, you're awake," she said. "You have a visitor or two."

Tempus trotted into the room, followed by the brothers. James could hardly believe how well they all looked. There were greetings all around and handshakes and hugs as the three of them recalled events over the past few days.

"We've been the talk of the tower since we arrived. With you all in bed, I've had to tell the tale so often my head's begun to spin," joked Bartholomew.

"Or is it the tale that's spun?" asked Solomon, winking at James.

"Where exactly are we?"

"Why, this is the Western Tower that sits at the heart of Lauderley Forest," Bartholomew said. "It's an ancient forest which spans a hundred leagues from east to west, and marks the edge of the world where the sun sets. The tower was built many millennia ago by the Guild as the regional seat of power, and is famed as a center of learning."

Eager to finally receive some information at last, James listened quietly as he continued. "But with the passing of centuries, the power of the Guild has declined. Where once a dozen wizards worked in the tower, now we have but one." Bartholomew's voice had fallen to a near whisper. "Though he is of greater importance than any wizard before him."

"To be sure," agreed Solomon.

"A wizard!" exclaimed James.

"Ssshh, boy," warned the brothers, looking about to see if they had been overheard, even though the room was otherwise empty.

"Like we said earlier, the Guild are the most brilliant minds in the world, many of them wizards," said Solomon. "Once their ranks were counted in the thousands, but now they are few in number, two hundred at most. Many wizard towers have been abandoned and fallen into disrepair, but the Western Tower still has Sibelius."

"Why are you whispering?" asked James.

"Because our wizard lives upstairs." Bartholomew pointed.

"Yes," the nurse's voice interrupted, "he's right upstairs. But he's far too busy to eavesdrop. You can tell him everything at your meeting with him tomorrow." She shooed the brothers from the room to let James rest awhile longer. Tempus hid until they were shepherded out. Then he jumped up and lay on the bed. The dog seemed fully recovered from his injuries. James reached forward and gave him a scratch behind the ears.

"Up a bit. Aaaah yes, that's it."

James's hand froze. He stared at Tempus.

"I can talk," the hound said matter-of-factly, "though I'd prefer if you didn't make it public knowledge."

James stared and then laughed out loud. "I heard the bear speak that night he killed the dragonspider, but I thought I'd just imagined it. Do all animals talk in this place?"

"No, only those that haven't forgotten the ancient lore." The dog's voice was low and husky.

"A land of talking dogs and bears and wizards! So magic really does exist?"

"Of course, though animal speech is not magic, strictly speaking. We call animals that still have the gift of speech 'parls': parlanimals. I prefer to think of myself as a hound. So I am a parlhound, but hound will do."

"Well, it's nice to make your acquaintance, Tempus parlhound," said James.

"And yours. Now, if you'll just continue scratching behind

my ears, I'll be happy to answer more of your questions."

"How did animals learn to speak?"

"In the lore of the parlanimals, Creation bestowed gifts to all living things. To animals was given speech; to the fish, silence; to the crawling creatures, society."

"You said only some animals still have the gift. Why have others lost the power of speech?"

Tempus raised his head and looked at James.

"At first animals cherished their independence and their gifts. But with time most fell under man's influence, accepting his domination over all other life. Some animals became domesticated and no longer had the need of speech. They began to lose the gift. Those who would not accept man's rule took to living in the wild. In the depths of the forest, they had need of other skills to survive and to escape man, who took to hunting all things wild. They too began to forget the gift of speech.

"Nowadays most men consider talking animals the result of dark magic, servants of the enemy. We speak only to those we know and trust. So we are all slowly losing the gift."

James shook his head, overwhelmed by the feeling of loss. "Do the brothers know you're a parlanimal?"

"They are dwarves, entirely different from men. We keep my parl a secret amongst ourselves. It has proved useful on occasions. Men of your world would surely react badly to talking animals as well." Tempus sighed. "Please excuse me, but talking makes me very tired. I need to rest now." And with that he laid his head down and was soon fast asleep.

Feeling well enough to leave his bed, the last thing James

wanted to do was sleep, so tiptoeing barefoot out of the room, he set off to explore.

He entered a large circular hallway at the center of the tower. In the middle a spiral stone staircase corkscrewed up through the vaulted ceiling to the floor above. There were three other doors leading off from the hall at opposite points of the compass. He heard singing coming from behind one of the doors, and he lifted the latch to investigate. As he looked around the doorway, the singing stopped. He found the nurse from the ward busy at a desk.

She looked up. "James! I'm pleased to see you up. How about getting dressed and we'll go for a walk?"

James hurried back to the ward to change out of the hospital smock. As he started back across the hall, Tempus fell in beside him.

"Mind yourself, she has a way that will turn your insides to marrow jelly."

"Thanks, I'll bear that in mind."

As he and the nurse descended the central stairwell, with Tempus at their heels, James noticed that the steps appeared to glow.

"Yes, the stone traps light at the top and channels it down the spiral to illuminate the tower," she explained.

They passed down through many floors, most of which were silent and empty. Turning off the stairs, they crossed to a wooden door set in the exterior stone wall. The door swung open, and in front of them a narrow wooden causeway stretched into the distance, the far end resting on a grassy knoll.

"This is the Rose Door, leading into the gardens."

James gazed at the parkland spread out before them like a beautiful tablecloth with splashes of color lovingly sewn on. It reminded him of Hyde Park in London, only more peaceful.

The nurse guided him into the gardens, where she pointed out some of the different types of roses. Her warm, willowy voice entranced James.

He had no idea how long they walked together, but eventually he found they had returned to the causeway. He stopped and looked up at the tower for the first time. The graceful line ascended five hundred feet or more, dominating the countryside. Its white granite gleamed clean and fresh in the daylight.

"It impresses you. Do you not have such buildings in your own world?"

"I've never seen anything like it."

"The Western Tower is but one of many in our land. It was built in a time when miracles were possible, and the necessary skills still existed." She contemplated the majesty of the structure. "This world will never again build something as wondrous as Faldamare."

James turned to her. "Faldamare?"

"The name given to this tower by the elves who built it."

That night when he climbed into bed, James realized that he had been too awestruck to ask the lady her name.

"Tempus, are you still awake?"

"Unfortunately."

"What is the nurse's name?"

"She isn't a nurse. She is Lady Orlania."

"Oh."

After breakfast the next day James and the dwarves set off for their appointment with the wizard. They climbed and climbed, passing endless floors, accompanied by nothing more than the echo of their own footsteps. After a dozen floors the spiral of the stairwell would reverse in a tricky feat of engineering that perplexed the eye.

"It's a defensive measure," said Solomon. "It forces an attacker to change sword hands, putting him at a disadvantage."

At last they reached the top. It was like arriving inside a rainbow. There were no walls or windows, simply bands of color and light arcing high above their heads and twisting into a spinning top of loops and curves. James looked down to find himself standing on a pool of aquamarine water, with vividly colored fish gliding beneath him. When he lifted his eyes again, the rainbow was fading, replaced by a blue-black sky powdered with stars. Finally the spectacle faded completely to be replaced by nothing more than a stone vaulted ceiling.

James saw that the room was a library, its walls lined with oak bookcases. Shelves were filled with books of every size, mounds of manuscripts, bundles of scrolls, and haphazard stacks of charts. There were books as big as James, others embossed in what looked like real gold, and a few even glistened with encrusted gems. The smell of old leather haunted the air. A stillness permeated every corner of the room. The place seemed to shimmer with magical power.

Bartholomew turned to his brother. "Did you see it, brother? The Seat of Elder Mosenor and all the slain! What a pyrrhic victory that was. What splendor! What a way to cross to the far side." Bartholomew hopped from foot to foot as he shook his brother in happiness.

Solomon was equally excited but for a different reason. "No, no, brother. It was the most amazing battle banquet I have ever witnessed. They were up there." He gestured. "Old Axer Tollominos sat beside Borofeare the Enslaver. They were toasting the death of their enemies. There must have been a hundred dwarves celebrating." He threw back his head and roared a battle chant. James stood watching them, noting how the dwarves seemed to have a limitless supply of war cries.

"Come up, come in," called a voice from above.

The brothers stopped in mid-embrace, remembering where they were. They shuffled apart and looked up the final flight of stairs.

"It's different every time. He always puts a good show on," Bartholomew murmured to James.

"Come up, come in," the voice repeated.

James followed the dwarves up until they were standing beneath a glass dome enclosing the entire tower roof. The room resembled an observatory, filled with strange apparatus and shelves of bottles, boxes, and jars. Chests and cauldrons stood on the floor. Plants with giant fronds arched overhead beneath the glass. Several climbing plants also grew up the inside of the structure. An enormous telescopic contraption on casters pointed a black accusatory finger skyward while other, lesser machines and devices crowded around it.

James glanced out of the dome window at the brilliant azure blue sky. It was as if the room were perched far above the world.

"Welcome, James Kinghorn." An old man walked forward

and placed a fatherly hand on James's shoulder before turning to the two dwarves. "Welcome, Solomon Brunel Bandamire and Bartholomew Shakespeare Bandamire, offspring of Splayfoot Teutonica Bandamire, warrior and prisoner-not-at-large, and grandspring of Borrowmason Goldenbeard Bandamire, whose fall at Highfall be remembered in lore."

The brothers beamed in satisfaction at these words.

The old man whispered to James, "Dwarves love this sort of stuff, as you know. Now, my good dwarves, what shall we be about? A cup of tea, and then I think we ought to explain a thing or two to our young friend here, who has been kept in the dark long enough."

The dwarves took two low-slung seats that were just the right height for them. James sat beside the old man and watched while the teapot poured itself. "And you like this sort of magic," the wizard murmured to him before announcing, "I am Sibelius, Principal Wizard of the Western Tower and representative of the Guild."

The wizard cradled his cup of tea. His face was at once young and old. His eyes glimmered with energy yet also told of a thousand lifetimes, were a man to live so long. It struck James how familiar Sibelius appeared to him.

"You entered the ancient world of Eldaterra by way of the Sea Arch, and you've arrived safely by the guiding hand of the Guild and, in no small part, by the brave and loyal actions of these two gentle warriors." This set the brothers grinning again.

"Your family has been of service to Eldaterra in the past, and we are grateful. But now we must call on *your* services." The wizard's tone grew serious. "It was in fact your grandfather, Sir

Neville, who aided us many years ago before you were born. I believe you never met your grandfather."

"No, I never knew him," James said. The wizard placed a hand on his shoulder again and, for the first time, the pain from the dragonspider attack was entirely gone.

"You can be very proud of him. Though we know little of his deeds, he has been influential in events between our two worlds."

"But still I don't understand—how can there be two worlds?" James asked. "Where am I?"

"This is quite an experience for you, I know. Eldaterra doesn't appear on any map you've ever seen, and it never will. Thousands of years ago wizards created the deepest magic to divide the earth in two. They hid the old world, the one we call Eldaterra, from the new world in the hope that the influences of change would not affect it."

James listened closely as the wizard continued. "When Creation placed life on earth, its work was as beautiful and intricate as anything that existed in the universe. The world was filled with marvels and astonishing diversity. It was to be a world of goodness. But the act of Creation can only take place when there is harmony, equilibrium. And for a state of balance to exist, there must be exact opposites for everything."

He picked up a measuring rule to demonstrate. "James, to balance this ruler across my finger, there must be equal lengths on either side. There are also extremes at either end—but together they balance each other out. Take one away, and the other will make the ruler fall. These extremes represent the forces we know as good and evil. And one does not exist without the other." The old wizard turned his hand and the ruler fell to the ground.

"When Creation placed life in the world, it sought to do so with nothing but goodness, but evil seeped in, seeking to return the world to a natural state of equilibrium. The balance begins to shift from purity to equality, good and evil in equal measure."

He took a sip of tea. James thought Sibelius had described the Garden of Eden in a way, but had not called it that.

"Among those gifts given to the world, *Knowledge*, an understanding of Creation, is the greatest of all. It is marked by the possession of a soul. Many creatures in the world possessed such a soul, and with it came all things we know to be good: love, loyalty, compassion, and freedom to think and be individuals. Yet as evil seeped into the world, many souls were corrupted. Life divided into good and evil. Everything that has a soul turns to one or other of these opposites. True perfection was lost forever." The wizard set down his teacup and looked at all three of them in turn.

"Oldest among the forms of Knowledge is what we call magic, though it was once deeper and more complex than what we know today. At the time of creation, all peoples had this knowledge. Much has since been lost, forgotten. Of all the magic that ever existed, the very first was that which divined life, but no one is allowed to use it. It was for Creation alone."

The room was perfectly still.

"I tell you this, James, because you need to understand that when the world began, magic was the oldest gift after life itself. Creatures used it to shape the world, for good or evil. Ever since those opposing forces have waged war, and countless lives have been lost. Eventually parts of the world were left with no magic, no Knowledge, no ancient lore. These places contained living creatures which Creation never intended. They possessed souls, but no longer understood their place in the ordering of the world. They created false gods and worshipped craven idols.

"The people who still wielded magic decided to act. They determined to create two separate worlds: one where magic would be protected; the other where it was all but gone forever. The world you know—the New World—has grown and developed without magic. Nearly everything gifted by Creation has been lost. Mankind, with its science and religion, has risen to dominate all else. Man stumbles down this path of learning where the distinction between good and evil is blurred and ill defined.

"Eldaterra is a world where one is *either* good or evil. There is no in-between. In your world all mankind is caught in the grayness that exists between light and dark."

Sibelius paused.

"James, your grandfather was a rare person, with such a depth of goodness in him. Sir Neville came to Eldaterra many years past, and for a brief time I knew of his purpose. But it was long ago, and I have heard nothing since. Yet now you have followed."

The dwarves looked at James. He had a question he wanted to ask but couldn't. Sibelius appeared to read his mind.

"We do not know which, but it is the possession of one of these extremes that allows you to pass between our two worlds. It was only through your grandfather's actions that we knew his place. In Eldaterra"—he spread his arms about him—"life is preordained in a design we may not fully understand, but that allows us some insight. We call this fate. Your world lives by its actions, by its will."

"If I am here, there is a reason?" asked James.

Sibelius waved a hand, and a map appeared and hung in the air before them. "This is the Lauderley Forest and the country that borders this region. To the west is the very edge of Eldaterra, and it was here that you crossed over. To the north, beyond the range of mountains, lies a desolate land. To the east lies a fertile region more populated than Lauderley. Farther east live strange races and beings that we have little contact with. To the south is where the Guild sits in Eldaterra's principal cities. Beyond there," he said, pointing to the very foot of the map, "the source of our troubles lies."

The room noticeably darkened. James looked up at the glass, but the sky remained bright blue. Sibelius scowled.

"By this darkness you see a hint of the powers that assail us. As the Guild's representative, this tower is my domain." His eyes flashed in anger. "For evil to dare intrude into my stronghold, let alone the Forest of Lauderley, is evidence enough that there is an imbalance in this world. I believe you have been sent to resolve this, to decide whether evil will breach the magic that separates our worlds. If this happens, Eldaterra will cease to exist. The science of your world will crash into the last of the true Knowledge, and it will be lost forever."

"But what am I supposed to do?" James asked anxiously. "And . . . if I'm supposed to help, why did we have to fight for our lives? Why didn't—why didn't you—help us?"

"Ah," the wizard said with a slight smile. "Magic leaves

tracks behind, a footprint that may be read by a skilled hunter. When you came through the Sea Arch, a ripple in the balance of this world took place. I sensed your arrival, and so have others. Like us, they do not yet know what potential you represent. I had the brothers Bandamire watch over you, and my spies informed me of your progress. Your survival was foreseen by the Fates, but only if you were determined to survive, which, happily for us all, you were. The most I dared were the fireflies to light your way.

"Until you encountered the Drezghul. For that magnitude of evil, I was forced to intercede. I'm afraid its presence tells me the enemy already knows just how important you are to us all."

6

More Questions than Answers

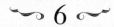

· *1895* ·

Corrick was busy with endless paperwork when a duty officer tapped on the door.

"Excuse me, there's a telephone call for you, we think, sir."

Corrick knew many of his colleagues were uneasy with this new technology, and some questioned the need. Some people did not like change, himself included, but he accepted it as inevitable.

"Hello, hello." The voice at the other end was disjointed by interference. "Chief Inspector Corrick?"

"Yes."

"*Bon.* This is Inspector La Forge. You visited our country on a police matter a few days ago?"

"Yes."

"*Mais oui.* I am calling from the telephone of Monsieur Barras, a very upstanding citizen of Zeebrugge." La Forge's delivery was slow and precise.

"Please, go on," Corrick urged.

"New evidence linked to the murder was discovered after your departure. You may wish to see it for yourself. It is, how do you say, very strange." La Forge sounded as if he were letting Corrick in on a secret.

That evening Corrick boarded a small steam packet carrying mixed cargo and a handful of passengers. The boat struggled with the weather conditions, pitching badly in the swell as she headed across the gray waters of the North Sea to the Lowlands.

"She's the wrong length for the swell," her captain said. "Must be coming down from Arctic waters." He had invited Corrick to join him on the bridge. A long night's steaming lay before them. "I'd be happier to tack across, as would all on board no doubt," the captain added, hoping Corrick would rescind the urgent official police request to steam directly to Zeebrugge.

But Corrick was silent as he gazed up at the black smoke curling away to the west, the steam engine thumping reassuringly below the deck.

Inspector La Forge greeted Corrick as he disembarked. "We meet in more favorable circumstances."

Corrick looked skyward. "The weather is definitely better."

"*Oui*, but I am referring to the absence of . . . your assistant?" The Belgian policeman was watching Corrick closely.

"So you weren't impressed?"

"That man was not your subordinate any more than he was a police officer. Do not take me for a fool, Chief Inspector. I had just decided to like you."

Corrick laughed a little and apologized for the ruse, which he said was not his doing. They climbed into a police carriage and headed for the city morgue.

"You see, Chief Inspector. It is most unusual."

"Very." They stood at a marble morgue table in the center of a cold, brightly lit room. The city coroner stood waiting for their questions.

Stretched out in a battered metal specimen tray lay a mass of convoluted flesh. It was discolored, with patches of brown and yellow, but mainly it was off white, as if it were bleached, washed out. Attached to it was a thick cord, perhaps two feet in length and frayed at the end.

"Please repeat your description, Doctor." Corrick wanted to check his notes.

The doctor shrugged. "It appears to be a placenta. Based on the weight and dimensions, one might say with certainty that it was from a full-term fetus. But it is not normal. . . . I have never seen one with so many anatomical aberrations. It is not my field of expertise, but to find that this has . . . a heart within it . . . this is impossible!"

An awkward silence followed as each of them pondered this. La Forge thanked the doctor, who quickly left. Corrick turned to the Belgian, but La Forge had anticipated the question.

"There will be no further investigation. This is unnatural, ungodly. It will benefit no one. She is *mort*."

As they left the morgue, he continued, "We checked the waterway thoroughly, but we have not recovered the infant's body." La Forge drew out a pipe and began to fill it with tobacco. He seemed to be weighing something in his mind.

"Chief Inspector," he pulled on the pipe, "we have interviewed many people. No one knew her. We do not even know her name. It was only when we found that 'thing' that the coroner examined the body a second time. It was then we learned that the victim had been pregnant at the time of the murder. The mutilation of the body disguised much, but the coroner was certain. Yet the placenta, he says, is not normal. How do we explain this?"

"Are you saying *that*"—Corrick gestured back to the mortuary—"is not connected with this case?"

"No, I'm afraid that undoubtedly it is. We do not find such things very often, you know."

Corrick sat in a deckchair as he recrossed the North Sea by boat, this time heading for Dover. Before he left, La Forge had advised him not to mention this trip to his "assistant."

"The less he knows the better" were La Forge's parting words. "Trust me, my friend; he is not what he seems."

Corrick considered the latest and most disturbing evidence. Could this new find be some sort of joke, a hoax on the part of the killer? Could it have been planted, or could the coroner be wrong? To find answers, he would have to get access to the other reported cases. That meant a trip to London—polluted, dirty London. At least his headaches seemed to have cleared up.

· *1910* ·

Rawlings sat in a booth at the back of the coffee shop just off Whitehall. He slid the envelope containing a crisp five-pound note across the table. The clerk drew out a small piece of folded paper and exchanged it for the money, his eyes darting left and right. Rawlings unfolded the note and checked it briefly. The clerk got up and left, sweat beading his brow beneath his scruffy bowler hat. They had not exchanged a single word.

Lady Jennifer was joined by her eighteen-year-old niece, Lady Amanda Brightmere, at the end of the week. Although the request by her aunt clashed with some of the most important events of the social season, Amanda knew that if her aunt said she needed her, there was a good reason.

Her aunt greeted her warmly, but Amanda could tell that something was horribly wrong. Jennifer explained about James's disappearance and that Sir Philip had so far managed to keep their trouble out of the newspapers. Amanda knew there was more going on than her aunt said.

They took to walking along the shoreline twice a day, whatever the weather. Amanda soon noticed that her aunt always walked the same stretch of beach. Was she looking for James? Was there something special about this place?

Rawlings had done his work well. Each page contained a short list of names, and each list was in a different handwriting.

Opening a desk drawer, Sir Philip took out a fifth page and an envelope. He passed the envelope to Rawlings and placed the new list with the others. "Now I need you to do one more task for me."

Sir Philip would never suggest meeting at his home unless it was extremely important. And that would mean a hefty fee. Rawlings smiled at the thought.

"Some years ago," Sir Phillip began, "I was a junior officer in the Excise Department, responsible for collecting taxes from overseas trade. An incident occurred which I'd like you to investigate."

Rawlings's interest was now more than financial. Sir Philip rarely mentioned anything in his past. Perhaps this "incident" would provide something of value for his own purposes, something that would let him retire at last.

Sir Philip handed him a larger envelope. "And if you wouldn't mind going out the way you came."

Rawlings stood up, tucking the envelope into his coat. Ascending the stairs to the third floor, he climbed into the roof space and passed along the adjoining terrace mansions before exiting via a side street.

Sir Philip looked through the lists. Each contained names of individuals working in various government departments, including Customs and Excise. He had compiled a separate list from his own department, the War Office. He was certain that the person he was seeking was someone with ambition, who would gravitate to these more influential departments.

He thought of the night when he and his wife had sat together deciphering the inscription.

Steady now your hand must act
And recall silence in your past

He'd now dispatched Rawlings on a mission that would address the silence in his own past, concerning the scandal that had resulted in his father's disappearance and that had also damaged his own career. It was an episode of his life that he had kept buried ever since. Now it had to be reexamined if it would help find James.

Your father's eyes you too may see
That which empire may not spy

Seek out the other in this pact
Who sifts for one in numbers vast

Lady Jennifer had made sense of the next lines, as far as anyone could. He and his father had shared a vision. They must look for another person who shared knowledge of the Sea Arch who might know of James's disappearance. And whoever that person was would be hard to find.

"Where would you hide but still have access to information?" Jennifer mused.

"When I want to get some work done, I go to the office and have my secretary tell everyone I'm out."

"Mmm, that would link with 'ministry' in the next line," Jennifer said.

And chase the wates in ministry
Or heralds forth a time to die

These final two lines had required more wordplay. Philip was reminded of his father. He had loved puzzles too. He had disappeared, fifteen years ago, without a trace. Now James was part of a puzzle, and it seemed his life depended on the outcome.

Jennifer had shaken him out of his thoughts by drawing out a traveling thesaurus. Together they listed reams and reams of words. Again it was his wife who made the connection—after twenty minutes of silent work, she presented him with two columns of words. Down one she had written every alternative for the word "chase." Down the second she had written every alternative for "waits" and "weights," since "wates" was medieval English and had fallen out of use years ago. She had seen the final lines as revealing a name, a very old name, or a very old individual.

So, with two long lists of words, they played at compiling a final list of all the names that could be made up with one word from each column. They narrowed the field by striking out any unusual name, since whoever they were looking for would be unlikely to draw attention to himself. On this last point Jennifer had also discounted the possibility of a woman. Although many women were employed in the ministries, none had significant roles with high-level access.

Now, with their final list of names and the department lists from Rawlings, Sir Philip searched each ministry for a match. His secretary had also "borrowed" certain employee files. With all these in hand, he began to study each candidate in fine detail.

The day after his visit with Sibelius, James sat with Lady Orlania in the rose garden enjoying the warm, sunny views and her company.

He and the dwarves had stayed with the wizard late into the night. Sibelius had given a rich and evocative history of Eldaterra, a world torn slowly apart by war. Yet now, as James sat and contemplated the peaceful parkland and gardens, he could hardly believe that anyone would wish to destroy such a beautiful place.

"I am grateful for your company," Lady Orlania said. "There are so few living in the Western Tower. Perhaps you can tell me something of your world, James. It must be very different."

For the first time James forgot the pangs of homesickness and enjoyed telling her of England and the world beyond. She was interested in everything. Tempus's earlier warning had been right, in a way. She did have a special sort of magic. Somehow being with Lady Orlania made everything seem better, calmer, more hopeful.

After a while the lady leaned forward, and taking his hand, asked, "Are there any questions you have for me, James?"

In truth there were many, but he felt flustered by her touch, and his cheeks burned.

"You wish to know more about Sibelius, and then, perhaps, myself," she answered for him.

He nodded slowly. She let go of his hand.

"Where does one start? There is his title—Principal Wizard of the Western Tower, Keeper of the Sword of Lind, and Master of the Shadows. And the fact that Sibelius has been a wizard for as long as I can recall, and I am ancient by your reckoning.

There are some who say he is the greatest wizard alive today, although there are many claims to that title. But Sibelius holds the Western Tower; it is only by his power that the lands hereabouts are kept safe. The war has sent hundreds of thousands of our people south to fight and there is but a smattering left to work the forests and tend the land. It is as if this war is gradually consuming us until there will be no one left to fight. Within the Western Tower there can be no more than three hundred, four hundred at most. If it should ever come to battle, we couldn't defend ourselves for long. Our wizard is our only defense for now."

She sighed. "And he is hard pressed, though you would not guess it by his manner. The demands of war draw ever more upon him, and the time he gives to watching our borders grows less."

She leaned forward and again placed her hand upon his. James's hand tingled. "It has fallen upon Sibelius to assist you in whatever you are here for. Had you entered our world by another portal, then it would have been a different wizard in a different tower with this responsibility. But it is fate that has brought you to Sibelius. Do not fail him . . . or yourself.

"As for me," she went on, "I am the daughter of Handrial, Once King of the Lauderley Elvenfolk, who fell in battle over five thousand years ago."

James was astonished. The Lady Orlania hardly looked more than a girl, and she did not look anything like the elves he had read about in fairy stories.

"Elves really exist?" he asked before he could stop himself.

She laughed. "Do I not sit before you? But I forget that in

your land these things are but myths and legend. The truth has been lost."

"I think that home would be a lot more interesting with elves and wizards and talking animals," James said.

"Though there are still elves in this world, we are far fewer than in days gone by. Many chose to pass beyond the realm of mortals millennia ago. The few that remain are scattered and divided. Some support the Guild and recognize the dangers of the enemy. But others have turned their backs and seek isolation." Her voice grew quiet. "And a few seek to reopen the route leading from this world to the *next*." James knew that she was not speaking about his world, but *another*. A feeling of fear came over him, and he asked no more questions on the matter.

Lady Orlania and James walked through the parkland until they came to a stockade and a gate. The gate swung silently open for them and they entered a farm enclosure. James could see all manner of well-tended animals, but no evidence of people.

"In this farm and many like it, we are growing crops to feed our armies in the south. But there is no one to watch over the place, only the animals."

He looked at her in surprise. "This is your work?"

"Yes, James, we all must help in whatever way we can."

He thought about his visit with Sibelius and wondered if she knew the details.

"Do these animals have any . . . magic?" he asked.

"No, they have long lost their magic and any other gifts. We accept that these animals remain to serve us. But though we are their masters, we must not mistreat or abuse them. Those few that still have the gift of speech must be very careful, for there are many who would harm them. Even in this world parlanimals are not safe."

Returning to the tower, she was about to bid him good night when she stopped and squeezed his hands once more.

"This world is in mortal danger, James. I feel it."

James wondered whether his earlier feeling was due to her own fear, that a boy from the New World might make the wrong choice in deciding the fate of Eldaterra.

~ 7 ~

The Warkrin

"Thank you for coming to see me again."

Sibelius stood at the top of the spiral staircase to greet him. This time James found himself in an open park, near a bandstand. A military band played as light streamed through the trees. King George V stood on the podium saluted by soldiers marching on parade. James's father stood close by. Flags waved, people cheered, and James felt the excitement. War! He came out of his dream to find Sibelius humming the tune.

"You were there too?" James asked.

"Occasionally I find it a pleasant distraction to look in on other's dreams, particularly if they are entertaining. As you've witnessed, this room is a dream generator. What you see is your subconscious, amplified in a way to appear real."

He gazed intently at James. "It also has another, more meaningful, purpose. Everyone produces a dream that reflects their inherent nature. For those who have fallen into the darkness, the dream generator is a very deadly weapon, for they are assailed by dreams as dark as the souls they possess. It is an ancient type of magic, rare nowadays."

"My dream was of war. What does that mean?"

"It could be a combination of many aspects of your world we don't yet understand, the influences of religion, science, and others. Sadly, we don't know enough to interpret them. Dreams are easy to observe, difficult to understand. But the music was good." He hummed again as he ushered the boy onward.

They ascended into the glass-domed observatory, where James was as enthralled as on his previous visit. He walked around the room, studying objects and reading the spines of books. Most of them were in languages made up of strange symbols and squiggles.

"We must talk more about the reasons for your being in Eldaterra," Sibelius said.

The wizard sat at the desk and James found a stool.

"When the wizards of old separated the worlds, they left doorways between, portals that were guarded and secret. The Sea Arch is one of them.

"The portals received powers greater than any single wizard would ever possess. They became like living creatures—almost, but not quite living—for it never shall be within our grasp to create true life other than as nature intended. The portals can show themselves or remain invisible as they choose, deciding who shall pass through and who shall not. They can also communicate messages—"

"Yes," James interrupted, and then felt his face flush. He stumbled on. "There was an inscription, but I didn't understand what it meant. It was poetry of sorts."

Sibelius nodded calmly. "I hope you will share this with me.

But I would need to give you a mild memory potion to restore the exact wording. We must know as much as we can to prepare for the fight ahead. And you should know that the enemy is led by the Warkrin. They are necromancers, beings cast down from the sky to make way for the stars, or so the story goes. We believe they possess many, if not all, of the powers of Creation. But, in truth, we have been able to uncover little about them.

"*'Where Death treads warily, so dwell the seven Warkrin.'*"

At Sibelius's words the brightness of the sun faded. "There is danger even in the name." He crossed to the windowed dome and gazed out.

"Last night I was in communication with a colleague in the south. We have captured a spy. He is being taken to the Tower of Cruxantire, some three hundred leagues to the south. Once there the wizard Ptarmagus and I will facilitate the prisoner's journey here. What we have learned so far is that this man is from your world."

The wizard held James in his gaze.

"This tells us two things. That the enemy has discovered the means of passing through the portals, something we have long feared. And that they would appear to be in alliance with someone from your world. From this we may conclude that your arrival is a counterbalance."

The wizard's eyes shone. "You are here to help the good!"

A broad smile lit James's face. "Well, I'm glad to hear that news."

"It also means that the enemy needs to stop you."

James's smile faded as he felt the weight of fear return.

"The Guild will do all we can to protect you, and we are not without considerable powers. But first you must decide."

"Decide?"

"Whether you wish to help us."

"I . . . But how?"

"There are many paths to choose from, and with each, new choices open before you." The wizard looked wistful. "That is one of the freedoms of your world that you bring with you into this one. Our lives are already written, our fate and destiny sealed. Yours is written as you live it. But our way is not without benefits too. By studying our past we may learn something of the future, glimpses of it, and I see hope where others may not. You are that hope, James."

"Can you influence my fate, Sibelius?"

"I can try to influence your choices. But any influence I have over you is already ordained. You always have the power to choose."

"So I choose my destiny?"

"Fate and destiny are two separate things. You may choose your fate, but you fulfill your destiny, whatever it may be. Let us leave your decision till later." The wizard rose from the chair.

"Now, there is work to be done."

Half an hour later, after James had swallowed a small vial of silver memory tonic, the two of them were poring over the inscription:

The roaring seas are silent now
And secrets are themselves once more

Complete the earth and fill the void
To mark the time when earth was whole
Locked are these gates to keep the vow
To end a world on barren shore
Protect a place to be destroyed
By man's belief, a lack of soul

Yet stand a vigil and wait a time
When stranger from the stranger land
Before the gates, behind the sun
Gives passage to the unsouled son
To pass to wild and pass to grime
The places split by sea and sand
Where one is slaved beneath the gun
The other stalked, evil begun

"It tells us little," Sibelius said with disappointment. James agreed. The words described everything he'd learned since entering Eldaterra.

"There is something else I need you to remember. Bartholomew told me of your encounter with the Drezghul. He said something strange happened between you and the creature. Can you tell me more?"

James thought for a bit.

"It looked at me, and it was like I was in a dream. There were three princes. . . . Each had a large hole in his chest. There was also a boy in the shadows, watching as hundreds of faceless people walked by, and there was fire, lots of it. . . . When the Drezghul looked at me, it felt like looking into a very deep hole. Then I thought it said something to me, but I don't remember . . . even with the tonic I can't. . . ." His voice froze in panic.

"James, you have already faced what few could. The Drezghul is one of the undead, a *mortalator*. Until now they were only rumored to exist; yours is the first sighting. They have been raised up by the Warkrin's blackest necromancy to be their loyal servants. But you have shown us there is indeed hope." The old man smiled at James.

"I will consider your dream. We may never know its meaning, but let us wait and see. Now, I have other business to attend to. Please return at sunset when we must decide a course of action."

They sat on their haunches beneath the low-hanging branches deep in a stand of pine trees. All were exhausted from a hard night's marching. The light was strengthening from the east. They would make no more progress today, not until the sun sank beneath the horizon again.

The leader swiveled on his flat, splayed feet and looked at the company. They numbered perhaps forty. Each handpicked; the fittest, most aggressive, and most skilled fighters in all the army. They wore the armor of their kind, heavy leather jerkins bound with plates of a fibrous material pummeled into a smooth hard shell and attached to a coat of coarse chain mail sewn on to the jerkin. They had helms of black iron with lethal spike and blade embellishments. Each carried a short halberd with a cruel sicklelike cutter and reverse spike. They were experts of war. They were *olorcs*, warrior servants of the Warkrin.

"We rest here till dusk. Get your heads down and no talking. The enemy will be watching for us."

The troop roused themselves in the dying light of day, anticipating another night of hard marching. The last of their provisions of dried flesh were stowed away and their drinking skins slung on their backs. The leader, Kagaminoc, berated one of their number for tardiness. "Get your pockmarked backside moving or I'll kick it into your gob," he snarled.

Kagaminoc was a large, powerfully built olorc who had risen in rank by mercilessly killing off all would-be rivals. Only the strongest, most evil, and most cunning could command, and there was none more so than he.

The olorcs had come from the empty lands far to the south. They lived in a place where the sun beat down and dried the ground until it cracked and screamed, where the land turned to dust and sand, and the only thing that flowed was a thick, black ooze from deep within the earth. The olorcs made their lairs underground, digging deep in search of the ooze that nurtured and fed them above all else. It filled their bellies when there was no flesh to be had. They called it shol.

Kagaminoc swung a halberd over his shoulder and the troop set off in single file at a pace that would have quickly exhausted a human. As they left the temporary camp, two stayed on briefly to destroy any evidence of their stay.

The troop headed due north, toward the Forest of Lauderley.

In the tower chamber Sibelius held a long, worn staff of ebony in his outstretched hand facing southeast, in the direction of Cruxantire, with the sun almost behind him. His head was lowered as he spoke an incantation of summoning. Across the great distance the wizard of the Tower of Cruxantire repeated the same words, and together they formed an unseen bridge. With this bridge established, the wizards anchored it to a fontlike stone structure called a vallmaria, which would hold the spell until it was either released or broken.

Sibelius stepped back and waited. At the other end of the bridge, the wizard Ptarmagus would be preparing to send the prisoner, rendered unconscious for the journey.

In only a few short minutes, the crumpled figure lay on the stone floor of the Western Tower. Sibelius sent silent thanks to his friend and broke the spell.

It was a man in dirty, worn clothes. He looked like a corpse. Sibelius prodded the inert body with his ebony staff and the man, startled out of his condition, sat up and looked around.

"Where am I?" he cried in a thin voice. He spoke in German.

"You are here."

"Ach, that is worthless information." He got to his feet and glanced about. Seeing they were alone, the prisoner straightened his disheveled clothes and addressed Sibelius.

"Old man, tell me where I am."

"I think it best if I ask the questions."

The prisoner said nothing.

"What is your name?"

Silence.

"You are already familiar with the means by which we can extract information." Sibelius watched the man flinch at these words. "Although I dislike the methods, I am very effective at interrogation."

The prisoner blurted out a hasty reply in German. "My name is Otto Freislung."

"You are Prussian?"

"*Nein*. I am Swiss, but my family is originally from East Prussia."

The wizard nodded, picturing in his mind a map of the New World. It would place him far to the south, corresponding to enemy-held territory in Eldaterra. An image of the two worlds superimposed on each other gave clues to where the enemy had breached the portals.

"And how did you get here?"

After a moment of hesitation, Freislung replied.

"I came through a tunnel in the alpine district of Bern Oberland, near the base of the Wildstrubel Mountain."

Sibelius knew little of this region. "Who are you working for?"

Freislung shook his head.

"Come now, we will discover everything."

Freislung swallowed. "They will kill me if I tell you anything. . . ."

"And they will kill you even if you don't." Sibelius could see the man was near the breaking point. Then Freislung's will suddenly failed him, as if a blow had flattened his defenses. Stifling sobs of despair he pleaded, "You must help me. I can never go back!"

Gently Sibelius promised to help him, but added a warning, "Turn again to the darkness and you will be lost forever."

When James met the wizard at sunset, Sibelius related some of what the prisoner had recounted:

"I have worked all my life at the Kulbinz Bank in Zurich, counting their money and stamping bits of paper with their official seals, making my employers rich while I remained poor.

"Then one day I was plucked from obscurity and escorted to the boardroom, where I was introduced to a client named Herr Dorpmuller. He described himself as representing a group of individuals working for a better world. He had learned of me through a recommendation and requested to interview me. Naturally the directors obliged. Before the interview they made it abundantly clear that I was to agree to any request. And so I was taken on as an employee of Herr Dorpmuller.

"For my first assignment I was ordered to meet him at his mansion in Bern. When I arrived there was a dinner party in progress. The butler took me to an alcove off the main entrance hall and went to locate Herr Dorpmuller. I heard two people walk down the main stairs. One of the voices I recognized as that of my employer. I didn't recognize the other.

"Herr Dorpmuller said, 'He is waiting for me in my study, Frau Colbetz. Tomorrow I am traveling to China. Should I instruct him to contact you?' The woman replied in the negative, and I received the impression she did not want me to know of her involvement and that Dorpmuller acted as a go-between and nothing more.

"After that the butler returned, spoke with Dorpmuller, and then took me to the study. Presently Herr Dorpmuller came in. I was given a small portfolio and a set of instructions. I don't think I was meant to have overheard the conversation. But Dorpmuller looked nervous, as if he suspected I had.

"I was more than compliant since I was now on a salary five times greater than I'd earned at the bank. I was also able to enjoy more leisure time to pursue my hobby of taxidermy.

"As per my instructions I traveled into the mountains to a village called Lenk. There I proceeded up the southern valley that led to the lower part of Wildstrubel.

"I was surprised to find a gate and fence at the far end of the valley. With a key Herr Dorpmuller had given me, I gained entry. Farther up the mountain there was a tunnel entrance. I walked into the tunnel as instructed. After that I found myself in some other place, which I thought must be on the other side of the mountain.

"There I came upon strange, repulsive creatures. They fell upon me and put me in chains. Held prisoner and tortured by these horrific beings, I believed I had stumbled upon a network of anarchists preparing to overthrow the Swiss government.

"Once they had had their fill of kicking and beating me, they examined the papers I was carrying. Eventually I was hauled before their leader, General Balerust, handed a letter, and told to deliver the message to my master."

Thus Freislung completed his first trip to and from Eldaterra. He returned twice more in the course of three years, each time subjected to inhumane treatment but rewarded with increasing quantities of money in Bern.

On his fourth and final trip, there was no return message. He was thrown out and left to wander in the desolate lands. Unable to find the tunnel, he stumbled about, crazed and starving, until captured in the marshes of Turmalor by soldiers of the Guild.

"Why did the enemy just abandon him?" James asked the wizard.

"His usefulness had come to an end. That he was not killed was an unusual act of mercy. . . . Now we know the enemy has been in communication with the New World for the past three years, at least. Maybe other couriers have preceded Freislung. Maybe he is simply the first to be released rather than executed. . . ."

"Sibelius, why did they choose this man?"

"It appears that Frau Colbetz is the one who first knew of the Old World and recruited Herr Dorpmuller and then Freislung. As for Freislung, he is unimportant in your world, but this woman was able to see his potential for evil." Sibelius tapped his lip with his forefinger as he contemplated this point. "I shall investigate, but in the meantime we must assume that Frau Colbetz is the prime concern."

Lady Orlania entered the room, looking worried. The wizard and James rose to greet her.

"I am sorry to intrude." She turned to Sibelius. "The forest is whispering. The trees speak of an enemy that has entered our domain from the south."

She looked at James, and Sibelius nodded for her to continue.

"It is a small force of olorcs that entered yesterday soon after sunset. I fear the message has waited until this morning when I was able to visit the parkland."

"What does this mean?" asked James.

Sibelius turned to him. "The Warkrin are searching for you. They have sent a force of fierce warriors to capture or kill you, the latter most likely. Now we know their plans reach across the portals—it is certain they will not let you cross back.

"You must choose now." James felt the weight of the wizard's words upon him. "Will you accept a fate from this world and embark upon an undertaking for which you have been chosen? Or do you wish to return to your own world and leave us to ours?" The wizard and Lady Orlania watched James closely.

"But I can't escape the Warkrins' plans no matter which world I'm in?"

"That is true. But you can raise your hand against the enemy, or stand aside and let them do as they will."

"But you could make the choice for me," James pleaded. The wizard shook his head.

"No, James. Only you can change the fate of our world."

James thought of the Bandamire brothers and their recent battles. He remembered the terror and the excitement of victory. He had felt more alive than at any other moment in his life. His loyal friends, and now the wizard, and Lady Orlania, they had all become so important to him.

"I want to help."

Kagaminoc halted the troop and motioned to an olorc who was a *sensii*, able to read and interpret their surroundings through the ground, a very rare and useful skill. The olorc placed his face to the earth. His large, squashed nose with its excessive wrinkles of skin now became a tool. He breathed deeply, taking in vast quantities of dust and fetid air from the soil. The sensii exhaled slowly and repeated this. Then sitting up on his haunches, his hands gesticulating in numerous directions, he reported to Kagaminoc in the crude language of the olorc.

The leader barked out orders, splitting the raiding party into two groups. One was under the command of Kreesang, a suitably unimaginative and ruthless deputy. Kreesang would cross into the next valley and close on the enemy fortification, set up the transmitter device, and protect it until its task was complete. Kagaminoc would lead the other group north to their second objective.

Noiselessly, the troop parted.

High up in the tower, the final arrangements for James's departure were set.

"I don't know what awaits you on the other side of the portal, but I believe that it is where you must go. You must find Frau Colbetz."

James nodded slowly, and Sibelius continued. "The enemy

has not attempted to enter this forest for many years. You must leave at once, and I am sending the brothers back through with you. Troops will try to intercept the enemy, but I must remain here to guard the tower.

"Understand, James, this is the last opportunity the enemy has to seal your fate in this world, and they will try with all their might to kill you before you reach the Sea Arch. My network of spies, my Shadows, inform me that the Warkrin are up to something."

James nodded again. He did not trust himself to speak, afraid he might change his decision.

"A portal cannot let living magic pass through. That is why the enemy needed Freislung. We can expect Frau Colbetz is a witch, or worse." The wizard studied James's face. "But do not be overly alarmed. In your world magic is scarce and long diminished. You recall stories of Merlin? He was in fact a minor wizard who at the time of division elected to pass through to the New World where there are only sorcerers of limited powers, the remnants of the past. That much we know."

Sibelius held out a small bundle. "Take this. It will be useful to you. Inside are two items. One is an Antargo stone for seeing the enemy, and the other is a pocket edition of *Talmaride's Answers to Questions*. You will find them both helpful."

Sibelius guided the boy to the top of the stairs. "I think we shall take the fast route."

With that, the whole spiral staircase began to corkscrew, whisking them downward to where the cavalry and soldiers were marshaling.

"Make haste, make haste!" Solomon cried when he saw them

arrive. In their four days at the Western Tower, his shoulder had completely healed, and he and his brother were eager to depart on another adventure.

The inner courtyard was full of bustle. A troop of horsemen were saddling up, their lances with the white, gold, and red colors of the Western Tower pointing to the vaulted roof. A group of elves, among the few that were allied to the Guild, had already left to track and shadow the enemy. James saw Bartholomew among the throng, awaiting assistance to climb onto the back of his mount.

The captain of the guard, a striking figure with a jet-black mustache, clad in shining chain-mail shirt and uniform, caught sight of Sibelius and cried out: "Company, present arms!" The men came to attention.

Sibelius waved his hand above his head. "Good people, brave soldiers. The hour of battle draws near. Though we are far distant from the war in the south, the enemy seeks this boy." James felt himself pulled to the wizard's side.

"He has placed his life in our hands and we will not fail him, as he will not fail Eldaterra." Sibelius's voice thundered into the chamber, and the people of the Western Tower responded as one.

"We may not meet for a while, James," the wizard said through the cheering. "But we will meet again."

"The tower!"

The olorc gestured toward the stone edifice. Kreesang

struck the back of the creature's head with a sharp crack of his halberd. "Fool! As if I don't know where the tower is. Don't think, or I'll beat your snot-brain until it pours out your ears." Kreesang was on edge. He did not like sneaking around on secret missions.

Give me a massacre any day, he thought. None of this skulking and tiptoeing in the shadows.

He turned to the olorc that was carrying the transmitter device. "Place it in the open ground. Set it firmly upright and away from trees or overhanging branches, or it will be the end of us all," he snarled. "The rest of you, form a defensive ring."

The transmitter was made of heavy iron almost three yards in height with a spike driving into the earth. A large copper dome was attached at the top by alchemical magic. Around the dome ran a crown of short copper spikes. Two olorcs were ordered to stand guard over it.

In a corner of the room where he was being kept, Freislung hugged his knees to his chest and slowly rocked, his eyes squeezed shut. His nerves had got the better of him since he had been left alone.

"I wish I was back home. I wish I'd never got into any of this," he said in a wretched voice.

Freislung didn't realize these thoughts were keeping him alive. As he sat there with his regrets, he held the darkness at bay. Eventually, however, thoughts of a different nature returned. He wished himself at home, not to forget or to make amends. Rather, to escape back to his own vices.

"I'll quit my job and get on with my hobbies." He could settle somewhere quiet, somewhere where he could go about his nasty habits: the slaughter and dissection of animals; stuffing and mounting of creatures. He found them irresistible. Yes, he would go back to being himself.

Despite Sibelius's warning, Freislung allowed darkness to bleed back into his heart. And it became like a conducting rod.

Far to the south black clouds boiled in the sky. The volcano Vomigragna spewed a giant mushroom of filth, heavy and laden with choking poison, into the eye of the storm. Deep within the roiling banks of darkness, a spell was shaped and cast. It rippled and spun within the eye, gaining power and intensity before it cannoned outward.

It took form as a lightning bolt, stabbing forward with blinding energy to connect the first transmitter. Instantly the bolt arced onward to the next transmitter on the distant horizon, and then the next, and the next, all placed by the olorcs as they marched northward.

Freislung stood and crossed to the window. *Something was calling to him, something. . . .*

A flash of energy blazed in the clearing and then it was gone. When their light-blindness faded, the olorcs could see the remains of their companions who had been standing guard over the transmitter. They were nothing more than black, frizzled piles of dust and twisted armor.

The bolt of lightning sheared through the atmosphere, crackling with surplus energy, searching with unimaginable speed for the point of grounding. Striking through the window and blasting into Freislung's face, it catapulted him across the room. At the same time his head and upper body exploded in a spray of flaming crimson.

The tower was rocked to its foundations. The courtyard was in turmoil; men and women shouting and screaming, horses whinnying, riders struggling to calm their mounts.

Sibelius shouted above the clamor. "They have struck at the traitor. They have murdered their own." The wizard waved his ebony staff above his head. "Be gone," he cried. "Ride out and find the enemy. Go!" He turned to James. "Can you ride?"

"Yes, sir."

"Then up on your mount, quickly. I fear the enemy is already at hand." He helped James with his stirrup and then reached up and clasped his arm. "Remember to hold true to that which you believe in, and you will not go wrong. Now be off!"

And with that the gates swung open and the cavalry thundered out, streaming away to the south. James, the two dwarves, and an escort of lancers headed off to the west with Tempus running behind.

～ 8 ～

A SURPRISE IN THE DARK

· *1895* ·

Upon his return from Zeebrugge, Corrick headed for Scotland Yard, where he made inquiries about the other cases that Harrington had mentioned. After some delay, the clerk returned with a worn manila folder with METROPOLITAN POLICE printed in large black capitals across the front.

The folder was empty. Corrick studied the scribbled notes on the exterior, recording details of each file's movements and usage. He could make out the words *Essex murder—file never arrived.* An "Officer D. C. Pallbrook" had last accessed the folder, and it was he, Corrick assumed, who had forgotten to return the contents.

"Look here," Corrick pointed out.

The clerk feigned surprise.

"I'll make a note of this immediately, sir, and we'll chase up the culprit. What is the world coming to? Now, if I could have your details again for the records."

Corrick leaned over the desk and brought his face close.

"I don't think you need to record my details. I didn't, as it happens, get to see anything." He brandished the empty file below the clerk's nose. "Let's just concentrate on finding this paperwork."

The clerk gulped down his sudden nerves. "Yes, sir. I shall see to it at once."

Leaving the Yard, Corrick was oblivious to the light rain beginning to fall. Something particular was bothering him. The note said Essex. . . . What did that mean? Burnham wasn't in Essex. . . . And then it struck him.

Half an hour later he stood outside the premises of Holbeck & Newton, "Cartographers to the Empire." Corrick entered the premises and an elderly gentleman approached. Corrick said he was trying to locate Burnham.

"Would that be Burnham on its own or with an addendum?" inquired the shop assistant.

"I'm not too sure. What are the options?"

"Well, there's Burnham in Buckinghamshire, of course. And then there's Burnham Deepdale in Norfolk, Burnham Green in Hertfordshire, Burnham Market, Burnham Overy and Burnham Overy Staithe in Norfolk." He counted them off on his fingers as he recalled them to mind. "And then there's Burnham-on-Sea in Somerset and . . . oh, I forgot, Burnham Thorpe, that's in Norfolk as well. And there's one more. . . ." He squinted at the electric lightbulb and clenched his hands together in professional anguish as he struggled to complete his mental map.

"Ah, yes. Burnham-on-Crouch, in Essex!" the assistant

declared. He looked back at his customer, but Corrick had already gone.

That afternoon Corrick caught the train to Maldon, the nearest town of any size to the village of Burnham-on-Crouch, which lay on the north bank of the River Crouch. It was likely that any investigation would be staged from here. Apart from a traction engine clanking from one farm to the next, the countryside was empty.

This stretch of the Essex coast was a frequent haunt of smugglers trading across the channel, and the Maldon police station held jurisdiction over most of it.

It took only a moment for the duty sergeant to locate the case file, which consisted of nothing more than a bundle of unsorted papers tied up in string. But they were not lost. Corrick asked why it had not been sent to Scotland Yard. The answer was refreshingly straightforward.

"Our governor came down here for a quieter life. He knows what they're like in London. Send them something and that's the last you'll see of it."

Corrick laughed with him. "If I promise not to leave the premises, may I read it?"

"I think we could allow that, sir." The sergeant smiled. "Would you like a cup of tea?"

· 1910 ·

Sir Philip had reviewed the employment records of every name he and Rawlings had gathered and searched for the names assembled by Lady Jennifer from the last riddle of the inscription: *And chase the wates in ministry*.

Chase = harry
    hunt
    track
    go after
    hound
wate = weight (?) ounce
    pound
    hundredweight
    ton
    deadweight

The employment records were all pretty bland and revealed little. Except for one. The one whose name fit the riddle best. *Harrington*.

Harrington had enjoyed a long career in various departments. What singled him out was that he had the hallmarks of outstanding ability and yet his career was too uniform, too dull. Sir Philip spotted a potential mole. He was sure Harrington was working for his own agenda, or someone else's.

He stood and crossed over to the tall windows. His intuition told him they had found their man. But would Harrington lead them to James? And where was their son? Was he all right?

He called his private secretary in the next room to arrange a meeting with Harrington's boss, the foreign secretary, Lord Grey. He would have to move very carefully but quickly. He could feel somehow that time was getting short for James.

It took a little over an hour for the Guild's cavalry troop to run down the band of olorcs that had placed the transmitter.

They struck hard and fast, charging down the enemy, lances finding olorc flesh.

Kreesang watched helplessly as all around him his command disintegrated under the onslaught. Half his force were dead before the battle had begun! He gave a roar and raced into the fray, bellowing at the survivors to regroup. Olorcs leaped up and sprinted back to join him. Together they formed a new defensive line, halberds at the ready. When a horseman came within striking distance, the olorcs split and gutted the charger in seconds. But outnumbered as they were, they stood no chance.

"Fall back to the treeline!" Kreesang yelled. The half dozen olorcs with him kept up a fighting retreat, warding off riders with pikes and halberds. In the distance two isolated olorcs fell to the lancers, who then turned to pursue Kreesang's dwindling troop. One rider came too close—in an instant the horse's head was lopped off and his rider cut out of his saddle. Infuriated, the lancers charged.

"Into the trees. We have served our masters. Scatter!" Kreesang screamed, and promptly turned and ran.

His warriors were slower to respond. One or two followed their leader, but he had a good head start. They ran through the woods as fast as their fear could carry them. Behind them, hooves grew louder. The lancers were gaining.

❖　❖　❖

Kreesang fell to the ground, his chest heaving as he struggled to catch his breath. He rolled under a thorn bush. His armor and tough hide were impervious to the long thorns. He had run for three straight leagues. The sounds of the enemy and dying olorcs were far behind. He crawled farther into the bush, pulled his helmet off, and listened. Jamming his face into the ground, he attempted to mimic the expert sensii with his own basic skills, drawing in odors from the earth to interpret them. There were no horses or men nearby, only the scent of dead olorc, and that at least half a league back. No, it smelled clear. Except for a trace of something, too remote to discern. He had smelled it before . . . where? What was it? He rolled over on his back to rest and think. His eyes adjusted to the light and shadow of greenery above him. As his brain strove to distinguish the different sensory information, an image overhead swam into focus. It wasn't a branch. It was a longbow. Kreesang finally identified the smell as two arrows slammed into his chest. An elf!

James's group had been riding steadily for six hours, stopping only to lead the horses over the steep Col. From there they'd ridden hard to make it to the upper valley lodge.

The dwarves' front door was smashed from its hinges and the mantraps sprung. Oily blood trailed along the path and off into the trees. Solomon dismounted and cautiously entered the lodge. He called out the all clear and emerged carrying a bloodied olorc foot in each hand while kicking a third before him.

"Clumsy creatures," he said, and threw the two appendages

over the wall. A well-aimed kick carried the third in the same direction.

"So we know there were at least two of them. You got two left feet and one right," joked Bartholomew.

"As like as not they've been killed by their own kind. That's the way of these vermin. They'll not be far off," the captain of the guard declared. James noticed him for the first time since their mad gallop from the tower. He could see now the captain was older than he'd thought, with a weather-beaten face that marked him as a veteran. James felt reassured by his bold confidence.

Solomon rubbed his saddle-sore backside before using the low wall as a mounting block to scramble back onto his pony.

"Our orders are to get the boy to the Sea Arch. We'll light our torches at dusk. Move off," the captain ordered.

They had barely gone a hundred yards when they were set upon. The first of the lancers had just trotted through a narrowing of the path when a halberd lunged from behind a tree, gashing the flank of the mare. The rider tumbled to the ground and the horse skittered and sank to its knees, neighing in fright. The next rider immediately kicked on to meet the threat, dropping his lance tip. The lance caught the olorc as it stumbled from behind the tree, its progress impeded by the lack of a foot. The point took the olorc in the shoulder and pinned it to a trunk. As it screamed and lashed out with its weapon, the olorc was finished off by a second lance.

The horse was lost, and so the lancer doubled up with James, the lightest rider of the party.

They rode on, more vigilant than ever. Solomon spurred ahead and caught up with the captain.

"They didn't kill their wounded." Solomon lowered his voice. "That can mean only one thing. They intend to use every means at their disposal to kill the boy."

"And that makes them all the more dangerous," said the captain. "They'll use their wounded to delay us while the rest prepare an ambush."

"The other wounded are probably just around the next corner," Solomon warned.

"Yes, I've sent two riders ahead to flush them out. They will not catch us unawares a second time. I thank you and your brother. They would have planned an ambush for us at the lodge if your traps hadn't ended that plan. Take my hand in friendship. I am Dolmir, of the city of Narima."

"Well met, friend," the dwarf replied, clasping his hand.

· 1895 ·

The last train to London had left Maldon hours ago, so Corrick was obliged to book into a hotel for the night. The next morning, as the carriage swayed from side to side and smoke from the cheap coal passed down the length of the train, filling compartments and eyes, Corrick mulled over what he had learned.

Firstly he had tracked down the Burnham case to the proper location. He was able now to see that all the murders had occurred within close proximity to the coast.

Next he'd learned the Burnham victim was found in similar circumstances to the others. No newborn infant or fetus was mentioned in the report. But no autopsy had been carried out since the deceased was of questionable moral character. Instead the mortician had been paid to conduct an appraisal of the body rather than enlisting a forensic expert. Yesterday Corrick had interviewed the mortician.

He'd walked to the funeral parlor and stood outside the front window, the company name—Grimend—painted in gold on the glass. Why was it they always had appropriate names? He pushed open the door. A bell rang, and a somber man in black glided between the heavy black velvet curtains.

"May I help you, sir?"

"Perhaps one day. But for the moment I am here to interview Mr. Grimend about a recent corpse."

"Deceased."

"Yes, the body was dead," Corrick said dryly.

"No, sir, we refer to each customer of ours as the deceased. It conveys more respect, in keeping with the Alun Grimend and Family tradition." And with that the funereal man glided back behind the curtains. Corrick studied the craftsmanship on a display coffin sporting rather fine interior coachwork.

"Good day to you, sir." A deep voice spoke from behind the coffin lid. Mr. Alun Grimend stepped around the display and made a slow bow.

"I am Chief Inspector Corrick. I'd like to ask you some questions concerning the mortician's report you provided for a young woman murdered last month."

Grimend was a short man with a face like wax. His mouth seemed disinclined to move and his eyes were half open, or perhaps half closed. It was, Corrick observed, like speaking with the dead.

"Ah, yes. I recall the work, of course. No one takes greater care of the deceased than Alun Grimend and Family." He encompassed the room with his arms. After a respectful silence, the funeral director continued, "The young lady died from a number of causes, including massive hemorrhaging of the lower body organs."

The science of examining dead bodies was quite a recent advance. But somehow the mortician's description sounded vague.

"Your report did not go into great detail."

"Chief Inspector, in my experience the average policeman is incapable of distinguishing a retina from a rectum. Furthermore, the reports I provide reflect my modest fee. Needless to say," he went on, "we provide our services for the benefit of the deceased, not the living."

"Mr. Grimend, can you recall any more detail? This is most important."

"Not for us," he replied. But he listed some other observations before adding, "It was a sad end. We conducted the funeral. She was never identified by the police and she went into the ground without a single mourner present. And it was a double tragedy."

"What do you mean?"

"The woman was gravid."

"Meaning?"

"She was with child. Full term. The evidence was fairly obliterated by the attack, but without question she was pregnant at the time of the murder."

· 1910 ·

The horses stood blowing noisily, their flanks lathered with sweat. They had ridden hard since the last footless olorc had been beaten from the bushes and put to death.

Pine trees hemmed their troop in ever closer. Captain Dolmir called a halt and they lit torches, the new moon thin and veiled. Tempus, his tongue lolling from the side of his mouth, kept silent as he caught up with them.

"By night the enemy has the advantage," Dolmir told his lancers, many of whom were new recruits. "Their eyes are suited to the dark, for they live mainly underground. With torches we will see what assails us, but the light also marks us out. Do not separate." Dolmir then turned to Solomon. "How far now, Solomon Bandamire?"

"The Sea Arch is no more than three furlongs up this trail." Dolmir rubbed his stubbled chin. The last stretch would be the killing ground. He needed a plan.

"Bartholomew, you and James have half an hour to make your way around to the north," he said. "I'll provide a couple of riders as escort, but stealth will be your best protection. After that I will lead the remainder of the troop forward. Once we engage the enemy, we'll make a slow fighting withdrawal and act as the decoy. The olorcs will be intent on killing the boy, so if they see him they'll follow in pursuit. Solomon will act as the boy's double. In the dark they are unlikely to spot the difference. Let's pray this deception works, for there is little else we can do."

Half an hour later the main body of riders set off at a steady walk up the trail. Dolmir ordered the troop to trot, and then to canter. With luck, the enemy would concentrate their forces for the ambush and leave their flanks unguarded.

Farther up the valley James could hear the troop bravely

riding the last furlong to the Sea Arch as, no doubt, could the enemy.

"Wait until they're close, real close," commanded Kagaminoc in a low growl that carried to every olorc. They could hear the riders from the other side of the valley. This was going to be a beautiful slaughter.

"The stupid humans are carrying torches. Must be scared of shadows, especially if the wounded did a good job farther back there. Pity to lose them, but a footless olorc is a near useless olorc." At least he had given them the chance to taste blood one last time, and not their own. He would have sooner split their gizzards for stepping in the traps in the first place, but he needed to buy time. Now the setup was perfect.

Kagaminoc checked to left and right. The line was bunching a bit. He knew it was nerves; excitement, really. They could see the riders coming up the hill now. There would be plenty of human and horsemeat for dinner.

"You!" He elbowed the olorc next to him. "What did I tell you about bunching? Now get back and guard the portal. Make sure no one reaches it."

The olorc began to protest, not wanting to miss the ambush. Kagaminoc bashed its face with his fist. "Get going," he snarled. The olorc, growling in pain and anger, slunk away into the dark.

A cry went up as the enemy rushed the horsemen in the darkness. Horses whinnied in fright, men called out, and metal crashed. The captain barked orders above the yells of the attacking olorcs. Torches flared and flailed, one falling to the ground, then another.

The commotion began its slow retreat back down the valley as Dolmir had planned, the lancers maintaining contact with the enemy to encourage pursuit.

"An olorc with his blood up can be trusted to run down the length of a lance," Dolmir had promised his men.

As the noise of battle faded, Tempus led the other group of riders through the trees toward the dark outline of the Sea Arch.

The dog gave a howl and leaped at a shadowy figure. The olorc whirled around and aimed a clawed foot, catching Tempus in the side and knocking him away. Then the creature turned and faced the two lancers on horseback carrying James and Bartholomew. The olorc slashed at a horse with its halberd, and the beast went down, tumbling the lancer and Bartholomew over its bowed head. The olorc had reversed the sweep of the weapon to bring it down on the prostrate dwarf when a lance caught the creature in the throat and tore its head from the still standing body.

"Bartholomew, are you all right?" James called, struggling to retrieve the lance from the dead olorc. Bartholomew moaned, stunned by the fall. Ahead, no more than twenty yards, James could see the gray outline of the arch against the starlit sky.

He slipped off the horse, calling back to his rider, "Don't worry. I'll get Bartholomew and we'll head for the Sea Arch."

In the darkness the olorcs were whooping and hollering as they fought with the cavalry. Despite the clamor of combat, Kagaminoc heard the brief fight behind, near the portal. Why were the horsemen not disengaging and retreating quickly, or driving through to reach the portal? Realization dawned on his ugly features. *He'd been fooled!* The horsemen to his front were merely a diversion, and he had fallen for it. For a second he lost control, slashing at everything that moved. "Back! Back!" he screamed, but his orders went unheeded in the frenzy. He grabbed the nearest olorc, hit it squarely in the face to break the bloodlust that ran through its veins, and screamed, "We must secure the arch! The enemy is at the portal!"

The dazed olorc nodded understanding, and the two of them ran back at full pelt. In the shadowy distance Kagaminoc could see two figures on the ground and a third in the saddle. He leaped forward, but his accomplice let out a battle cry and gave away the advantage of surprise. Two lances cut the olorc down. Kagaminoc immediately avenged his fallen comrade with a swift chop that beheaded one of the lancers. The second, still in the saddle, spun his horse around and drove it forward to shield the boy. Kagaminoc brought his halberd up and the horse died on its feet. The reverse sweep clove the rider from his saddle before the horse had fallen.

Kagaminoc rounded on James as he kneeled over the dwarf. James's hand scrambled to draw the dagger from its sheath. He was too slow. He saw the cruel blade swing up high over the olorc's head, the edge already notched and blunted from recent use.

Suddenly the darkness behind the olorc exploded, and his halberd went spinning into the black night. An enormous clawed hand raked the side of Kagaminoc's head, tearing off his helmet and an ear. The olorc let out a spine-wrenching shriek cut short as its head disappeared into a pair of enormous jaws.

James was numb with shock. "Get up!" a voice called. Tempus was licking his cheek. "The arch, make for the arch. Come on." Tempus grabbed James's sleeve in his teeth and began pulling, but James could not move.

"Please, James, please. They're coming back." James staggered to his feet and stumbled forward. Behind them the noise of the olorcs was growing louder. Tempus kept pulling at him, but James knew he was not going to make it.

All at once an enormous arm swept around and lifted him off the ground. The angry howling of the olorcs came in waves. He was being carried. The enemy was right behind. The distance closed, and then they were through.

~ 9 ~

FOOTPRINTS AND CLAW PRINTS

James felt the slap of wet sand on the side of his face as he dropped to the ground. His ears rang with the roar of the surf. He rolled over, pushing an arm under to lever himself up. Behind him loomed the dark mass of the Sea Arch, the gates chained shut.

He sat up, brushing sand from his face and arms. A shadowed mound sat a short way off. *Thank goodness Bartholomew is here*, he thought.

Getting to his feet, he stumbled forward, spotting Tempus sitting nearby.

He collapsed next to the hound, wrapping an arm about the dog's neck, and turned to thank Bartholomew for rescuing him. But it was not the dwarf.

"You've decided you can walk after all," said the black bear.

James could only gasp.

Tempus spoke. "This is Baranor. He's the one who rescued you, again."

The bear looked down his long snout at the boy. He had

brown, intelligent eyes and even sitting was as tall as James.

"So this"—he leaned closer to James—"was what all the fuss and bother was about." Rows of sharp, yellowing teeth flashed in the dark.

James wanted to back up but was afraid to offend the bear. "How many others came through, um, Mr. Baranor . . . sir?"

The bear stared at him and then burst into a low rumble of a laugh that made his fur shake. "Others? There were no others, only the foul-tasting creatures—what do you call them? Olorcs?—but none of them made it through the gates. And you very nearly didn't either. If I hadn't been within a bear leap of you, there'd be no cheer in Sibelius's cup tonight. And to think that old charlatan talked you into this." The bear rocked back and forth in laughter.

Tempus put his head next to James's and whispered, "Be careful. Bears can be awkward and ill-humored. They don't generally have much to laugh at."

"What's that, dog? Nothing to laugh at?"

"My name is Tempus, and I have heard tell of the sorrow of bears."

"Mmm. So you say, dog. But tell me, how do you know this? Do you go hunting bear?" The bear leaned forward, sniffing in a threatening manner.

"My bloodline is bearhound, but I've never hunted your species. I speak only of legend."

"What legend is this?"

"I think," James interrupted, "that we should get away from the Sea Arch as soon as possible. If we've returned to my world, we'll need to hide before the sun comes up." He cast an eye to the east. Fortunately dawn was still some way off.

"Why, boy?" asked Baranor. "I do not fear those little black creatures that taste of the ground. And as to this land, what dangers will we face that a bear cannot overcome?"

Baranor was indeed an impressive animal, but James knew that in his world survival would be no laughing matter.

"Mr. Baranor, sir. In this world bears do not exist. Well, not *here* anymore."

"How is that? Did Creation never make them?" The bear looked about him at the quiet, darkened coast. "Sandy beaches, clean seas, and I smell plenty of farms inland, too. It seems the ideal place for a bear to dwell. Mmm, probably Kodiak. They love the water." He looked at James for an answer.

"Well, there were bears once. It's just that . . . a long time ago bears ceased to live in these parts."

"So they left? Where did they go? It must be quite the perfect place wherever they went. It takes a lot to persuade a bear to move house."

"They were hunted." James looked pale.

"Hunted. Yes, we all love hunting," declared the bear. "But hunting is about winning some and losing some. 'The doe may be gone so far lately but we'll bag a roe,'" Baranor sang.

James felt faint. "No, sir. They were hunted, all of them . . . to extinction."

The bear stopped his humming. His eyes grew threatening. "Are you telling me," he said in a very low growl, "that every last single bear in this world is a trophy?"

"No, sir! Not all of them. Only in this place. It's an island, a quite small one, actually." James's mind leaped ahead. "And there are some bears still. They live in zoos."

"Where is 'zoos'?"

"In the cities, sir. They are like . . . like . . . homes where bears can live safely."

"Oh," said Baranor. "That sounds sensible. Especially if everyone is hunting and the bears are outnumbered." He scratched an ear. James saw the claws flash. "Nice that they can have a place to rest and catch their breath. Hunts should be fair, evenly matched. Mmm, yes."

James wondered whether he should correct the misunderstanding. He decided to leave it for the present. "So we'll need to find somewhere to hide during the day."

"And we'll need something to eat," said Baranor.

James and Tempus looked at the bear anxiously.

"Oh, you two are safe with me," he said, "but I do have to keep my strength up. Winter is always just around the corner. Mmm. I smell mutton. And lamb. *Mmm.*"

"But Baranor, we can't go eating sheep from the farm," said Tempus. "It will alert the hunters to our presence."

"So we must eat and be away before they can catch us." The bear sniffed the night sky expectantly.

Tempus turned to James. "How far must we travel?"

"I'm not sure where we're going yet. I need to think." James frowned, trying to come up with options. It was too dark to read any message on the arch.

"The enemy could come through the portal anytime. We need to get as far away as possible," Tempus answered for him.

The bear agreed. The two animals looked at James. His two legs were not built for speed.

"You carry James upon your back, Baranor. That will allow us to go at your pace," Tempus said.

The bear growled. "You think yourself faster than me, dog? I could outrun you, even with a human on my back. Even with a human on my back and a belly full of mutton. So watch your every canine step!"

"Well then, Baranor, the biggest of black bears. What say you to a fine leg of lamb, and then a sporting race?"

"Sounds good to me."

Tempus had persuaded the bear to carry a human, something bears never did.

The bear paused. "Do you really think me slow?" Then, turning his attention to dinner, he sang a tune James vaguely recognized: "'Do a ram for my tea but cook it rea-lly slow,'" and ambled off into the night.

"Bears like to hum and sing when they are contented," whispered the hound. "And our Mr. Baranor will be quite contented with some mutton in him. His dander was up with the fighting, and he needs to let off steam."

"I always thought bears were sad animals too, living on their own as they do," said James.

"Maybe not," replied Tempus. "I don't suppose they're often asked how they feel."

"Tempus, why is he here?" James asked as he shared the rations from his squashed knapsack, which had somehow stayed on his back.

"Because Sibelius sent him."

❖   ❖   ❖

Corrick had changed his mind and his ticket, returning to Cambridge instead of London after his visit to Maldon. He checked through his messages at his office and then went home, where he'd lived alone for several years. Only the housekeeper kept the place in any sort of order.

He was still awake at three in the morning, considering Grimend's additional comments on the postmortem. The man had revealed two remarkable points: that the victim's lower body cavity had what looked like multiple blade slashes, and that there had been remarkably little blood remaining.

Corrick was more intrigued, however, by the mortician's comment—"One could tell a great deal more if the organs could be recovered."

Corrick vaguely remembered the tattered remains on the bed at Purbeck Hall, but the start of another headache distracted his thoughts. The Purbeck victim's body was still missing in transit to the Natural History Museum, but there were the remains of the Zeebrugge cadaver available for further examination.

The next morning Corrick outlined his recent conclusions:

1. The murders all took place near a river or coastline. (Query: a seagoing suspect?)
2. All the murder victims died as a result of massive injuries. (Query: evaluation of organ remains—Zeebrugge)
3. All victims pregnant (?). Newborn missing. (Query: second sample from Purbeck; query: Natural History Museum, Oxford)

4. Evidence of attacker using a sharp implement. (Query: markings on body—Zeebrugge, Burnham)
5. Victims' blood drained prior to death? (Query: blood content—Zeebrugge)
6. Evidence missing. (Query: D. C. Pallbrook, Metropolitan Police Harrington??)

An hour later Corrick had dispatched a note for the personnel file for D. C. Pallbrook of the Metropolitan Police, station unknown. He had also reached Inspector La Forge in Belgium by telephone after a lot of difficulty. La Forge agreed to have the body reexamined by a suitable specialist, the expense to be reimbursed by Cambridge police, specifically for details concerning the internal organs and indications of wounding. That left the Oxford museum.

· 1910 ·

"Here. I saved this for you," said the bear as he threw down a mutton leg. Tempus thanked him and licked the joint.

"Now. Where to, boy?" The bear swung his head at James.

"We should head for a quiet place west of here, to the moors," James said. "But I also think I should head south to Newcastle, a big city, to find out what I'm supposed to be doing here."

"Good reasons for both directions. But where is your home? Can't we go there to consider the options in comfort?" Baranor asked.

"I'm afraid I live far to the south, in Oxford, many hundreds of miles away."

"Well then, it seems that we are on a hunt of sorts," the bear said. "The Sea Arch has brought us here, so it would seem we are meant to be here and not Oxford or Newcastle. Let's lie up somewhere and see what kind of trail we can unearth."

And with that, Baranor waved a shovel-sized paw at Tempus and instructed James how to climb aboard. "I once gave a lift to a fair forest elf, a beauty she was. She knew how to ride bearback, but I don't suppose you do, boy. Let your legs hang loose around my shoulders. Don't squeeze them. Grab tufts of my hair and twist your hands in. Go on, tighter. That's how you ride! Now off to the west we go." Baranor let out a mighty roar of exhilaration and bounded across the sand, Tempus racing beside him with the fresh joint of meat clamped in his jaws.

"What was that?" whispered Amanda Brightmere to her aunt. Awakened by a roaring sound, Amanda had rushed to her aunt's room. Polly, the maid, crowded in after her.

"Whatever it was, we'll investigate in the morning," said Lady Jennifer. "But we should all sleep in here tonight."

"This will do nicely," said Baranor as he pushed aside the dense hedge and James and Tempus crawled in beside him. They were high up in the fells of Northumberland, where the farms gave way to open moors and occasional stands of wind-bent pine. The bear lay down and his head sank to the ground. With one eye already shut, he said to James, "We'll talk later. Now we rest."

❖   ❖   ❖

Lady Jennifer looked at the clearing sky. The barometer in the farm had risen overnight, and the weather promised to be better.

"I'm ready now," her niece called from the top of the stairs.

"Good. Let's see if we can discover the cause of that ghastly howling last night." Lady Jennifer set off, and Amanda had to run to catch up. She wondered what on earth compelled her aunt to investigate wild animals' noises. Could it really have something to do with James's disappearance?

They walked down to the beach and then turned south, with the sea to their left as was their usual route. They stopped and stared. An enormous set of animal footprints appeared out of nowhere and made a line across the wet sand before vanishing among the dunes. A set of human footprints ran parallel to these, and what could only be a doglike creature had left a third set. The women followed the tracks back down to the flat expanse of sand where they began. "It's as if they materialized out of thin air!" Amanda said with excitement. Despite a good search, they found nothing else unusual on the beach.

Returning by way of the inland road, they heard raised voices. Struggling over a sty and through muddy fields, they made their way toward the commotion. From a distance the women watched a farmer cussing and flaying the long grass with his walking stick. Two farm laborers joined him. One of the men ran off toward the distant farm, returning after ten minutes with a heavy bundle. Then they unfolded a tarpaulin and covered whatever lay there.

After returning to the rented farmhouse in silence, Amanda

decided to confront her aunt.

"What has really happened to James?" she asked.

Jennifer was on the verge of sidestepping the question entirely, but then stopped and looked at her niece. These events were so extraordinary that Amanda was probably as capable of handling the facts as well as any adult. But still she hesitated to tell her niece all their secrets.

"Polly heard that the farmer lost a ewe during the night. Apparently the poor beast was savagely ripped apart. The farmer is so angry he's demanding the police be called out to search the countryside. Some say it's a pack of wild dogs, but others think it looks more deliberate."

"Surely, this has nothing to do with James?" Amanda led her aunt to the couch, where she studied her closely.

"The footprints we found are connected with James's disappearance. I cannot explain them, but I know they are connected. If the farmers or the police find the tracks, it will make things more difficult. You must believe me." Although the words came out calmly, Lady Jennifer's face was white and still.

"But what are we to do about them?" Amanda asked.

"We must erase them."

After Amanda accompanied her back to the beach and they had carefully erased all evidence of the footprints, Lady Jennifer called her husband. The connection was very poor, probably routed through half a dozen switchboards up the length of the country.

"Philip, something has happened. We found tracks in the sand." He hoped it was the hundreds of miles that made her voice sound so hollow and ghostly.

"Tracks? What sort?"

"They looked to be three sets—a boy, a dog, and a wild animal, a large wild animal!" There was a short pause. "Amanda thinks they may have been made by a bear."

Sir Philip sat forward in his chair, thinking quickly. "There are no more wild bears in this country. It was probably a large dog, and the local constabulary will deal with it. Please keep the door locked at night, and don't go wandering too far. I'm sure this has nothing to do with James."

"But Philip, the footprints came out of nowhere, in the middle of the beach, and I think they led from the Sea Arch!"

The sun was lowering into the west when the three companions awoke. They had covered over ten miles the previous night, and James felt sure the local farmers would be unaware of events at the coast.

Tempus sat up. "James, I think Baranor is right. Fate has decided this is where we must be. That is why the Sea Arch was revealed to you in the first place."

But what do we do now? James thought. He didn't want to say that traveling through the English countryside with a big bear meant they were highly likely to be shot at.

"Listen, Tempus, Baranor . . . you need to know some things about this world. Things that will keep you alive here." He saw they were listening and continued. "We have no magic, but we have science, and there is such a thing as a gun.

It can shoot bullets—small pieces of metal—faster and farther than an arrow. It is a very powerful weapon that can hurt and even kill you." The dog and bear exchanged questioning looks, but remained silent. "This is what they used to kill all the bears." He looked very seriously at Baranor.

"I understand this gun is a terrible weapon. What must we do to avoid it?" Baranor asked.

"There is not one gun. There are many. And any human we meet could be carrying one. So we must be very careful. It is best if you stay hidden during the day. Tempus, dogs are under man's rule here, as you know, so you're not at risk. But remember, no animals talk in this world."

James pulled the velvet pouch from inside his traveling cloak. "I have these gifts from Sibelius. They might help. This"—he held out the crystal—"is an Antargo stone. He said I could see my enemies with it, but I'm not sure how it works exactly. And this book is *Talmaride's Answers to Questions*. Sibelius promised it would be useful." James opened the pages and found them all blank.

"How is this useful—?" he started, but Baranor interrupted him.

"If you want answers, why not ask it a question?"

"Go on, James. You have nothing to lose," Tempus said.

James shrugged. "If you say so." He didn't want to anger either of them by explaining how a book should really work.

Halfheartedly he asked, "What should we do?" But the page before him remained blank. Then, faintly, four words appeared.

Use the Antargo stone.

~o 10 o~

ABROAD IN THE LAND

· 1895 ·

The next morning Corrick was at the Oxford Natural History Museum when it opened.

"I wish to inquire after a specimen that may have been delivered to the museum for investigation," he began.

"Very good, sir." The young man behind the desk opened a large, cumbersome ledger and leafed through the pages. "Would you have a date of delivery, sir?"

"The beginning of February of this year."

"Any idea on the nature of the delivery?"

"I'm afraid not. The specimen was supposedly being sent to London but got diverted here instead."

"Ah, I see," said the clerk. "Things have been in a bit of a muddle lately. Well, here we are. 'Anatomical specimen, attention of curator.' It was delivered to the storeroom pending examination, a large sealed specimen jar." The clerk continued reading. "'It arrived at the same time as a delivery for the Pitt Rivers Museum.'"

"The anthropological museum?"

"Yes, sir, it's located in the rear of the building. That was entered as being a 'human anthropological' specimen. A pine coffin sent to the labs. It would appear to be for dissection or teaching purposes. A specimen won't keep for long under those conditions."

Corrick was looking to track down a body. But what was in the specimen jar? Something in the far reaches of his mind was trying to come forward. The note he had written down? The one about . . . *a second body?*

He asked if it would be possible to inspect the large specimen jar first. He was taken into a musty but brightly lit room with tall windows down one wall and workbenches set out in ranks.

"Hello," a bespectacled man in a white laboratory coat greeted him. "I am Professor Pollen. They're just bringing it in now." He turned as a brown-coated porter staggered into the room, his arms wrapped around a large, thick-walled, glass specimen jar. The top of the jar was an enormous glass dome, and the lid was sealed with a wax rim.

The porter placed the jar carefully on a workbench and wiped his brow. The contents rocked backward and forward in the briny solution.

Professor Pollen referred to the packing notes. "A 'large rodent creature.'" He shook his head. "Not much of an attempt at cataloging or identification. And it doesn't say who's responsible for the labeling and preservation work. Very careless indeed." He looked at Corrick. "Shall we see what we can make of it then?"

As Corrick looked closer he saw that floating behind the distorting glass was a large creature, the likes of which he had never seen. Surprisingly Professor Pollen felt the same.

"This is not a rodent of any sort. Superficially one might think it a member of the order *Rhinophidae*, but it is much too large and the bone structure is not correct. No, this is something quite different."

"Could you tell me exactly what it is then, Professor?"

"We will need to examine it more closely. Should have an answer for you within the hour," he said, focusing his attention back on the specimen.

At the Pitt Rivers Museum Corrick found another scientist happy to assist him. He was led to a low-roofed vault under the main exhibition hall where another brown-coated porter searched through a large array of cases stashed in long piles along the floor and on shelves along the back wall.

"It must be in the preservation room, sir."

They walked through a narrow, whitewashed tunnel into what looked like a workshop. It contained giant copper kettles and heavy-looking tin baths. Marble workbenches were covered with brown and green glass bottles, and metal utensils lay ready for use.

"This is where we do the preservation and embalming, and through there"—the scientist's arm waved to a flight of steps— "is where we do taxidermy and fine detail work."

The porter again rummaged through various crates and peered into several of the covered baths. At last he stopped at a metal container, perhaps six feet in length, placed on a low bench to the rear. "This is the one. No notes were received with it. One of the staff may have decided to use it for practical work with the students."

Corrick leaned over the container and lifted the lid. Inside the body lay stretched out, glistening from the effects of preservative fluids. A searing stench rose from it. Corrick gagged and stepped away. The porter quickly replaced the lid.

"Is there any way we can get a detailed examination of this corpse?" Corrick asked.

"It may be best if you were to speak to the curator directly."

After convincing the curator that it was a vital police matter to have the corpse examined, Corrick took a cab to the main police station to use the telephone.

Inspector La Forge answered. "I have the findings of the examination you requested. It is indeed interesting. The pathologist expressed the opinion that the tissues were torn with a sharp instrument, or perhaps more than one. The markings are best described as claw shaped, rather like the marks of a wild beast, or perhaps a trident spear or something similar.

"And these same markings were found in the organ remains, as if the body and its contents had been slashed from within. Finally, the pathologist noted an abnormally high blood loss at the time of death." His voice went quieter. "At the scene in Zeebrugge, there was a lot of damage, but much less blood. I believe you have a theory concerning this, yes?"

"I have a lot of theories, Inspector, but very few facts," Corrick said.

· *1910* ·

"I should like to see the place. I am told it resembles Bavaria, but without the mountains," said Frau Colbetz to the fawning man beside her. She gazed out the window of the private railway carriage heading north through the drab gray of the Ruhr Valley, the industrial center of Europe. "Oh, to escape this little human world." Her accent was as heavy as her perfume.

"Yes, Fräulein. England is beautiful, if not quite as beautiful as your homeland." Julius Dorpmuller held her hand in his and lightly stroked it.

"Don't try to worm your way any deeper into my affections, or you may regret it." She accented this warning with a flash of her perfect teeth.

Frau Colbetz was a most unusual woman who reportedly could trace her ancestry back to the times of the High Court of Chivalry, when Noble Minnesanger in Germany rivaled Britain's King Arthur. The Colbetz line was rumored to be descended from Charlemagne, and some said even Attila the Hun, which might explain the mix of her thick black hair and ivory skin.

"I shall need to meet with my colleague Frau Feder. We shall of course travel together." She fixed an icy stare. "Julius, make the necessary arrangements. This meeting must go off without a single mishap. There can be no mistakes."

He shivered in delight, loving the waves of fear that rose up inside him and made him feel faint. "Yes, Frau Colbetz. Everything will be as you desire."

James and Tempus made their way down to the road. They had left Baranor sleeping in their hideout.

Pulling the Antargo stone from the pouch, James held it to

his eye, squinting through the clear, blue-tinted jewel. He could see pale blue fields and pale blue trees. A cart drove past and James begged a lift from the driver, who was heading toward a small town a few miles to the south. James studied the driver's pale blue back through the jewel.

When they arrived at the market square, James climbed down, Tempus at his heels.

"Remember, in this world animals can't talk."

"But the humans have a curious habit of talking to animals," Tempus muttered under his breath.

They found a place at the top of the town hall steps, where James could spy on the busy market through the jewel. Everyone he studied remained a shade of pale blue. They moved to a new location near the railway station. Here they sat and ate some of their provisions, while James checked every passerby.

A passenger train arrived, big billows of white jetting up above the station roof. Passengers disembarked on the southbound platform as rail porters in red and gold marshaled luggage and hatboxes for the first-class travelers. A motor car rolled up to the front of the station. The driver called out, "Guests for Cragside! Guests for Cragside!"

A stream of baggage was loaded into a waiting car. James watched as an elegantly dressed woman was helped into the rear, her baggage piled high about her. A metal rod was inserted into the front of the car by a porter and turned, cranking over the engine until it fired up and, with a wave of thanks, the driver slowly edged through the crowds. James raised the jewel to his eye, wondering if the burgundy car would look better in pale blue.

He was shocked to find himself staring at a tall creature, sitting erect and imperious in the backseat, its tail making lazy coils in the passing breeze.

"It's a . . . a . . . it's a dragon!" James choked on the words as he struggled to think. "Go back to Baranor, quickly. I'll try to find out more, and I'll meet you on the road south. We have to get to Cragside!" Tempus gave a wag of his tail and sped off.

James was barely able to hold the jewel steady as he watched the station. Another train pulled in, this time heading north. Passengers boarded and left, but none of them changed shape in the eye of the Antargo stone. Finally he set off to meet his friends.

Tempus came bounding up to James with his tail wagging. "I've got him. Follow me!"

The two of them raced away. They rounded a hill where a tumbled-down stone building sat by the side of a stream. Two gnarled, stunted trees grew in the lee of a wall.

Beneath the trees they found Baranor with the carcass of a newly killed sheep.

The bear looked up. "I brought dinner with me." He looked wistful. "I reckon it's so long since a bear roamed these parts they have forgotten to be afraid." He prodded the dead animal with an outstretched claw. "This one just watched me amble right up to it."

James looked at the sheep with a mixture of hunger and revulsion. "Well, we cannot risk traveling in daylight, and I am starving. I'll make a fire if you like."

The bear nodded and said, "I am partial to cooked meat, it

must be said. The smell of roast mutton makes my mouth water like a rain cloud. But I'm less taken with fire, boy. Mind how you manage it."

In the waning light they sat around the flames, picking at the last of the meat. Baranor had a leg bone between his teeth, cracking it and sucking on the marrow. James leaned on the big bear and despite the worries mounting in his head, enjoyed the warmth of the shaggy fur coat. Tempus lay with his paws before him, alert to the noises out on the moors.

"Don't worry, dog. All's quiet," Baranor said.

"Yes," said Tempus, "and it's time we were going."

Later that night James and his two companions passed into Rothbury Forest, to the east of Cragside. They found a suitable place to lie low, beneath an overhanging escarpment where a cave ran a good way into the cliff face. The entrance to the cave was well hidden by bushes and small trees. Baranor had brought new provisions, although James was less than thrilled to share the ride with yet another dead sheep. The forest was remote and quiet, and James lit a small fire. That night the three of them huddled together; it helped to ease their fears. All slept as soundly as bears.

Unknown to their enemy, a second, much larger band of olorcs had set out the day after Kagaminoc's troop. Led by Goramanshie, an experienced fighter and a thoroughly unsavory character, they numbered four hundred. Goramanshie's orders were to use a circuitous route, striking west and then north, to ensure they arrived at the portal undetected. When they could no longer conceal their movement, Goramanshie drove the olorcs underground, crawling through a crack in the rock, deep into the bowels of the earth. They found tunnels and crevasses, and slowly, deviously, drew nearer to the portal.

· 1895 ·

"We have a most unusual situation here," the curator of the Pitt Rivers Museum greeted Corrick on his return. He was ushered into the department for human anatomy, where a small group of white-coated men were waiting for him. "This is the body of a young female . . ." The curator paused. "I will ask my colleagues to explain."

"I am Doctor Spratt, head of the department," began a short man with a slight list to one side and a left hand that remained in his coat pocket. "With me are Professor Kingston, head of biological anthropology, and Professor Rees of the medical school." Dr. Spratt looked over his glasses and pulled at his earlobe as his voice drifted off.

Professor Rees cleared his throat. "My findings are that this female died from gross destruction of the lower anatomy, probably the result of an attack by a wild creature. Evidence proves that she was pregnant. Judging by the concentration of the attack around the central portion of the body and the total removal of related material, we conclude that the creature sought the removal or destruction of the unborn infant."

That is the causal link between all the murders, Corrick concluded. He cursed under his breath.

"Furthermore, the attack resulted in the blood being drained from the victim by means unknown. And therein lies a dichotomy. A wild creature could not drain blood from a victim unless it was some sort of giant bat." The scientists looked at one another.

"And then there are Professor Kingston's findings," continued Dr. Spratt.

"I was only asked to consider the biology of the victim in case there were any anthropological issues," said the third academic. "And indeed there are. The evidence forces me to conclude that this female is not from any racial grouping known to science. Although she appears to be, she is not, in fact, even human."

When Corrick went back to the first room, Professor Pollen was clearly unprepared for his return.

"What we are looking at is something . . . most unusual. I wouldn't want to rush into giving you incorrect information." Corrick offered to give them a few hours more and went off to sit in a nearby coffeehouse.

When he returned to the Natural History Museum it was closed, and he had to knock on the wooden entrance doors to be let in. Professor Pollen had been joined by a large group of fellow scientists. There was a buzz of excited voices around the laboratory workbench as Corrick approached. The crowd made way for him to join Pollen in its center.

The professor spoke without formalities.

"What you see here is quite the most bizarre specimen the University Museums have ever received." Laid out upon the marble table was what looked like an enormous bat. Its wingspan was fully four feet and its tail hung over the end of the bench, dripping preservative fluid on the floor. The head hung over the far side, out of sight.

"Note that there are six finger bones making up each wing. This means the creature is not a member of the bat family, since bats have only five. The creature is not a bird, since it lacks any feathers whatsoever. One might presume the specimen to be of a more ancient order, a new discovery perhaps. However, three aspects should be considered. First, the tail is a skeletal feature one would associate with mammals, with a high degree of muscle and bone to enable it to act as a limb. Second"—here, the professor used a small wooden rod to lift the head into view—"one may see that the head consists of a birdlike cranial structure, but without a conventional bill. Instead this creature has a soft palate and a prehensile tongue as one finds in certain higher orders of Mammalia, the dromedary for example. Also note the complex and highly developed dentition, marking it out clearly as the teeth of a predator, similar to a crocodile.

"Third, and most conclusively . . ." The professor nodded to a technician who stepped forward and, with heavy gauntlets on his hands, maneuvered the creature's body around the table.

"Please note that below the upper-wing limbs we find a pair of highly developed legs, capable of grasping, and the possession of an opposable fifth claw, similar to that in primates." A gasp went around the room. Corrick, too, was stunned at the information, although he had no real idea of its implications.

Professor Pollen paused while the room filled with discussion. He tapped his stick on the marble surface for silence. "We do indeed have a creature that is not of the group Insecta, yet has six working limbs. There are a number of other observations that are of interest, but of less importance." He waved the stick over the specimen.

"In summary, we have a specimen before us that is an extraordinary amalgam, mammal-like and yet not mammal-like, batlike and yet unlike any bat—or any flying creature, for that matter—that science knows of, birdlike without feathers, predatory in nature with dentition that is closest in type to the ancient order of Reptilia, possessed of six working limbs in a similar arrangement to certain groups of Insecta but sharing no other similarities with that order, and finally the creature has an opposable fifth claw—finger, if you like."

The group burst into uproar. Corrick stood quietly alone in its midst. The wooden stick beat down upon the bench.

"Gentlemen, please. I would like to thank Chief Inspector Corrick for bringing this magnificent example of a Hydra to our attention." His words were slow and clear. "I am of course speaking of a mythical creature. Here today we may all learn the importance of sound scientific research—for this, gentlemen, is nothing more than a *hoax!*"

The laughter rang out as Corrick turned scarlet and elbowed his way from the room.

Corrick knew there was no choice but to confront Harrington with the information and somehow extract the final pieces of the jigsaw.

He stopped briefly at the local police station and wasn't surprised when Harrington came straight on the line, as if he had been expecting the call. Corrick gave him a cursory greeting and demanded they should meet at New Scotland Yard the next day.

"Of course, Chief Inspector. But would you join me first on one more trip? It will help a great deal to explain everything."

～ 11 ～

THE *PARSIMONY* PARADIGM

· *1895* ·

Corrick was at the Pool of London at eight o'clock sharp. The waterway was never busier than at this time. He watched the black masts and spars that rose above the docks, like trees burned by forest fire. The China clippers, the coal barques and down-at-heel East Indiamen of a previous century crowded the water. Amidst the sailing vessels there were also the harbingers of change—steam and paddle. The noise and grim filth of this newer breed clung over the docklands like the smog of war: scientific applications of power versus nature and her elements.

Harrington was waiting for him. Despite himself, Corrick smiled and shook the man's hand.

"I have arranged for a different vessel on this occasion, something of a treat, really," Harrington said. They passed down a gangway and reached the gently rocking deck of a long, sleek craft. "She's His Majesty's Ship *Parsimony*, and a more aptly named ship you'll never find."

It was clean and brand-new, still in the process of being

fitted out, but there was nothing particularly special to see.

"The economy is all belowdecks, in the engine room. This vessel is the first of her kind, twin propellers but only one engine. She uses a new type of gearbox and has excellent maneuvering. It's particularly useful when chasing smugglers close inshore."

Harrington waved up to the captain, who was on the open bridge, calling out orders.

"Let go aft. Bring the helm around. Let go for'ard. Push away. Put your back into it, man! Helm to midship." The crew worked the vessel into the midstream and eased her nose toward the open sea.

Harrington and Corrick were offered steaming coffee and stood sipping from enamel mugs as the commercial world of the docks slipped past.

"I know you're keen to question me." Harrington smiled over the lip of the mug. "But can we wait until we've reached our destination?" Corrick nodded. He would bide his time a little while longer. Besides, he was enjoying the view. Corrick watched as the cityscape fell behind and the riverbanks emptied to reveal a gentle green horizon of farmland and wilderness on either shore. To the north a dark smudge on the horizon hung above the gasworks. To the south a string of little fishing harbors dotted the shore, with Chatham naval docks just off in the distance.

Corrick noted the towering thunderhead of a Channel storm to the southeast.

"We should be there and back before we get into any bad weather," Harrington said.

By eleven they stood off the Essex coast. They had just

passed through a line of buoys stretching northeasterly.

"They're artillery range buoys," the captain explained. "The navy use Foulness Island for gunnery practice."

Behind them the southern horizon darkened. Captain Gilchrist turned to Harrington. "We're on a rising tide. If the storm should break, we'll be in harm's way."

"And that is precisely why we are aboard this able vessel today, Captain." He turned to Corrick. "We're going to make landfall just along here, once the men have cleared a boat for us."

Presently they were seated in a small wooden rowboat in the lee of the larger ship.

The captain called down to them, "Be sharp about your business, gentlemen."

Harrington looked up. "You will stay on station until you recover us." Corrick saw that for some reason Harrington exerted authority over the captain. Still the captain's face was red with indignation as he turned away.

"Now, Chief Inspector, I'll row while you ask your questions," Harrington said.

Corrick considered where to start. "The crimes, in chronological order, were Burnham, London, Southend, Purbeck, and Zeebrugge, all on or near the coast. Each victim may be linked in some way to the sea. You tried to hide these details from me. Why?"

Harrington gave a pull on the oars. "I didn't hide anything from you; I merely failed to correct the mistakes of others."

"Why?"

"It was important that you investigate each of the cases as

thoroughly as possible rather than simply reading reports and listening to the opinions of others. I needed you to tease out the clues and facts. In discovering them firsthand, you would come to see the truth. And I do believe you were able to learn more from the evidence than I ever could." The little boat rode up and over a wave like a cork, and spray hit Corrick's face.

"But the evidence was not always available. When I went after the corpses taken from Purbeck, they had disappeared—or almost, I should say."

"Yes, they would have thrown up too many questions had you examined them early on. You might not have continued with the case. So I had them spirited away, for you to find once you had ended other avenues."

Their eyes met in understanding.

"Yes, Chief Inspector, I am aware of your second trip to see La Forge. It was clear he wouldn't talk while I was there. You policemen do seem to stick together, and he saw through my charade immediately. That's one of the reasons I didn't want to waste any time on the first trip." He leaned on the oars. "So, what did he tell you?"

Corrick hesitated before answering. "He showed me a portion of anatomical evidence that had been found later." He watched Harrington closely. "You knew the victims were all pregnant women. But did you know it was *because* they were pregnant that they were attacked?"

Harrington nodded as he pulled on the oars. "Yes, you discovered enough along the way to comprehend the truth on your trip to Oxford. You saw what you saw, not what the scientists wanted you to see. You believe the unbelievable!"

"The victims weren't normal women?" Corrick yelled above the crash of the surf. "The scientists said the body from Purbeck wasn't even human. They'd never seen a being like it before. That's why you had the bodies disappear."

Again Harrington nodded.

"So without a human victim, it was never really a murder case. But that still leaves many unanswered questions," the policeman said as the boat grounded on the beach.

· *1910* ·

"Guten Morgen, Frau Colbetz." The officer gave a rigid, formal bow as his guest stepped aboard the warship. "His Imperial Excellency Kaiser Wilhelm the Second extends his most gracious welcome and requests that I place myself and my ship at your disposal."

"Why, thank you, Captain," Frau Colbetz purred as she looked around her. "My! Isn't it a wonderful ship. What do you call it?" She took his arm and led him away for a personal guided tour.

An hour later they were on the ship's bridge, Captain Raeder giving orders for their departure.

"As I understand it, Frau Colbetz, we are to convey you and your party to Britain for a conference of some international standing."

She gave a naughty grin and flicked an imagined piece of thread from the captain's arm. "You are almost perfectly correct. We are on something of a 'mission' for Kaiser and country. If you could deliver us safely, and wait, we won't be very long."

"Your wish is the wish of my Kaiser, Fräulein."

"In that case, Captain, could you arrange for those lovely

men in uniform to accompany us? I do like to make a grand arrival." She pointed to the Bremenhaven dockside, where a company of naval marines was marching.

Once at sea the German cruiser *Ausburg* made for the coast of northern England under full steam, her bows cutting through the unusually calm North Sea waters. Belowdecks Frau Colbetz held court in the captain's wardroom.

"Well done, Julius. You have exceeded yourself today." She ignored his delight and turned to her traveling companion, Frau Feder. "Now, Eva, we are expecting how many . . . ?"

"There have been two hundred and eighteen replies to the two hundred and twenty invitations we sent. Frau Schwerin is expected to attend, although she is arriving directly from Egypt. And we have no knowledge of Mrs. Sedger of Hartford, Connecticut."

"Good, that will be a near complete attendance." Frau Colbetz looked down the list. "We can all be accommodated in the grounds of the estate?"

"Yes . . . Helga." Frau Feder addressed her informally with a degree of caution. One could never tell; so much depended on Frau Colbetz's mood. "I've arranged to have the entire estate and surrounding countryside cleared of occupants the week of our conference, using a little money as an added inducement, of course."

"Much more convenient. Herr Dormuller informs us that the venue is large and enjoys splendid isolation—it even has its own fire-fighting equipment and power supply—quite handy! Now, I have asked our nice young captain to drop us on the coast near Cragside. We shall disembark the Benz and motor up to the house, the boat will wait for us to return, and then we'll scoot back home to a hero's welcome, I shouldn't wonder." In early celebration she helped herself to the contents of the captain's drinks cabinet.

· 1895 ·

They dragged the dinghy up the beach out of the crashing surf, getting their shoes and trousers soaked in the process.

"See anything?" Harrington yelled.

After looking up and down the beach, and across the low rugged tundra that backed onto it, Corrick shook his head.

"Tell me then, what are your unanswered questions?"

Corrick fixed on him. "That creature, the other thing found at Purbeck, disappeared with the victim. When I eventually found it, it was declared a hoax. But it isn't, it's genuine." Harrington didn't argue, so Corrick continued, "There seemed no rational explanation for the Purbeck murder. All the evidence was there, but I couldn't put it together. And then I started having headaches and forgot details. But now I see it was the creature, that abomination, that killed the woman. It was growing inside her. It literally clawed its way out!"

Rain began to fall.

"Chief Inspector, look around you," Harrington commanded.

Corrick turned and stared down the beach again. An enormous gateway stood a short distance away, its gate open, shrouded in the rain.

He would swear it was not there a moment ago. He looked back to Harrington.

"It was there all the time, but you couldn't see it." Harrington held on to the boat gunnel to steady himself in the rising wind. "To know the truth, you must first learn it. Your investigations have led you to a great secret. Behind that gateway are the perpetrators of the murders. I know it sounds fantastic, but listen to me." The wind picked up more still and he had to shout. "The creature at Purbeck wasn't of this world. None of the victims were. That is why your scientists refused to believe it was real. You were the man destined to unravel the mystery." He paused. "I know all about your past, Corrick. I know you were once married, and that your wife died in childbirth, and you lost your son, too. I know of the pain you've suffered at every step of this investigation, and how determined you are to find these murderers. That's why you've gone to the lengths you have."

Harrington lost his footing. He glanced around and saw the *Parsimony* at sea disgorging black puffs of smoke against the inky blue-gray of the storm clouds. The ship was struggling against wind and waves, dropping anchor to hold herself.

Harrington turned back to face Corrick.

"The victims came from through that gate. There may be other gates, other victims, but they all come from one place. If you want to avenge their deaths, you'll have to cross on to the other side of the portal."

"What are you telling me? Why didn't you try to stop it?" yelled the policeman.

"There was nothing I could do. I need you to pass through the gateway. I am unable to, because of who I am. Remember those blinding headaches? I was the cause of them. By blocking certain memories I was able to steer your investigations so you weren't overwhelmed by the implications too early. You would never have accepted the evidence as real. Science would have made the facts unbelievable."

As soon as he heard the words, Corrick knew they were true. Immediately after leaving the crime scene, he had forgotten key details. He'd even had difficulty understanding his own notes. It was only when he saw the specimen in the Oxford laboratory that he connected it all.

"And you were D. C. Pallbrook, hiding the files from me?"

Harrington nodded.

"What must we do?" Corrick asked.

"If I passed through, I would die. You have to go, alone."

Corrick looked back at the gateway. It appeared to lead nowhere. He could see the beach on the other side.

"You have to trust me. And what do you have to lose if I am wrong?"

The open gate was menacing, yet strangely forlorn. It did not make sense. But he felt compelled to do as Harrington said. That feeling of being under another's influence was now familiar.

"All right. I've come this far; I'll walk through the gate. But when I return you'll tell me everything!" His threat was lost in the storm.

Harrington reached into the dinghy and pulled out two bundles. "You'll need these." One of them was a bandolier of bullets, the other a heavy rucksack.

Corrick shouldered the items and trudged along the wet beach, leaning into the wind and rain. Beyond the gateway he could see the waves surging over the sandbanks that made this coastline so treacherous. Then he walked through the gate and was gone.

· 1910 ·

The *Ausburg* stood a mile offshore in the night. The moon had risen early and now lay against the horizon, making it unlikely that the ship would be seen from the shore. Captain Raeder was with his passengers.

"Two of my crew will remain on the beach to facilitate communications during your visit. My ship will retire to international waters until the signal for the pickup is made, in three days' time. I trust you will find the brief crossing invigorating." He looked at his watch and then at Frau Colbetz.

At the ship's stern the crew stripped off the tarpaulin covering the Benz automobile, which was lashed to the deck under the raised gun. The long barrel was then used as a makeshift crane to lift the vehicle over the ship's side and onto the steam-driven motor launch. It was lashed in place again, the wheels hanging over the gunwales, threatening to sink the little vessel. Captain Raeder bade farewell to his guests, kissing Frau Colbetz's hand as she stepped down into the second waiting boat.

"Until we meet again, Fräulein."

The journey to the beach went without mishap. The vehicle was cut free and pushed along special wooden stirrups up over the bow and onto the wet sand. Then the ladies were carried through the gentle surf by burly sailors.

Frau Colbetz climbed into the driver's seat as Dorpmuller cranked over the engine. It fired on the second attempt and they were soon on their way, motoring through the dunes and off into the dark.

"Funny," observed one of the officers, "they drove off without any lights."

"Yes, very dangerous," replied the other.

"James. James, wake up." Tempus was licking the boy's face.

"Yeeuck." He sat up, wiped his face with his sleeve, and rubbed his eyes. Dawn glimmered overhead.

"If we're going to investigate Cragside House, we need to go now, before it's too light," said the hound.

Baranor was already awake, scratching himself and no doubt thinking about breakfast.

"Are we going to take him?" James asked Tempus.

"Who is 'him,' boy?" asked the bear.

James, still grouchy at being woken up, turned to Baranor and asked, "And who is 'boy' or 'dog,' for that matter?"

Tempus looked on in amazement.

Baranor's body began to shake with laughter, a deep and joyous sound. "Yes indeed. I have been a bore of a bear to you both. Please forgive me. I have been in the forest on my own for far too long." He sat with his legs before him, his forepaws dangling in the air, and looked like an oversized teddy bear. It was easy to accept his apology.

Baranor lumbered onto his hind legs and stretched with a tremendous yawn. "Shall we be off, then?"

They found a rocky outcrop with sufficient cover where they

could observe the main house at a safe distance.

"Cragside. Mmm. The name's appropriate," said Baranor.

"Imagine if we'd had to spy on a house called Swampside?" James said, to prove he was in a better mood. They settled down to watch.

With the help of the Antargo stone, James identified the woman he had seen the day before. They took turns with the stone to watch the strange sight of the big fat dragon squeezing in and out of the front door, while her human form harassed the departing servants. The house was being vacated, or perhaps prepared for new arrivals?

After the three friends had shared the remains of the mutton as a meager lunch, things became busier at the house. A fleet of cars and buses began to arrive. James's hand shook with excitement as he watched them through the stone.

All the passengers were ladies, and all the ladies were dragons!

· 1895 ·

Harrington watched the policeman disappear through the gate, then looked out to sea. In the gray distance the *Parsimony* was just visible, plunging and rearing in the North Sea swell. Sheets of rain obscured the ship one moment, only to reveal it again in the next. The horizon was black in every direction, bringing night to the day, except when jagged lightning lit the sky like the arc lights of London's Crystal Palace.

He leaned against the dinghy and gave it a push, but the keel was stuck fast. He would be stranded for the duration of the storm.

Five-hundred yards out, the *Parsimony* lurched drunkenly and Captain Gilchrist worried. North Sea storms were some of the worst on the planet, with contrary winds that can change the sea in the blink of an eye. Any ship close to shore was in serious danger. It was too late to move the ship farther out to sea. They had to drop the solitary sea anchor where they were, paying off as little cable as they dared, to ride out the storm. Now the ship was battling wind and sea with barely enough water beneath her keel. "By the mark, a quarter fathom," cried the deckhand from the bow. Captain Gilchrist looked around, but there were no lights to gauge their movement.

"Prepare to winch on the sea anchor," he called. "Make full steam, bearing one-twenty degrees." He had to do something. He'd attempt to pull his ship along the sea anchor cable, away from the threatening shore. The *Parsimony* was supposed to carry no fewer than three anchors, but he had been ordered to sea today, despite having only one. "Make haste! Make haste!"

Harrington sat in the lee of the dinghy with his knees drawn up, watching the *Parsimony* struggle. The storm had blown up so quickly. Was it because of Corrick's passage through the portal? Did there still exist that much power in this world? Or was it the power of the gateway itself? The black smoke from the ship's funnel changed to gray and then white before stopping altogether. Harrington watched with something like sadness.

"She's gone out, sir!" roared the voice pipe. "The boiler fire's gone out!" Captain Gilchrist stared at the mounting seas. Without power, if the anchor dragged or was lost, they would be wrecked.

"Can you reset the furnace?" he yelled back down the pipe, his voice choked.

"We'll need to clear out the water. The bilge pumps can't cope. It'll take ten minutes at least, sir."

The storm-tossed waves were breaking over the ship's side in every direction. Minutes without engine power could spell disaster. Without the electric pumps, the ship would fill up with water and sink, if she wasn't battered to pieces first.

It turned out they had even less time than they thought. As the men belowdecks struggled to relight the boilers, the anchor cable parted, throwing the vessel broadside and signaling the doom of the *Parsimony* and her crew.

The surf pounded the sides of the vessel. Captain Gilchrist looked over the side in horror as his ship began to break up.

From the beach Harrington watched, thinking: *Perhaps it's for the best.*

· *1910* ·

The spy had found his man, the first name on Sir Philip's list.

Rawlings had trawled the dockside bars and listened to the gossip over pints of watered ale. Eventually he'd found a land-lord who knew the rumors on almost every seafarer who'd passed through London in the last twenty years.

"He took to being a recluse, a lighthouse keeper," the landlord recounted. "Loved the sea, but never went back."

Next Rawlings visited Trinity House, home of the British maritime authority, and checked the records. Among the names was one in particular, a long-serving employee. Almost fifteen years. A long, lonely time. A man who was escaping something. A man who had something to hide, something to fear.

⚏ 12 ⚏

BREAKING AND ENTERING

· *1910* ·

"Good day, sir. I am here to see Mr. Weatherburn."

"Ah yes. Unfortunately he is no longer available, but Sir Philip, his superior, will meet with you."

A few minutes later Harrington was ushered into a formal room. Heavy ornamental silverware gleamed from the table center. Imposing oil paintings of long-dead men stared down from the walls.

The doors at the far end opened and Sir Philip strode in. He was taller than Harrington, and many years younger.

"Sorry to keep you waiting." He ushered Harrington into his private office and directed him to a leather chair. "I think we shall be more comfortable in here."

"I understood that this was a meeting to determine committee selection. . . ." Harrington began, but Sir Philip waved this aside.

"Please forgive me . . ." Sir Philip looked down at the file in his lap for the man's first name, but it had been omitted. "There seems to be a detail missing from your file, *Mr.* Harrington."

It was apparent that Harrington realized he'd been duped, but he recovered quickly. "It's not missing. I chose many years ago to forgo a first name. It helped simplify matters."

What is he hiding? Sir Philip chose his words carefully.

"The thing is, Harrington, I've been studying your file for some time, and I think you're the man I've been looking for."

"It is good to know I'm in demand, Minister. But what in my file is so interesting?"

We could be at this all day, Sir Philip thought. He closed the file and placed it on a nearby table. "Do you know my role at the War Office?"

"Yes, you are a senior official handling financial administration for the army and Royal Navy."

"Surely you've been in governmental service long enough to see behind that and hear the rumors that circulate."

"I have heard that you run the War Office intelligence service," Harrington replied.

"Good. And I've a feeling that you are in the same business." Harrington didn't answer.

"Now that we've got that clear, perhaps it's time for you to retire?"

"If Sir Philip thinks that appropriate" was all he would say to this threat.

"The file is correct in stating that you are sixty-two?" Harrington could have passed for fifteen years younger.

"Yes, but young at heart." Harrington had to be very careful. As head of the Intelligence Services, Sir Philip had a wide range of methods available for dealing with him, including summary execution.

It was clear to Sir Philip that Harrington had no intention of being bullied. He would not get this man to talk against his will, and he preferred to avoid the other ways of extracting information. He wondered what else might work.

"Would you like to come work for me?"

Harrington gave a visible start.

"So, you're interested?" The offer must be extremely tempting. He would be able to work from within, accessing sensitive material with greater resources at his disposal. *Does this mean that he is secretly ambitious or a spy?* Sir Philip wondered.

"Might I know the reason for your offer?"

"Let's just say I believe we would work well together. I will speak to your superior this evening. I would like you to be ready to travel the day after tomorrow."

"Very good, Sir Philip." Without another word, Harrington departed.

Sir Philip realized he still didn't know what this man's motives were. He would have to keep a very sharp eye on Harrington.

The seaside town of Lowestoft sat at the very eastern edge of England, where the flat fenlands of East Anglia jut out into the gray North Sea. This remote part of the country had a breathtaking starkness. In mid-May the changeable sea and sky make for seascapes that fascinated artists. To Rawlings it was a windy, barren land that no one in their right mind would bother to visit, let alone live in.

He detrained at Woodbridge and then traveled by cart

through a string of villages until he came to Orford, on the Suffolk coast. He trudged out of the town, past the Jolly Sailor pub to the dock and took a ferry across the River Alde to the far bank. The boatman was unwilling to take him any farther, so Rawlings had to walk across the marshes until he reached Orford Ness. Flocks of seabirds thronged the desolate beach, their angry cries marking Rawlings's passing. Ahead the lighthouse waited, its white walls the only vertical object for miles.

Rawlings gave a cursory knock on the door before pushing it open and stepping inside. The ground floor was filled with upended barrels and coils of rope. Around the inner wall, stairs wound up to the next floor.

"Hello?" he called into the cool, peaceful interior. Above him he heard footsteps. A man appeared at the top of the stairs. He had a full beard and wore a thick, navy blue woolen sweater, canvas work trousers, and boots. In his hand he carried a paintbrush that looked like the kind used by artists.

"I don't often have visitors. Come up and I'll put the kettle on. Then we will see what you've come for. Of course, I knew you were coming. I saw you from miles away!"

It was much later by the time Rawlings said his good-byes. The keeper had been a happy host, although his seascapes had inspired Rawlings even less than the real thing. As he trudged back over the shingle, disturbing nesting birds as he went, he reviewed what he had learned. Was it an eyewitness account of murder, or the excuses of a broken man? He wasn't sure. It certainly wasn't much to go on, the word of a broken man: Captain Gilchrist.

Goramanshie led his troop of olorcs out of their underground shelter to the foot of the arch. Scattered amidst the undergrowth were the decaying bodies of the first party. They found Kagaminoc next to a dead horse. Wild animals had eaten the horse's body but avoided the bitter taste of olorc flesh. They performed the ritual debasement of a hated commander's body, and chopped it into pieces. The olorcs ate heartily that night as they camped by the arch, feasting on the flesh of the fallen and sucking on the bones.

Frau Colbetz was the last to arrive. Although she possessed excellent night vision, she and Dorpmuller proved incapable of reading a map. They got lost among the many country roads before they reached Cragside.

All day James counted, tallying over one hundred dragons at the house. But it was impossible to keep track of them as they shuttled between the main house and the various estate lodges being used for accommodation. By late afternoon all the estate staff had left. James could not see a single person through the Antargo stone who remained pale blue and human. But when the last automobile drew up at the entrance, a limousine carrying two distinguished-looking lady dragons, James gasped. The driver was as brightly colored as any of the dragons, but still a man!

James and his friends discussed the meaning of this new development.

"Perhaps the stone is telling you that the man is an enemy, but not a dragon," Tempus suggested.

"Perhaps he is an enemy, but from this world," said James.

They all agreed that this made sense and that these last arrivals seemed particularly important.

"But what are they all here for?" James asked as he placed the stone back in the pouch and tucked it inside his cloak.

"Well," Baranor said, "when a bear hunts, he searches for spoor—clues. I think tonight, we go hunting!"

Light exploded from every window at Cragside as the guests were entertained with a welcoming dinner dance in the sumptuous ballroom. Music and chatter drifted up the hillside to where the three companions waited. While the guests were occupied, Tempus led the others cautiously down into the formal parkland, with Baranor bringing up the rear.

At the back of the house, a number of buildings and garages were built into the cliff face. Tempus went off to investigate the main building while James checked the sheds and greenhouses. Baranor snuffled around the ground. They met again a little while later.

"Over here," whispered Tempus. The others joined him.

The big wooden doors of a coach house stood open, and several automobiles had been parked in the dark interior. At the rear a wooden staircase rose into the gloom. Tempus and James climbed the tread warily, leaving Baranor among the silent automobiles. They found themselves in a cobwebbed roof space from which a tiny window looked out on to the rear courtyard below. The attic appeared to be used for storing canvas car covers and tarps. They heard a grunt from below. When they went back down, Baranor had his head crammed under a vehicle, which rocked noisily on its suspension.

"What is it?" James hissed.

"There's a draft coming from under this," the bear said, slapping his paw on the car.

Tempus crawled under. "Yes, there appears to be a space underneath. It's covered with wooden beams, but there's more than meets the nose down here."

"We'd better find out where it comes from, or leads to." James jumped into the car and released the handbrake. Then he directed Baranor to push the vehicle backward so they could pull up the wooden floorboards. Beneath, they found what looked to be a mechanic's pit. Tempus didn't hesitate. He darted down and disappeared.

The bear and boy waited. It seemed like ages before Tempus came running back up the stairs with his tail wagging. "There's a tunnel. In one direction it runs toward the house, and in the other direction it runs in a wide semicircle with lots of doors leading from it. The end is down by the ornamental lake. There's a metal-railed gate that's locked, but a big fellow could bust right through it," he said, looking at Baranor.

"Right," said James. "I'll cover our tracks and then head toward the house while you and Baranor see to that gate. We could use an escape route."

James replaced the wooden boards, leaving a gap big enough for him and Tempus to slip through, and pushed the car back into position so that it partially covered the entrance, in case anyone should glance in. Then he squeezed through to the darkened tunnel where the others were waiting for him. They said their "good lucks" and went off.

James shuffled forward in the dark, edging along crumbling walls, until he felt his way barred by a door. It was bolted shut from his side, and he had a tough time freeing the rusty bolt.

The low-roofed cellars were extensive, and full of discarded objects. Baby carriages, old picture frames, and other family heirlooms lay piled everywhere, cloaked in cobwebs. James was soon covered in a gray veil of the stuff, but he ignored it as he crept through the dark labyrinthine. Then he sensed something looming over him. For an instant he was sure he saw the terrifying eyes of the Drezghul. James fought down his fear and inched forward. A thin band of light shone in the distance. It was enough to make out a tangle of lamps and hatstands leaning crazily across the aisle. Making his way toward the light, he deduced it came from the jam of a door at the top of a flight of stone stairs. James climbed up the uneven steps until he stood facing the wooden door. He pressed his eye to the rusty keyhole, but saw nothing. The he pressed his ear to it.

Somewhere in the interior of the great house, voices were raised. He listened for quite a while, but the noises never moved closer or farther away. Gathering his courage he lifted the heavy latch and pushed the door ajar. It opened into a scullery that led off from the ante-kitchen at the back of the house. James guessed this was the service quarters. Having studied the house all day, he felt sure no staff remained in the building. The dragon-ladies didn't want nosy humans in the house during their stay. Slipping noiselessly around the door, he pushed it closed, careful it did not lock behind him, and made his way into the building.

He saw that in addition to the main rooms and hallways, there were boot rooms, gun rooms, a sewing room, multiple pantries, and many other rooms, as well as what seemed miles of connecting corridors running behind and between the walls. He knew these were for the servants to move quickly and discreetly in their tasks. And they were also handy for spying on the household.

At the front of the house, the formal rooms were set around the main hallway, with an enormous staircase at the center. James found he could, if very careful, walk through the servant areas without meeting the houseguests, who preferred the luxurious front rooms. Once he had to dive into a cupboard to avoid a guest who had taken a wrong turn, but she quickly returned to more sumptuous surroundings.

James slipped over to a doorway leading from the back of house to the drawing room. A lot of noise carried through, and he placed his eye to the keyhole.

The colors of a painter's pallette paraded before him: silver and gold, vivid blues and emerald greens, tiny delicate scales of pink, shiny broad scales of sunshine yellow crowded his vision. James rocked back on his heels. Without using the Antargo stone he was seeing *a room full of dragons*! They had transformed out of their human forms and into the most spectacular display of rainbow-colored leather. He needed more than just a glimpse. He would have to find a better vantage point to spy on this amazing scene.

James found the servants' door to the dining room. Peeking through this keyhole he could see the dining table prepared for a banquet. The table was enormous, stretching all the way down the room before disappearing off to one side. It literally groaned with food and drink. This would be the perfect spot to spy on the dragons.

Baranor and Tempus made rapid progress. The tunnel led down a slight incline, and they stopped at the first of a number of doors.

"Lean on it," suggested Tempus. The bear did and was rewarded with the splinter of wood and the hinges ripping from the frame. Tempus darted in, only to reappear seconds later. "Paint store," he said, and they moved along.

The next door received the same treatment. This time the room contained a mass of metalwork and instruments with dials and funny workings that neither could understand. They went on. After several more disappointing discoveries, which included a room containing a giant red contraption with ladders and hoses attached to it, they came to the end of the tunnel. Baranor dealt with the metal gate and they stepped outside to find themselves in a small enclosure, hemmed in on three sides by rough stone walls. The fourth opened out to the lakeside. Cut into one of the walls was a flight of steps leading to the top of the rock face.

"Should we go on?" asked Baranor.

"We need to know where it leads. Let's go." The dog raced up the long flight of steps, the bear following behind.

❖   ❖   ❖

James settled down by the keyhole to watch for developments. His waiting was rewarded when a gong sounded in the main hallway and dragons began filing into the banquet room.

"Ladies! Ladies!" a male voice cried above the chatter. "Please study the seating plan and find your place in the dining room. There are rather a lot of us, and we must respect social rank!"

James had a good view of the far end of the room where a scrum of tails and wings formed around the seating plan pinned to the wall. After a lot of maneuvering, and a good many grumbles from dragons unhappy with the pecking order, the horde took their seats. James found he was looking over the shoulder of a garish orange and pink dragon. Everywhere he looked, long muzzles of teeth flashed, bejeweled claws waved, and scaly tails curled. Large, lumbering dragons with great canopy wings barged past smaller ones with their wings neatly folded. Some had tails that ended in a diamond, others had two tails with spikes, and some tails were shaped like armored cudgels. A green and yellow dragon even had two sets of wings. James counted more than sixty dragons in the room and knew there were many more out of sight.

There was a rapping noise. One of the dragons was knocking a long, slender claw against a porcelain bust to get everyone's attention. The head fell off the bust in a shower of pieces, but no one minded.

"Lady dragons," called the voice. James recognized the man who had driven the motorcar that afternoon and had appeared in color through the stone. He stood at the head of the table. Next to him sat a very important-looking dragon, one of the two James had observed in the limousine.

"Welcome to the seven-hundredth meeting of the Exile Club of Dragons," said the man. "On behalf of the planning committee, may I say how pleased we are by the turnout." He turned from side to side and smiled at his audience. James saw the dragons did not smile back. "To start the evening I would like you to welcome our entertainment manager, Frau Feder."

A medium-sized dragon bedecked with white and red scales and matching wings stood up to light applause. It was the other dragon from the limousine, who now spoke.

"Thank you. Welcome to you all. We expect this meeting to be our most successful ever. We have the run of this lovely estate for the next three days, and I hope you'll all enjoy your time here." The dragons clapped politely. "We have some excellent fun and games designed to bring us together as one big happy family. As well as a range of seminars on topics such as"—she glanced down at a list she held in her claw—"Cooking with Humanity, Fashion Tips from the Guru We All Love, Christian Gore, The Monster Diet Program, and How to Have a Holiday in Hell. Enrollment is in the reception hall afterward.

"Finally, I know you will all enjoy the lecture by our honorary dragon, Herr Dorpmuller, on the future prospects of human and dragon relations." A patter of applause greeted this announcement. The honorary dragon bowed his head in gratitude. "Now, without further ado, I would like to introduce our chairdragon and host, Frau Colbetz."

Frau Feder had worked the crowd well. The room filled with clapping as a very tall and slinky dragon, covered entirely in flashing scales of gold, silver, and blue, rose at the head of the table, directly across from James's keyhole.

"Thank you, ladies." She flashed a jaw full of spiky, sparkly white teeth, tossing her head back to accentuate the long muscles of her scaly neck. "I know all you ladies are looking forward to a weekend of fun, and we all have very old friends we want to catch up with. But there is an important side to this conference. A decade of our time is like a day to humanity, but time stands still for no one, not even dragons. Change is all around us. Humanity is on the move. And so, at last, are we. Tomorrow I will be revealing our most exciting plans for the next millennia!"

Frau Colbetz stopped and looked slowly around the room. Her eyes came to rest directly where James sat crouched behind the servants' door. The dragon's steely gaze seemed to lance through the keyhole, piercing James's head with withering pain. He fell back into the dust of the corridor, clasping his head. As the ache eased, he heard her words continue from beyond the door.

"For now let me tell you that I have a plan to free us all from the ceaseless grind that is our lot in this world. We will drag evil from the darkest corner and overthrow humanity. No longer will we be forced to live in the shadow of mankind's Science and Politics and Money! No more the secretive lives of disguises and denial! We will be liberated!" There was thunderous applause and several dragons rose to their hind feet. "So now, let us have a toast. *To the Exile Club of Dragons!*"

At this, every dragon threw back her head and jets of flame flew up to the ceiling.

❖   ❖   ❖

James sat nursing his head, reflecting on the scene he'd just witnessed. It was clear that his fate, as Sibelius had referred to it, must be linked in some way with these dragons and their plans. James and Tempus would both eavesdrop on the big announcement the next day. Baranor, too large to sneak about in the house, would guard their exit.

He listened awhile longer. Each speaker stood and gave her name and a brief summary of the most recent happenings of her particular branch. Most consisted of dull summaries; lists of sheep killed, cattle rustled, petty theft, and occasional grand larceny. But some were more memorable.

There was Rianasorine Pettyplunder, who had a tendency to rob pensioners in Birmingham. Everyone agreed that she was supremely spiteful, since the elderly don't usually have much to steal. Then there was Garanolaura Savagespitter, who never kicked the habit of eating forty stray dogs a day. She was badly received, which pleased her enormously. James was particularly revolted by a most hideously fat dragon called Ballasifimor Crazychainsaw, who still rode over the American prairies burning up the buffalo, and had the slide show to prove it!

James was about to set off to find Baranor and Tempus when the voice of Frau Feder carried over the party hubbub.

"Ladies, please get ready for the midnight hunt! Everyone has been given a number and you will be paired with a partner, one hundred and ten teams in total. We'll be flying according to the revised Lambton rules. The objective will be to capture the sheep that corresponds to your number. They have all been prepared. It's one sheep per dragon, please. And remember to keep clear of town for the sake of good relations with our neighbors. Ten minutes to takeoff, ladies."

James froze. Two hundred and twenty dragons! Hunting! Sheep were practically the only animals to be found on the moors, but two hundred and twenty was a lot. And there was no mention of other animals being off limits, in particular dogs or bears. If his friends were caught in the open, they would be killed instantly just for sport. James had to find them!

He raced back to the cellar, leaped down the steps, and stumbled through the dark to the tunnel. He ran into the wall and banged his knees as he tried to hurry in the gloom. When he made it to the broken metal gate, he saw no one around. Without stopping he climbed the steps.

Tempus and Baranor were standing at the top of a wall, looking out over a reservoir. The man-made dam stretched between the sides of a ravine high up on a hill behind Cragside. At one end of the dam stood a small building, its door locked. Baranor flicked a paw and opened the lock. Inside they found yet more dials and strange metal instruments.

Tempus looked out of the window and saw James puffing and panting as he staggered to the top of the steps. "Trouble," he gasped as they ran to meet him.

"A hunt! They're having a hunt. We've got to get under cover." As James spoke, a sound like a thousand rugs flailed by a thousand housemaids in a thousand courtyards rent the air. The dull crack and thump of the mass beating of leathery wings reverberated in the valley. They spun around and looked over the roofline of the house below. In the moonlight the dragons were rising en masse from the front lawns. It was a spectacular and ominous sight.

"Quick, back down," cried James. Tempus flashed past the boy and down the steps with ease, while behind him James and Baranor crashed recklessly down the stairwell in the rush. Above them dragons circled in the night sky. James was afraid that they had been seen, but the stairway proved dark and protected, and the dragons too enthralled to notice the three spies.

"We have got to go back and discover their plans," James said. The three of them were safely inside the tunnel. Baranor was to guard the cellar door while Tempus and James set off for the house. They slipped through the domestic quarters, up the back stairs, and onto the main landing. The house appeared deserted, the dragons off to ravage sheep in the dead of night.

James tried a door that looked promising. It opened into a suite of rooms that he thought was the master bedroom. Dresses and other clothing lay everywhere. He crossed over to the desk, but found nothing. Then he looked in the cupboards. They were filled with more clothes of all descriptions, including feather boas and furs. Dozens of shoes littered the floor. The room reminded him of his mother's dressing room—although she had far fewer clothes than Frau Colbetz—and for a moment he let himself think of his parents. Where would they think he had gone to? Was his mother worried sick? He pushed the thoughts away before his courage failed him. He noticed the bear rug by the fireplace and was thankful Baranor wasn't there to see it.

Suddenly the door opened. James dove to the ground and rolled noiselessly under the bed. He watched as a pair of men's shoes crossed the room to the bedside table.

James sighed with relief after the man turned and left, closing the door behind him.

He waited a minute before pulling himself out from under the bed and going to the table. There was a map on the top. It looked similar to one he had seen in Sibelius's library. The map showed part of northern England and part of Eldaterra where the two worlds met at the Sea Gate. He studied it for a while longer in the moonlight from the window, careful not to touch it. Then he crossed to the door and tapped once, very lightly. He heard scratching—Tempus's signal that the coast was clear.

~ 13 ~

IN THE LAND OF THE MARKED

"Stop!" The voice carried across the hallway, and every muscle in James's body obeyed the command. He was halfway to the servants' door under the stairs, following Tempus's tail, when, unseen behind him, the front door swung open and Frau Colbetz entered. She stood on the threshold with the carcass of a dead sheep hanging from her mouth.

James turned slowly toward the voice and realized his body was being controlled by the dragon's magic. He found Frau Colbetz standing in front of him in her human form. She appeared slightly disheveled but otherwise quite normal. The dead sheep had gone, and the front door was closed behind her.

"What are you doing in this house?" she demanded, her voice rising.

Out of the corner of his eye, James caught sight of his grimy clothes in the mirror.

"Excuse me, ma'am. I'm looking for the butler. I've chores to do and I must find him." He tried to make his voice sound as small as possible.

The woman took a step closer. "The staff have all been released for the week. What chores are there to be done? Answer me this instant."

James cowered in genuine terror. "I'm the chimney boy, ma'am. I go up the chimneys and clean out all the soot from the stacks."

Frau Colbetz studied him before saying, "You're a bit big to be a chimney boy, aren't you?"

"Not here, ma'am, on account of the chimneys being so very large. I've grown up in these chimneys."

"Well, your services aren't required at this time," she replied. The main door opened again and Dorpmuller entered.

"Herr Frau, the drag—" His words halted when he saw James.

"This is the chimney boy." Her voice sounded dangerously sarcastic. "Perhaps we may find employment for this young soul elsewhere?"

Something passed between the two of them. The man smiled. "Yes, we can use a healthy lad. Come." He signaled James to follow. James looked first to the woman and then the man, trying to decide who was more dangerous. He caught sight of a trail of bloody footprints behind Frau Colbetz. He ducked his head and obediently darted after Dorpmuller, escaping any further scrutiny from her cold eyes.

They reached a small study at the end of a hall where James was pushed into a hard leather chair. "My boy, your appearance here is timely for the entertainment of our guests. I will make arrangements shortly, and I believe you will find them"—he searched for the right word—"extraordinary. But first, please explain how you came to be in this house. All the doors are locked, and tonight the house has been very full. How did you get in unnoticed?"

James knew that if he pretended one of the ladies had let him in, the man would know he was lying, since the ladies had been in dragon form the whole night.

"I didn't, sir. I live in the cellar," James said innocently.

In the hallway Frau Colbetz moved slowly to the servants' door under the stairs. Putting her face to the half-open door jamb she breathed in a lungful of air. Slowly she released it. Something called to her, like a long-forgotten memory struggling to be found again. She shut the door.

James was left in the study while Dorpmuller went off to make plans. He heard the rasp of the key in the lock. When he was sure the man had gone, James stole over to the wooden paneling next to the fireplace. He fumbled about for a bit before finding the hidden handle and pulling the servants' door open.

Tempus sat waiting. "I followed you."

"The man was suspicious about how I'd got into the house, and I had to tell them I live in the cellar." The words poured out of him in nervous excitement. "It's important that you and Baranor stay out of sight. They may check the cellar to confirm my story, so you'll have to drag some blankets down there. Quick, I hear someone coming." Tempus padded back down the corridor. James closed the secret door and returned to the chair.

Dorpmuller returned with Frau Feder and another woman, who was dressed in pink. James could hear only snippets of the hushed conversation from his seat. "Yes, we could do that. No, no one will notice. Not immediately. An exciting climax, definitely!" The ladies stared over at James. Pink-dress dabbed her eyes as she said, "Such a sweet boy. Just the right age. Strong, yet tender." The women whispered among themselves and then left.

Dorpmuller lit a cigar and puffed on it. "You're going to have a wild time tomorrow, my boy, a wild time."

It was almost sunrise before Dorpmuller had finished a cursory inspection of the cellars and left James there to sleep until he was called for. The man also gave him something to eat. As expected, the doorway at the back of the cellar had not been discovered, the piles of junk and paraphernalia discouraging investigation. James heard the key turn as Dorpmuller closed the cellar door. Minutes later he was down the secret passage with his friends.

"They want me to be involved in the entertainment tomorrow," James told them and realized he was shaking.

Tempus growled and put his head between his forepaws. "I don't like the sound of that. There isn't any entertainment dragons indulge in except the killing kind."

Baranor agreed. "I've never met with a dragon, but what I know of them is not to their credit. As I recall, the dragons were exiled from Eldaterra a long, long time ago, back when the worlds were first divided. Nothing good will come of this."

"But if they don't find me in the cellar, they'll be more than suspicious and we won't stand a chance of discovering their plan."

"What about that book of yours? Maybe it's time for another question or two," said the bear.

"And some answers I hope," said James, reaching for the pouch.

Tempus asked the book the first question: "What is the history of the dragons?"

The reply appeared in handwritten script on the page:

The dragons are of the Origin (Old World) and were amongst the first to be created, from the fabled birthpit, before natural procreation took over. They were given the gifts of flame and rainbow (the ability to change coloration at will) over all other creatures. When Creation became corrupted, dragons were found to be most susceptible of all to the effect, as the negative aspects of the rainbow were revealed: pride, avarice, wrath, and envy. When the Great Divide took place, all female dragons were exiled from Origin. The remaining males, devoid of the pleasures of female company, took to brawling among themselves, which led to a drastic decline in numbers to the point where there are no known surviving male dragons in Eldaterra. Female dragons have remained in exile since that time. Current status, unknown. Further reading: Origin of Species by I. Land, Creatures Extinct and Exiled by M. Thatcher.

Baranor asked next, "What do dragons do for entertainment?"

Dragons are difficult creatures at the best of times (for reasons, refer to Deadly Sins: pride, avarice, wrath, and envy), and occasions for social interaction are few. No official holidays or celebrations are recognized by their kind, and family structure usually lasts for two minutes after birth of offspring. However, history shows several recorded occurrences of formal entertainment:

1. The brief collective hunt of 11,256 B.C. (local time).

"That's the entertainment they enjoyed tonight," said James.

2. The tournament talon grab of 11,247 B.C. (local time).

"That might be what they plan for tomorrow?" He gulped.

3. The raffle of 11,232 B.C., 11,011 B.C., and 10,996 B.C. (local time).

"Well, that one sounds okay. What is the raffle?" James asked.

On the rare occasion of a dragon social function, a raffle for all participating dragons was arranged (absentia applications were rejected). The prizewinner of the first recorded raffle, Desmoraktor of Macedonia, won the privilege of single-hunt status.

The prizewinner chose to hunt a large under-mountain warrior. Hunt duration: seven minutes. Time to kill: two minutes, thirty seconds.

Postscript: The final hunt of 10,996 B.C. led directly to the exile of the dragons when the choice of hunt was a wizard representative of the Guild.

This did not look good for James. "And what is the tournament talon grab?" he asked.

Talon grab is a game that consists of combat between two dragons. It is lethal.

"I suppose that one rules you out at least," said Baranor. James felt nauseous. "That leaves the raffle as the likely entertainment, and I'm going to be the prize!"

Tempus gave this some thought and then asked the book, "How can you stop a dragon from hunting you?"

There are seven theoretical means to stop a dragon. All require the death of the dragon in question. Four have proven fatal to the individual attempting to stop a dragon, one has proved near fatal, and two have proved that the theories do not work.

Only one of these has provided a suitable means of stopping a dragon.

The success of the theory led to it becoming known as the Promalski Principle, named after the individual who proved it.

The Promalski Principle requires the individual to be attired in 100 percent flame-retardant armor, then enter the esophagal passage via either the nasal or mouth cavity and assault the soft inner tissues. Persistent assault is required to stop the dragon.

No theory on exiting a stopped dragon has ever been proven.

Tempus quickly asked another question before James had time to digest the last answer: "How can one survive a dragon hunt?"

1. Dragons use magic to hunt (as well as flight, fright, scent, and sight).
2. Instinct and the auditory sense play less significant roles when a dragon is at leisure—for reasons refer to pride.
3. Dragons do not use reason.

This did not seem to answer the question, so Tempus asked it again. "How can one survive a dragon?"

Dragons do not use reason.

They thought about this for a while. "If dragons don't use reason to hunt, then maybe that's exactly what the hunted must do," James proposed. So he asked next: "How can one use reason to survive a dragon hunt?"

Reason can enable the hunted to satisfy the hunter's require-ments without need for a victim.
Example:
Hunter—Purpose to hunt: hunger, revenge, boredom, satis-faction of blood lust.
Hunted—Purpose for being hunted: food source, revenge, stupidity, naturally selected victim.

Reason will seek to satisfy all the relevant hunter purposes listed above while seeking to avoid satisfying any of the hunted purposes.

Additional reason will seek to satisfy all irrelevant purposes that may also exist.

Out of time and questions, James returned to his bed in the cellar to await dawn and the "entertainment." He was exhausted and needed to sleep for the day ahead, but he couldn't. Instead his mind churned away, thinking over what the book had said.

"Sibelius, I believe we have made a terrible error," the wizard Ptarmagus said. His grave image hung over the vallmaria at the top of the Western Tower. "We have allowed the enemy to grow unchecked in the south for too long. Reports tell of their gaining numbers every day. They spawn new hordes while we are diminished by every inconsequential battle."

"We can only act as we have always done," Sibelius replied.

"I have spoken with other members of the Guild, and there is wide agreement that we must seek the help of new allies."

"Who would those be?" Sibelius knew the Guild was tempted by a certain prospect.

"There is much debate about help coming from our descendants in the New World," Ptarmagus said cautiously.

"I take it the Guild has no means to persuade the other races in Eldaterra?" The Guild knew that Sibelius felt it was made up of more politicians than wizards these days, relying ever less on magic and the power of the Good to undertake its bidding. Ptarmagus, Keeper of the Tower of Cruxantire, was close to the central cities where the main body of the Guild gathered, and was not immune to their pressure.

"Every single member of the Guild respects your opinion on this matter—"

"The portals exist to separate two incompatible worlds, not to bring them together," Sibelius cut in. "The Guild is panicked and would seek to open Pandora's box. Do they not fathom the depths of power they plan to tinker with? The wizards of old were sorcerers in the truest sense. Some were so magical they were divined without body. Mages of spellbinding stature worked the deepest magic to create the great divide, and we who remain should never be compared to them, not even spoken of in the same breath." He shook his head, his voice charged with anger. He had argued with the Guild too often to recount. For these last hundred years, Sibelius had fought and won every time. If not, Eldaterra would be a dying world rather than a wounded one. But at some point, when the temptation and the need were too great, he would lose the argument.

Ptarmagus looked helplessly at his old friend. "Dear brother, I know they will bring up the debate again at the High Council. I will help your cause as much as I am able, but I cannot undermine my own position. That would hurt your situation even more."

The politicians wielded such power they could threaten to unseat even a senior wizard, and it went unspoken that Ptarmagus would be obliged to follow the majority if it came to that.

"We will rue the day the Guild was opened to non-magi. They will be the undoing of this world," Sibelius said quietly. "Ptarmagus, there are things afoot that the Guild is not aware of. Portents that concern the Shadows. They will transpire soon enough and show good reason why the portals must remain closed."

"I trust in you, Sibelius. But the Guild considers your Shadows no more than ghosts."

"I do not expect them to believe. It is beyond the Guild's understanding. The Shadows are relics from the past, yet their time will come again. This Drezghul is in some way like them.

"But I need more time," Sibelius continued. "Would you delay the calls for a meeting of the High Council?" He knew he could ask this much of his fellow wizard. To delay the meeting was simply to postpone the moment when Ptarmagus would face his friend in public and be forced to vote against him. He would put this off as long as he could.

"Very well, my brother. Your Shadows have their time. Make good use of it."

"May your wisdom guide you," Sibelius bid his friend farewell.

"And your wisdom save us, Sibelius."

· *1895* ·

Corrick stepped out from under the gateway just as the portcullis crashed down behind him. He looked back. The storm-swept beach was visible through the bars, but on this side it was a different scene altogether. The gate stood at the bottom of a flight of worn stone steps lit by torches. The walls were black, covered in centuries-old grime, and the smell of decay hung in the stale, dense air.

Somewhere in the distance came a low wail of desolation. Corrick felt the floor tremble. His whole body flooded with a sense of loss and inevitability. His knees began to sag, and the pack on his back dragged him down, suddenly too heavy to carry.

The noise faded, and as it did, Corrick recovered. The very sound had sapped him of his willpower. Everything about this trip was unreal, a nightmare. He leaned against the wall.

"I've got to stay alert and focused," he told himself.

He investigated the provisions that Harrington had provided, which included spare clothes and a handgun, the type with a big magazine to hold plenty of bullets. Corrick never carried a gun in his daily work, and its presence now felt as threatening as the unknown dangers he faced.

Putting the gun in his coat pocket and the rucksack on his back, he studied the gateway, looking for clues. With no way to raise the portcullis, he would have to find another way back. Harrington's words just before he stepped through came back to him. Harrington had known that Corrick would not go back until he had justice for the victims, humans or not.

Examining the gateway he found a black metal plaque set into the stonework, bearing an inscription:

Let us speak of evil deeds
That at present nurture here
Its scaly curse to plant the seeds
In divided worlds for those to fear

Seek out the canker of these crimes
Before this place forever falls
To those all counted in the nines
Turned up and on by deathly calls

Know that you stand alone as first
And last to follow is the younger
Together seek those whose accursed
Knowledge drives this wicked hunger

Find them in their darkest dream
Before the alchemy is finished
The horror of this crime wiped clean
Or stand mankind to be diminished

Look to blackest heart of granite
Ancient in most secret magic
Science end this rainbowed birthpit
A weakened world the coin for logic

Unable to discern the meaning, Corrick moved on, mounting the steps carefully, his hand on the gun. More torches flickered at the top of the flight, where a roughly hewn tunnel led away. Gazing along it, he could see the distant glow of yet more torches. At its end he came to a crossways leading left and right, and decided to go left.

He slipped down the short passage, which ended at a closed door. Lifting the latch, he pushed against it and stepped onto an empty balcony above a cavernous space so wide he couldn't make out the other side. Figures moved about on the floor far below. Corrick couldn't see any details of the figures or the duties they performed, but it reminded him of the view from the top of St. Paul's Cathedral into the crowded, dirty streets of London.

Corrick realized he was watching a crude production line in the vast cavern. What at first looked like an incoherent set of actions by the figures below had slowly formed into a familiar pattern of repetition. He had once visited a shipbuilding yard to interview a suspect, and looking down now reminded him of the scene he had witnessed there, the systematic approach to building. The noise was deafening in both cases.

The creatures, which looked to Corrick like something from a Grimm fairy tale, rolled barrels into the cavern and stacked them in a holding area. Others then opened the barrels and drained off the fluid, leaving a solid material lying in the lower portions. Another group took the drained barrels and upended them; the large shining black lump that fell out was stretched and placed on a large conveyor belt that moved slowly over rollers. The belt ran the lump under a series of sprinklers before it was placed on a trolley-type device and wheeled out of the room by yet more of the laboring creatures. Corrick could not make out any form of security or guards.

There didn't seem anything else to learn from his spot on the balcony, so he retraced his steps and proceeded along the other passageway. Moving down steps that twisted this way and that through the rock, he eventually found himself at the cavern floor. He moved stealthily around the side, keeping close to the rock face. The workers seemed not to notice his presence.

Growing more confident, he stole closer to one as it was stacking empty barrels. He angled around it, intending to slip between two stacks. But as he started to move he jarred one of the stacks and a barrel toppled from above and crashed to the ground. The creature turned toward the sound. Corrick stared straight back at it, horrified.

Its eyes had been cut out!

Judging from the state of the wounds, the poor creature had been blinded deliberately. Inspecting several other workers nearby, he saw they were in the same state. Two gaping cavities were gouged deep into their skulls.

With the ceaseless din and stink from the barrel contents, Corrick felt it was unlikely the sightless creatures would be able to detect him. He was safe as long as he kept out of their way. He left the cavern following the loaded trolleys. The passage gave way to a second cavern. Here the systematized approach was again evident. Corrick crept against the wall and watched.

A different creature, one that still had the use of large, limpid, pool-like eyes, walked past the parked trolleys, inspecting each. Occasionally it would tap the shoulder of a particular worker, signaling to take that trolley to another destination. The rest remained in a long, silent line waiting for the trolleys to be hooked to a heavy chain that dragged along the ground and led down a smaller tunnel where showers of sparks and blasts emanated sporadically.

When the inspector's back was turned, Corrick slipped around a shoulder of rock where the singled-out trolleys had disappeared from view. Rounding the corner he walked right into one of the workers, bumping its meager body backward against the wall. As Corrick pulled the gun from his coat pocket, the creature cringed, its arms jerking up to protect its head. Mouth stretched wide in terror, it began to scream but no sound came forth. *Its tongue had been cut out too.* Corrick watched with pity as the creature cowered, shuffling this way and that to escape its unseen tormentor.

Meanwhile, oblivious to the incident, others of its kind continued with their own work. Corrick tucked his gun in his waistband and resumed his exploration with increased caution. Somewhere far behind, a loud bang echoed off the walls and through the tunnels. It sounded like a gate closing.

The next room resembled a slaughterhouse. An inert mass lay on a trolley nearby. Corrick crossed over and looked more closely. It was a grayish-black figure, lean and featureless at the front, with two long arms that ended in wide lumpy hands. Corrick noticed it had two protruding shoulder bones at the back. The legs resembled the arms, only longer. But the head and face were what held his attention. The broad face had wide-set eyes and a nose that resembled a foreshortened lizard snout. The skull was streamlined with tiny aural passages toward the top on each side. The eyes were closed, and the creature was not breathing. Ahead of Corrick was a row of trolleys where an inspector-type creature was at work on another of the bodies. It took no notice of him as he made his way carefully along the row. It was as if they were programmed to be interested only in their work.

Looking all around he saw that in fact the room was an enormous operating theater. A dozen trolleys were positioned in a line in the center, each with a small team of creatures hovering over it. The room was brightly lit, torches fitted with polished metal reflectors. Were they performing some form of medical examination? No, these were operations—and it looked as if they were cutting babies out of their mothers!

Corrick watched the team nearest him. First they cut open the victim and prepared the gaping wound. Next a large jar was fetched and the lid removed. Corrick stood frozen in fascination. The fetus they lifted from the jar was the same as the one declared a hoax at the Natural History Museum! And they weren't removing a baby from the mother—they were implanting one!

· 1910 ·

James was roused from his bed by a hand rocking his shoulder.

"Get up!" a voice ordered.

"Yes, Father."

"Not your father. Your new employer." James opened his eyes to see Herr Dorpmuller wearing a thin smile.

He was led upstairs into the servants' quarters, where he was told to wash. Next he was taken to the dining room where a frugal meal of leftovers from last night's banquet awaited him.

"Stay here until I call you," Dorpmuller ordered, even less friendly than the night before.

As soon as Dorpmuller left, the servants' door swung open and Tempus was beside him, hidden beneath the table.

"Any new ideas on how to stop a dragon?" James asked miserably.

Tempus laid his muzzle on James's knee. "We were awake all night trying to think of something. Baranor suggested using a sheep as a decoy, but the book never mentioned anything about dragons being stupid."

There was no way out. "This will be the fastest dragon-kill in history," James moaned. Then he jumped up, almost knocking his chair over. He had an idea!

"Ladies, I hope you've had a lovely morning at the various seminars," called Herr Dorpmuller from the dais. The whole room turned to him in anticipation. "Frau Feder will now announce the lunchtime entertainment."

"We have a special feature today," Frau Feder said in response to the brief but excited clapping. "We have been lucky enough to gain the services of a young human. So we will be running another exciting event—a raffle!" At this there was an audible gasp of delight from many in the crowd. "You will each be given a book of raffle tickets. Please put your name and guest number on the tickets and then pop them into the tombola barrel at the rear of the drawing room. We shall conduct the prize draw in one hour."

Tempus and James heard the announcement from behind the servants' door. After quickly discussing their options, Tempus rushed off to help Baranor with the preparations.

For James, locked in the study, time crawled by like a wounded slug. Even the clouds outside seemed to stop drifting. The hubbub of chat and occasional screeches drifted through the mansion while his stomach turned like a steam engine's wheel.

Elsewhere Tempus and Baranor carried out James's instructions as best they could. The plan required some nifty handiwork, and they made do with paws, teeth, and claws. At the last moment Baranor raced off over the hills searching for the final ingredient.

When at last the time came, James was taken to the ballroom.

"Up on the dais you go." Dorpmuller kept a firm hand on James's shoulder to deter any attempt at escape. The excitement in the room was palpable. It thronged with guests, all in their human forms.

Frau Feder called out over the craning heads. "The hour is upon us. I should like to call upon our host and president of the Exile Club to make the raffle draw." The cheers rattled the chandeliers.

Frau Colbetz stood next to the wooden drum as it was set slowly spinning. When it came to rest, the hatch was opened and she pulled out a green ticket and read it aloud. "Number one-zero-zero-three-two. Frau— Why, it's me!" she said in mock surprise.

All around the room there was murmuring of disgruntled voices. "Fix! Fix!" someone called from the back. Colbetz shot a withering look.

This crowd was not to be bullied. The hubbub rose an octave, and Frau Feder began to look flustered.

Dorpmuller leaned over to Frau Colbetz and whispered urgently in her ear. A venemous look crossed the woman's face. Dorpmuller whispered again, even more urgently. Then she grew still, her mouth becoming very small and her eyes dark slits.

"Ladies, I find myself unable to take advantage of this prize." Every word was dragged from between her clenched jaws.

"Therefore I am forced to make a new draw." The discontent eased somewhat, although the heckler risked another anonymous remark.

"I should think so."

The next number to be read out was 19897, belonging to Miss Mabel Ardlibuckle, who gave a growl of pleasure.

~ 14 ~

DOCTORED IN SO MANY WAYS

· *1910* ·

Armed with a pass from Sir Philip, Rawlings was able to gain entry to the Palace of Westminster to track the second name on the list. Once inside Rawlings found a bench in the main entrance lobby where he could study the crowd over the top of his newspaper. He had no interest in the splendid architecture or the government at work. To Rawlings this place represented everything he hated, a system where insiders greased the wheels of power. Ever since he'd been thrown out of the army, he had been an outsider in this world.

Each morning the man Rawlings was tracking followed a complicated route that would lose anyone attempting to follow. In order to follow the man once he was in the palace, Rawlings had to already be inside, ready for him. The man he was spying on was elderly, still preferring to wear an outdated brocade coat and the heavy muttonchop whiskers that had been at the height of fashion in the last century—a sure sign of a lifelong civil servant.

When the man came through the main entrance, Rawlings

stood up casually and followed him. The target walked to the end into the parliamentary lobby, where only elected members of Parliament and their staff were permitted. That was one place Rawlings could not go. He would have to sit and wait some more.

When Rawlings had seen enough to report back to Sir Philip, he left an envelope marked in red ink for his employer's attention with the note: "receipt for flowers." He dropped it into the postal box at the rear of the building.

An hour later Sir Philip opened his office window and placed a potted plant on the sill. The meeting was set.

Rawlings again arrived at the house by way of the connecting roof spaces. He appeared tired and out of breath. Sir Philip offered a whiskey, which he accepted as he slumped into a chair.

After a few hasty gulps, Rawlings caught himself and smiled sardonically. "I should be used to the servants' entrance." Sir Philip weighed the words of resentment carefully, but said nothing.

Rawlings tossed the rest of the fierce drink down his throat and struggled forward in his chair. "I've been to hell and back to crack this one for you. Orford in Suffolk, actually, but compared with London that is hell for me."

Sir Philip remained silent. That part of the coast made him think of his father, what they had shared and the loss he had felt when Sir Neville disappeared. And he thought of James. He shook himself out of these thoughts as Rawlings continued.

"It's where Gilchrist lives, as keeper at the Orford Ness

lighthouse. I had to trek all the way out to that ruddy tower in the middle of nowhere just for a chat." He saw Sir Philip was not interested in small talk. "Gilchrist was able to tell me a few things that were never put into any official report and never revealed at all, before now. It seems that there were some passengers on the *Parsimony* the day she went down. He talked of three men, one a policeman and another a civil servant, who left the vessel before it sank. He could recall only one name. But perhaps he didn't want to give the other. Anyway, he'd never met them before and never saw them again. His orders were to meet their every requirement. It came from high up."

He leaned out of his seat and lowered his voice. "He reckoned the orders came from the head of the Excise Department, Thomas Audrey. And that's who the second name on the list, your old boss, Tobias Skate, is now working for. He's a private secretary for Mr. Audrey."

This was news to Sir Philip, but he didn't show his surprise. The list he'd given Rawlings had been short, just two names, both connected to the event that had blighted his career. He had always wondered why Skate had not defended him at the court of inquiry. Now the finger of suspicion pointed to Audrey. There was no coincidence.

Rawlings went on. "As to the identity of the third, unlisted passenger that Gilchrist spoke of, well, he wasn't too sure. . . ."

Although Philip had already guessed the name some time ago, he needed it confirmed. He hadn't even dared tell Jennifer his suspicions, not until he knew for sure.

Rawlings's black eyes gleamed. "The thing is, Phil, I could

use a bit more in the way of a pay raise. A bonus shall we say."

Sir Philip waved a hand to signal that he would agree to the demands.

Rawlings pressed his luck. "Five hundred pounds."

Sir Philip did not argue.

"It was your father, Sir Neville, on the *Parsimony* that day."

"Now that we've announced the winner of the raffle, I would like to welcome our young huma—boy to the party. His name is—" Dorpmuller bent down and hissed to James, "what is your name?"

"Smith, sir."

The man nodded and said aloud, "Please welcome Smith." And with that he pushed James to the front of the dais. James was dizzy as he looked out over the sea of faces. If his plan did not work, he would be lunch for one of them.

"Now I will explain the rules so that Smith and all our guests understand." He grinned at James, but his eyes were cold and gray under his top hat. "Our prize winner, Miss Mabel Ardlibuckle, has won herself a little game of hide-and-seek with Smith." Dorpmuller chose the most simple, inoffensive words to explain the principles of Hunt and Kill. James knew he was to be the bunny to Miss Ardlibuckle's shotgun. He looked at his adversary. She was an older woman, a bit smaller than him though somewhat rounder, with delicate little hands and a soft, sweet face. She looked like anyone's granny. Her modest dress certainly did not stand out in this crowd. Perhaps he was in for a lucky break, a nice little old dragon to chase him? But her sharp teeth suggested otherwise.

"Smith, you will have ten minutes . . . no, we'll be generous and make it more entertaining; we'll give you fifteen minutes to run off and hide somewhere. Then when the time is up, we'll relea— send Miss Ardlibuckle after you. If she finds you within one hour, she's the winner. And if you stay hidden for one whole hour, then you'll be the winner and you will receive ten pennies for your trouble. Now isn't that going to be fun?" His hand tightened on James's shoulder.

James had to stop himself from swaying with terror. He just prayed Baranor and Tempus had got everything ready.

Dorpmuller mentioned a few final rules: buildings were out of bounds; all the ladies were to wait in the drawing room for a full fifteen minutes at the start to ensure a fair game; and the winner was to return to Cragside at the end to collect his or her prize.

Dorpmuller coughed loudly to attract everyone's attention as he made a final announcement.

"Before I set Smith on his way, I think there should be one last incentive to ensure that he is full of competitive spirit." A few titters broke out as the crowd pressed forward in anticipation. Miss Ardlibuckle, standing on the other side of Dorpmuller, leered at James.

"Would you lovely ladies kindly reveal your true selves to this young man?"

James was off as fast as his legs would carry him. He tore around the back of the house, past eager dragon faces straining at the windows before he ducked out of sight. He ran to the coach house and dove inside, slipped into the gap between the automobiles and down the steps. Groping around in the dark, he caught the line that Tempus had strung along the length of the tunnel to guide him.

He set off, scared he might run into a wall, but every yard told him Tempus had done a good job. Twice he grazed his knuckles where the rope looped around a wooden post or jutting rock, but that was a small price. Three minutes after starting his run, he was at the broken gate and mounting the stairs to the top. Here he met with Baranor and Tempus in the pumping station, away from prying eyes. James quickly climbed onto the bear's back and they were off.

A bear can outrun a horse over a reasonable distance. Within ten minutes they were almost three miles from Cragside at the base of Shirlah Pike, where they had found the cave two nights ago. Baranor climbed to the top of the cliff, and James slid off his back. Below them Tempus kept a sharp lookout toward Cragside.

The dragons were hysterical with anticipation. It was a marvelous bit of last minute organizing, and it had been priceless to witness the look on the human's face. Miss Mabel Ardlibuckle was now Friedeswine Mountainscorcher, a splendidly large, red and green dragon with satisfyingly cruel claws, formidable dentition, and a bloodlust to match. She had to be physically restrained, but Dorpmuller kept the drawing room doors shut the full fifteen minutes in the interests of fair play. He always stuck precisely to the rules, and this would be a record-breaking attempt for the fastest kill ever. At the stroke of fifteen, the doors burst open and Friedeswine Mountainscorcher took to the air in a rush of wings and fire. Once aloft the dragon circled several times, her sharp eyes searching for movement. Next she scented, attempting to locate the boy's trail. She soared down to the coach house and smashed in the garage doors, wrecking a number of the vehicles inside. Scrambling over the automobiles she did more damage but failed to find him. His trail ended in a pool of engine oil.

Enraged, she flew skyward again and observed her fellow dragons crowded onto the front lawn of the house, all eager to watch the spectacle unfold. She grew angrier by the second. She would have to catch the little vermin soon, or be humiliated in front of the others.

"I see her!" called Tempus from below.

James looked at Baranor.

"Right, where do you want it?" Baranor asked, and James indicated his left cheek. He only had time to see a yellow claw whistle pass his face before the warm stickiness of blood ran down his chin and onto his clothes.

"Make sure you spread it about a lot," advised Baranor as James wiped the wound with both sleeves.

"I think she's seen you," Tempus called. "Yes! Yes, she has. Get ready!"

Mountainscorcher turned about, her wings working like oars. That boy had managed to evade her long enough. Then she smelled blood, human blood. There! She saw him, high up on a cliff a good way off. Her keen eyes narrowed as she watched. It was her turn to be amazed. The boy was battling a large, furry animal. "By all the black magic," she exclaimed. A bear! She hadn't seen or heard of one in these parts for years, and it was a magnificent creature. What a trophy! The dragon watched a few moments longer, unperturbed by the jeering from the crowd below. This would make an even better hunt, one that would go down in history. In the distance the bear felled the boy with a giant swing of its paw. Then they disappeared over the edge. Quick as a blast of dragon flame, she arrowed at the cliff face.

"There's no time to lose. Off with those clothes," Tempus said. James stripped off his outer garments and threw them to the floor. They were streaked in his blood. He ran deeper into the cavern where they had hidden the carcass of a sheep Baranor had killed before dawn. The head, coat, and hooves had been removed and left out on the moors. It was now just a large, bloody hunk of meat. James grabbed the rug they'd stolen from the house. He dragged it into position over a fragile wooden lean-to arrangement set against the wall, with the carcass beneath. Tempus and Baranor retreated to the very back of the cave. James followed, and together they hid beneath a tarp and waited.

Mountainscorcher beat her wings as she hovered at the cliff face. A trail of blood led down from the top of the cliff to a clump of bushes at the base.

That's where the bear took the wounded boy, she thought. She let a jet of fire fall on the bushes below. "A little wake-up call for Mr. Bear." She laughed.

Far off, the spectators oohed at the sight of flames. The hunt was heating up!

The dragon landed, pushed her way through the scorched bushes, and stopped at the cave mouth. She gave a roar and was satisfied to hear the bear's defiant reply. She stepped into the entrance, but the walls narrowed too quickly for her to make much progress. Her wings struck the sides, preventing her from entering any further. Frustrated, she let out another bellow, and the bear answered with one equally ferocious.

Mountainscorcher strained her eyes. She could just make out the shape of the bear in the pitch-black of the cave. She smelled the blood of the boy, who must be dead by now, his bloody clothes scattered at her feet. And the bear stank, a smell she had not smelled for years. She let out a blast of red-hot flame. It seared right to the back of the cave, catching the animal full on. She saw it burst into flames and collapse on the floor. Another blast for good luck and that would be it.

The dragon craned her neck as far as she could and managed to nip a tuft of scorched fur between her teeth. She dragged out her trophy. All that remained was a bear paw and a strip of skin. A lump of charred meat rolled out from underneath it and she gulped it down without thought, satisfied and smug with victory.

Rising up in the air, she triumphantly carried the meager trophy back to the roaring assembly. With a killing time of four minutes sixteen seconds, Friedeswine Mountainscorcher had not broken the record, but it was highly satisfactory and she had gained additional status—a bearkill was many times superior to a human, especially a young one.

James, Tempus, and Baranor looked over the top of the heavy tarp. The surface was scorched black and still smoldered. All three had frizzled hair from the blast of heat. They looked at one another and then burst out laughing. *Never try to reason with a dragon.*

· 1895 ·

Corrick had never felt so overwhelmed and helpless in his entire life. Behind him, at twelve operating tables, twelve implantations were taking place. It was truly more like a factory than anything else. They must have performed hundreds, perhaps thousands of implantations here.

A figure caught his eye, walking between the rows of tables, inspecting the work. Corrick ducked down between two trolleys and watched it come closer. It was a human, a man! The man marched purposefully along, stopping once to throw his hands up in despair at the operating staff, spending a few minutes correcting their procedure before turning back down another row and walking away. Corrick followed, keeping low behind a line of empty trolleys.

The man walked out of the operating theater, up a short flight of steps, then disappeared into a room. Corrick pulled the gun from his waistband and soundlessly followed up the stairs to the doorway. It was only partially closed. He looked through the gap into the room.

There were four men. All wore white laboratory coats over

stiff collars and ties. Two were talking together while a third sat in a chair reading. The one that Corrick had followed stood talking with a fifth figure. Corrick had never laid eyes on such a grotesquely fascinating creature. Standing a foot taller than the men and swathed in red and black armor, it looked like a fearsome and savage warrior, with ragged teeth, clawlike hands, and enormous booted feet. A wicked blade hung from its side.

Corrick stepped into the room with his gun leveled. The five occupants were stunned by his unexpected arrival. All, that is, except for the warrior creature. It made a grab for its long, jagged blade. Corrick didn't hesitate. Two shots crashed around the confines of the room. The creature staggered but kept coming, the knife now in its hand. Corrick aimed one more shot, and the body fell to the ground. Everyone else's attention was now fixed on the gun.

"We'll have no more sudden movement," he commanded. The men remained motionless. Corrick edged around to cover the door. "Are there any more of these things lurking about?" He nudged the dead creature with the toe of his shoe.

The men shook their heads. "*Nein*," said one.

Corrick looked down at the figure. "What was it?"

The same man checked with his colleagues this time before answering, "That was General Balerust, chief of the armies in the south. An olorc." The man had a heavy European accent but spoke English well.

"An olorc?"

"*Ja*. They are cruel and terrible creatures, but make for excellent slave labor, and they are fierce warriors."

Corrick made the men empty their pockets on the table and

then herded them into a corner. He kept the gun trained on them as they stood with their backs to the wall, hands on their heads. "Now then. You gentlemen are going to tell me exactly what is going on here."

· 1910 ·

After Tempus had checked that the coast was clear, the friends slipped cautiously from the cave. They went by a circuitous route back to the head of the dam and into the tunnel. Once inside they reviewed the recent events.

"So what made you think of that ruse?" Tempus asked.

"When I was in Frau Colbetz's room looking for clues, I saw the bear rug in front of the fire. I guessed she wouldn't notice its absence, especially with the way she keeps her nose in the air." He turned to Baranor. "I'm sorry we had to resort to such a ploy. It was disrespectful to have used that bear's skin so cruelly."

Baranor patted James gently. "It was a fine way for that bear to be laid to rest, helping us all to survive. And now that his hide has been given a dragon-flame cremation, there is nothing but dignity for the old fellow. And as for you, James Kinghorn, you took that wound like a warrior. You played the game like a true hunter and you have the cunning of"—he thought a moment— "the cunning of a human. A good human."

Tempus set off to eavesdrop on the dragons from the servants' quarters, since the smell of James's wound would arouse them. Baranor went to forage on the other side of the hill, and James lay down for some sleep. A while later the friends were back and woke him. They retreated to the outdoor stairwell and, under cover of the darkening evening, enjoyed roast mutton again.

Frau Colbetz sat in the study with Dorpmuller. It was as she expected. This little man had proved big on words, but when it came to the crunch, he was showing a distinct lack of spine. She pressed him further. "You must set off soon for the coast. Take my car. But"—she slid her hand to his knee where it transformed into a claw that grabbed him with just enough pain to make him whimper—"do not fail me."

Dorpmuller dragged the wreckage of the car from the coach house, kicking the board back into place over the mechanic's pit. "That dragon," he muttered. "That putrid lump of reptilian—" He cursed under his breath as he cranked the car, got in, and drove off.

Baranor stuck his head up over the top of the stairwell and saw the car's headlights along the drive. "One of them is leaving," he called.

"We had better know who it is," said James.

"Hang on, then. This looks fun," Tempus said.

The dog ran off into the dark to chase his first car. When he returned, panting and exhausted, all he could gasp out was "man."

If only we knew where he was going, James thought.

· 1895 ·

Corrick looked at his captives in revulsion. Three of them were surgeons. The fourth, Victor Brack, was the man responsible for the organization, but he would give no more information. He spoke flat, accentless English that gave no definite clue to his origins.

"How could you do these things?" Corrick demanded.

The young Polish surgeon named Mrugowsky shrugged. "They are not human."

"And what of the victims, the ones you placed those *things* in?" Corrick spat the word out.

"The first experiments were conducted on humans, one of the minion breeds that exist in this world, but they were not satisfactory carriers. These olorcs are more effective. They have a much longer gestation period, ten years or so, and it is more stable. They are of this world. Strange beings. The dead one"—he pointed at the corpse—"General Balerust, he despised them. He called them 'the marked.' They are similar to the workers, but a different species, and there was no need to remove their eyes for obedience. Balerust provided us with 'volunteers' for our research. We simply could not refuse this opportunity to experiment, to see what might be possible without the restrictions of our world."

Another doctor, whose name was Sievers, joined in. "The work we have done here represents a great step forward in medical and scientific discovery. Think how this knowledge may be put to use in our world." His young face lit up with a fanatical glow.

"And how exactly will this work benefit 'our world'? Aren't there enough mouths to feed without science creating more? For God's sake, can't you see our world doesn't need this, and neither does theirs!" Corrick watched their blank faces. These men had no idea of the consequences of their actions. They thought only of science and theories. They were as inhuman as the creatures they experimented on.

"But we give them the chance of a future," Mrugowsky said. "You see how they treat their own kind. This way they become *kindersegen*, blessed with children, and it is thanks to our work." He squared his shoulders in defiance.

Corrick cocked the pistol and pointed it at the surgeon's chest, trying to calm the rage that threatened to consume him. "Don't try to justify this butchery. You don't know what you've done. Where do you think these creatures go when you are through with them? What do you think they give birth to? Who do you think you're working for?" The men looked at one another but did not reply.

He rounded them up, drove them down the steps and through the halls to the gateway. He didn't know what he was doing. He just hoped one of his prisoners would know how to raise the portcullis. But when they got there, it was open.

"I don't make a habit of killing people in cold blood. So I'm going to turn you out of that gate, and you're going to get the hell out of England. Because, when I'm through here, I will search high and low for you. And if I find you, I will kill you."

The doctors recoiled at his threat, and Corrick had to push and goad them through the gateway. Brack calmly walked through, nodding as if he had expected this all along. When the last surgeon had shuffled reluctantly beyond the threshold, the portcullis fell with a resounding crash, and they were gone.

Corrick's work was not yet done. The portcullis had again barred the exit, and now the words of the inscription were beginning to make sense.

Seek out the canker of these crimes.

He had found the instruments but not the source.

He returned to the room where the general's body lay to make sure he had not overlooked anything. The creature's knife was gone. Someone had been in the room after he left. He continued through the tunnel complex, moving farther away from the gate.

· 1910 ·

Sir Philip was ushered into the palatial offices of the secretary of state for war. The rooms were high up in one of the corner towers overlooking the River Thames and the Palace of Westminster. He knew he would have to be very careful; one false move could compromise whatever situation James was in. Thomas Audrey rose from behind the titanic-sized desk.

"Ah, Philip, glad I could fit you in. How is it going with all that cloak-and-dagger stuff of yours?"

"We continue to turn up the truth occasionally, sir."

The secretary of state paused. "Good. So then, what may I do for you?"

"It is a rather sensitive situation." Sir Philip watched his ears prick up. "Something we wouldn't want to leak out, sir," he continued.

"I understand." Audrey had spent his career bartering secrets for personal gain. He leaned his girth over the desk in anticipation.

"Were you not at one time the junior minister at the Excise Department? And I was the officer beneath you, responsible for London?"

Audrey sat back, suspicious of this sudden change in tone.

"That is a matter of record. Where are you going with this?

If you think as head of the nation's intelligence service that it is your place to investigate me, you are very much mistaken." The secretary puffed up with his own importance. "I could take immediate steps to remove your authority, if I wish."

"Mr. Thomas Audrey, I have proof that your political manipulations led directly to the deaths of eleven seamen from the crew of the *Parsimony*."

The minister remained calm. "Kinghorn, you know very well that the original testimony of the captain proved to be worthless. That idiot drove the *Parsimony* onto a sandbar and paid the price. And you, as his immediate superior, paid the price too. You cannot change the facts as they've stood for fifteen years."

"Yes, Minister. And after fifteen years I have a witness, an unimpeachable witness. Someone who was there that day."

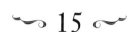

15

A LINE IS DRAWN

· *1910* ·

The automobile came to rest among the sand dunes. The clear sky gave a ghostly feel to the night, washing away the colors of day as sunlight still shone beyond the horizon.

Dorpmuller climbed out of the car and staggered up a steep dune, the going slow and awkward. At the top of the dune, he looked around for the two German naval sailors. He could not see anyone.

He called out in a low voice. Nothing. He repeated his call, this time a little louder. As he finished hollering for a third time, a voice piped up from the dark shadows of a sand dune. "Shut up. We heard you the first time."

The two uniformed men came marching out of the gloom. "We were where you left us, down the beach."

"Signal the boat that I must be taken aboard immediately."

The two men looked at each other and then trudged off.

"Where are you going?" Dorpmuller called.

"To set up in a suitable location for signaling the ship. We can't see it from here," one sailor said.

The other added: "Idiot."

An hour later a boat landed from the *Ausburg*, and Dorpmuller was conveyed to the warship.

"And why have I the pleasure of your company and not that of Frau Colbetz?" asked the captain tersely.

"She requests that you escort me down the coast a short distance where I may deliver a message."

"My orders from the Kaiser were specifically intended for the benefit of Frau Colbetz. I do not intend to be a glorified taxi for you."

Dorpmuller sighed. "In that case, you will be pleased to know that she will be here shortly."

Dorpmuller stood at the rear of the ship and placed a small silver whistle to his lips. He gave one long, noiseless blast.

Far to the west in her suite at Cragside, Frau Colbetz was still feeling slightly unsettled by something. *What is it?* she thought. *Something I've overlooked.* She was distracted by the blast of the ultrasonic whistle. It was inaudible to most creatures—like a dog whistle—except in this case it was inaudible to dogs, too. The sound also formed a pattern that only she would recognize.

She went over to the French windows, opening them to the deepening sky. Bathed in the copper-orange glow, she transformed into her true dragon-self—Komargoran Monarchmauler, self-proclaimed Queen-by-Violence of all Dragons in the New World and Deliverer of the Portal Lands.

She spread her silver and blue wings and rode the evening breeze, her golden underbelly flashing in the last of the light.

"I am sooo sorry to intrude."

Captain Raeder looked up from his papers and found Frau Colbetz at the door to his sleeping cabin. "*Liebe Fräulein!* I did not hear you come aboard." He rose from his desk and led her to a seat. *Come to think of it, I didn't hear the motor launch*, he thought.

"You were too deep in your thoughts to have noticed little me," she teased.

"Never, my lady," he said, intoxicated by her presence.

"I have come to plead the case of Herr Dorpmuller. It was rude of me to assume you would graciously accept my request." Her voice dripped with guile, but Captain Raeder did not hear it.

"Please accept my apologies. I will arrange to have my ship raise anchor and depart in the next few minutes, and may I say how pleased I am that you have returned."

"My dear Captain." She turned her face up to his. "I am afraid I cannot stay. I must fly."

A short while later Captain Raeder watched the launch return after dropping Frau Colbetz back at the beach. No one could explain how she had got on board in the first place.

James sat in the pale moonlight with *Talmaride's Answers to Questions*. Baranor lay gently snoring, and Tempus stretched out next to him. Today he had only just managed to escape from the dragon hunt.

"What are we going to do?" James watched the stars above and thought of his parents.

Sir Philip could help, but he was too far away. And he'd never believe James. Then by the time he did, it would be too late. It didn't seem that even Sibelius was aware of the dragons' plans. And if he was, how could he help from a world away? Certainly the wizard had made it clear that only James's actions could ultimately make a difference in fighting this enemy.

He looked down at the book.

You must finish the entertainment.

James stared at the answer on the page without understanding it. "What do you mean?"

The dragon entertainment.

"Why must I finish it?"

To halt the spread of darkness.

"This will stop the plot by Frau Colbetz? How do I finish it?"

This will halt the plot of Komargoran Monarchmauler whom you call Frau Colbetz. To finish the entertainment is to initiate the last activity, talon grab. This is the only proven means for a party to kill a dragon without the party being killed. For success it is vital that each of the following criteria are met:

1. Komargoran Monarchmauler is one of the participants of the talon grab duel.

2. Komargoran Monarchmauler is killed in the talon grab duel.

It was one thing to evade a dragon and quite another to come back from the dead to provoke a fight. "How do I initiate a talon grab?"

Use the weaknesses in all dragons. Refer to Deadly Sins: pride, avarice, wrath, and envy.

"Can you tell me anything more about initiating . . . please?"

You must provoke the enemy.

This was too much for James. Weary and worn out, he let his head slump down on to his chest and began to dream about Solomon and Bartholomew.

"We haven't got long. Shake a leg, sonny."

James opened his eyes to find a big, hairy face close to his. Baranor was up early.

"Oh, go away, you big bear." James tried to close his eyes, but a mug of tea was pushed into his hands. "Thanks, but I'm trying to sleep."

"Since when do bears make tea?" said a voice remarkably like Solomon's.

"Or let young lads lie in after sunrise?" added a voice like Bartholomew's.

James sat up, rubbed his eyes, and gave the dwarves a smile that showed what a happy surprise it was to see them.

Baranor and Tempus were lapping bowls of tea, a first for both of them. Bartholomew had recommended its revitalizing qualities, but Baranor just drank the tea because it had sugar.

"We've heard all about your adventures," Bartholomew said.

"So we'll share our modest tale," continued Solomon, who told how Captain Dolmir had rallied the remaining horsemen after the diversion. They had all galloped around the hill and into the woods to meet the enemy from a new direction. And once their leader was dead, the enemy's courage failed and they scattered. The captain ordered the recovery of the fallen, and it was then that they found Bartholomew lying in the dark, sound asleep.

"I was not asleep," Bartholomew interrupted. "I was knocked out. And I have the bear as a witness. He saw me fall."

They all laughed, and Solomon went on with the story. After Bartholomew had recovered his wits, the brothers decided to follow James through the Sea Arch the next night. Once they had crossed into this world, they had tracked the three companions.

"There was something strange going on. Your footprints had been erased, as if someone wanted you hidden. So we made sure our tracks disappeared as well." Solomon fixed on James as if expecting an answer to this mystery.

"Anyway, all we really had to do was follow the trail of dead sheep," Bartholomew said. "We finally found you when we caught a glimpse of a dragon in the sky. We knew you'd be there."

James told of his questions and the book's answers. The dwarves were quite excited about an opportunity for a Pyrrhic victory, until James pointed out that not everyone was quite so excited by that prospect. They all agreed it was a grave situation.

At least the morning weather promised a fine day. In fact, it was going to be a very hot one.

Captain Raeder had raced the *Ausburg* down the eastern coastline of England through the night. He wondered how Frau Colbetz had persuaded him into this mad dash and swore never to fall for such a woman again.

Dorpmuller was put ashore on the Essex coast. The captain informed him that the ship would be returning north immediately and that he should in future consider other modes of transport.

Tramping over the beach, Dorpmuller found the gateway in the early morning haze. Walking up to it, his resolve wavered. That horrid little wretch Otto Freislung had not yet returned from his last mission, and that worried him. Freislung should have brought word of final preparations being completed. But then he thought of Frau Colbetz and her terrible wrath. He stepped through the portal to deliver his message.

After the mild shock of changing from one world to another had worn off, Dorpmuller pulled a map from his pocket, prepared by Freislung. He wondered whether the man was still alive and decided it was probably better if he wasn't.

And besides, Dorpmuller thought, *I have the details of his Swiss bank account.*

Following the map he made his way quickly through the corridors and caverns up to the same room where Corrick had encountered the scientists fifteen years before. But Dorpmuller did not find what he had expected. All the rooms and caverns were empty. Fear crawled over his skin. He must find General Balerust and initiate their plans before it was too late.

· 1895 ·

Corrick broke down the problem before him. He had come through the gateway seeking justice for the murders of five women . . . victims. He had found the culprits, of sorts, but the hideous practices of the creatures continued. *He had to put an end to it, but how?*

The complex of tunnels and caverns led him to the lower floor deep underground. There, at the heart of the mountain, lay a dark secret—a volcano. It did not behave like most volcanoes, wild and unpredictable. Instead the enemy's powers had channeled its primal forces long ago and created a crime so original and so heinous that the energy of earth was utterly corrupted, unlike anything in its history. What was once molten magma had been transformed into a huge engine capable of creating motherless life.

The men had revealed the secret to Corrick before he had thrown them out. They had pleaded with him to let them stay and continue with their work. They honestly believed that they could conjoin science and sorcery. Corrick believed only what he saw. But now, as he stood and beheld the volcano, he understood its significance, and power.

"Now I understand," a voice behind him echoed his thoughts.

Corrick could barely tear his eyes from the spectacle before him. Slowly he turned and saw the man, a short way off, holding the blade taken from the fallen olorc general. He too was captivated by the vision.

The man appeared to be in his fifties but was strong and fit. He ignored Corrick and gazed out across the enormous cavern. A radiance of such beauty and clarity, like the sun, filled the void. Every color one could imagine shone forth, so rich you could almost feel them: yellows were soft silk; reds all the wine and fruits of nature distilled; blues were a million dragonfly wings all held in the curve of the iris. The room whirled with vitality. And at the very source they saw a small globe of light form and grow, capturing the colors and coalescing. Eventually the globe of light grew too large to hang in the cradle of rainbows and fell, slipping down a gentle incline and appearing to cool into a hard globe as it rolled. Then another globe of light would form and fall in the same way, slowly repeating, again and again. At the bottom of the gently sloping hill, the workers stood waiting to pick up the globes and take them away. It struck Corrick that the creatures would not be able to see any of this beauty.

"This is what the inscription talks about, in the poem," the stranger said.

Corrick tried to recall all the words, but so much had happened since then he was not sure. "Do you remember it?" he asked.

"Yes. All of it." The man began to recite from memory.

As he spoke, Corrick recalled it too. But where Corrick's message had five verses, this had a sixth and seventh, and one subtle change.

Let us speak of evil deeds
That at present nurture here
Its scaly curse to plant the seeds
In divided worlds for those to fear

Seek out the canker of these crimes
Before this place forever falls
To those all counted in the nines
Turned up and on by deathly calls

Know that you stand alone as first
And last to follow is the younger
Together seek those whose accursed
Knowledge drives this wicked hunger

Find them in their darkest dream
Before the alchemy is finished
The horror of this crime wiped clean
Or stand mankind to be diminished

Look to blackest heart of granite
Ancient in most secret magic
Science end this dragon birthpit
A weakened world the coin for logic

Accept a fate to wander wide
This bordered land in shadow
They seek you for the altered side
Down this path you must go

Or fall to that by choice makes free
To serve them by mere mortal sin
The snare is closed with subtlety
Then cast thy lot and serve Warkrin

"I followed you in. Through the gate." The stranger saw Corrick's confusion. "I was on the boat with you. You might think of me as an unofficial passenger."

The man did not volunteer a name, and Corrick didn't ask.

"Look, Chief Inspector . . . I don't admit to being very good at solving crimes, but I'm fairly good at puzzles. I think the verses contain clues. We've reached the deepest part of this mountain, a 'heart of granite.' The verse talks about alchemy and magic and that"—he pointed to the brilliant volcano—"is the most amazing display of both."

"And I believe those globes forming in that cradle are dragons, or at least the embryos of dragons," Corrick added. "Which makes this the birthpit."

"And so we need to think how science can end it," said the man. They stood silently considering.

"What do you have in your bag?" he asked.

Realizing he wasn't sure what Harrington had provided, Corrick swung it off his shoulder and emptied the contents on the ground. At the very bottom of the rucksack, hidden beneath the clothes, two hand grenades rolled out. Corrick and the man looked at each other. It seemed a remote possibility, but the grenades were the only real science the two men could hope to use. *Had Harrington planned for this?* Corrick wondered.

He stooped and picked them up, handing one to his new accomplice. "You know how to use one of these?"

The man nodded, and they checked the fuses.

Corrick judged the distance to be forty yards, a long throw even for a trained soldier.

"We'll throw together," Corrick instructed. "That way the combined effect may do some damage. On the count of three . . ."

When the grenades exploded it was like a sledgehammer hitting a crystal chandelier. Instantly the colors and patterns splintered into falling shards. The light faltered and failed, leaving only an afterimage in Corrick's mind.

The two men were silent afterward. They had destroyed a most extraordinary and beautiful thing which, despite its warped purpose, had somehow touched their souls.

They made their way back to the gateway. As they passed through the halls, they saw the workers continuing at their mindless labor until at last the whole process ground to a halt. And then the creatures just stood where they were, waiting for someone or something to come along and restart their work and their reason for being.

Perhaps even more than the beauty they had witnessed in

the birthpit, the men would never forget the wretchedness of the creatures known to be *marked*.

The gateway was still closed, and a new inscription awaited them:

Now Creation's fairest work destroyed
Ended the mountain of black dreams
Worlds step away this fate avoid
Push back the issue of these schemes

One step forward if one steps away
The path lies here and there one goes
But in this emptiness one must stay
To work in silence and shadows

"I know the meaning," said the stranger, and in his heart Corrick knew it too. They parted as friends, having shared in that brief time an understanding they could never explain to anyone else. Corrick also knew he would never reveal the stranger's fate to anyone. He gave the man the rucksack and provisions, as well as the pistol and ammunition. The portcullis rose noiselessly, and Corrick stepped through alone.

The late February sky was clear, with high clouds streaming in the upper atmosphere the only hint of the previous day's bad weather. Corrick walked along the beach. He was not sure how he was going to get off the island, but he would figure that out. Compared to everything else in the last two days, that would be easy.

Sir Philip met Harrington at the War Office very early that morning, and they caught a train north. Harrington was itching to know their errand, but Sir Philip would not reveal the destination. For some reason Harrington was unable to read this man. He resigned himself to watching the countryside from their first-class compartment.

"You never said why you were on the *Parsimony*," Sir Philip stated.

Harrington didn't respond, but his look at Philip revealed the truth. He sat back and sighed.

"I wasn't sure you were until now," Sir Philip said, but did not press the question. Instead he gazed out of the window, wondering what Harrington would make of his next surprise.

When they alighted at their destination, Sir Philip flagged down a horse-drawn carriage. Outside London the motorcar had not caught on yet. He gave an address in the small village of Hemingford Grey. Half an hour later the carriage halted outside a cottage with a sign at the gate: "Rainbow's End."

Sir Philip knocked on the door and a gray-haired man opened it. A young child peered timidly around from behind him.

"Good day, sir. I am looking for Chief Inspector Corrick."

Goramanshie, the olorc captain, saw the sun's orb sink behind the ridge of trees. At last, it was time to begin. He roused the troop with well-aimed kicks and sharp insults. They responded with mutterings of rebellion but made ready. It was a big command, with over four hundred warriors, far larger than Kagaminoc's party.

The captain spoke for the first time of their mission:

"Tonight we are the vanguard of a mighty invasion. We will pass through the portal and prepare the other side for our armies that follow. Beyond await our allies, the dragons in exile!" Several shouts of approval followed this news. "Our generals have worked relentlessly for many years to plan for this day. Now our forces will crush the enemy. The Darkness will swell and fill all earth. Our orders are to stop our enemies from using this portal. We will not fail." The olorcs stood silent. Words did not inspire them, only bloodlust.

Slowly they began filing through the Sea Arch.

Lady Jennifer awoke to the sound of gunfire. She ran downstairs to find the housekeeper clutching her apron to her face to hide her tears.

Amanda was up too, but trying to control her nerves. "I have checked that the doors and windows are locked, and stoked the fire."

Jennifer thanked her niece and crossed to the telephone. Her husband's office informed her that he was out. She rang off in annoyance.

"It could be farmers shooting?" ventured Amanda.

"I'm afraid not. That is rifle fire, quite distinct from the sound of a shotgun. And it's coming from the shore."

∽ 16 ∽

THE TALON GRAB

· *1910* ·

The olorcs infested the beach around the Sea Arch, spreading out among the dunes. Goramanshie gave strict instructions to stay hidden in this position until reinforcements arrived, either through the portal or from the dragons.

It was only a matter of minutes before an olorc, moving through the dunes, stumbled upon the two sailors in their camouflaged position. The olorc reacted first. It raised the scimitar in its hand and brought it down on the nearest man, cleaving his arm below the elbow. The sailor fell to the ground in a dead faint, but his comrade scrambled for his gun and shot the creature dead, and the next one, and the next.

Arriving at first light, Captain Raeder had the *Ausburg* stand close to shore. He ordered that the Imperial Flag of Germany not be flown. In its place they ran up the British White Ensign, a flag usually reserved for diplomatic engagements, or acts of espionage. Today would require subterfuge and guile if they were to avoid an international incident.

"Captain, reports of gunfire from the beach."

He raised his binoculars toward the shore and barked out orders. "Prepare to launch the marines in boats. We will hold the beach until our guests are here." Around him the men moved swiftly into action. Captain Raeder crossed to the map table. The nearest British Royal Naval vessels were based to the south. If they sent a ship to investigate, the *Ausburg* would be more than a match, but he would prefer to avoid any trouble.

"Is there a message from our men on the beach?" he asked.

"Not yet, sir."

Goramanshie looked down at the body of the enemy. The two had been waiting in ambush. One of them had killed five of his warriors with their magic, which left little bloody holes in the dead. It was not impressive, not like a sword slash, but it was effective—very. He cursed his superiors for sending him through the archway without some magic for protection, a shaman at least to accompany them. The olorc stooped down and picked up the metal rod that lay at his feet. It had wood bound to it, and complex workings on the top and underside. The metal was both smooth and rough, as if forged but not polished. Goramanshie could not understand its magic and let it fall to the sand.

Seaman Holtz fell panting in the grass. He had beaten off the attack, but not before his petty officer had been cut down and hacked to pieces. Holtz had remembered to grab the signal lamp as he ran. Now, amidst the dunes, he recognized the false sense of security they provided. The enemy could be just over the next dune, preparing to attack! He kept running.

Captain Raeder watched as his two larger cutters and the pair of smaller boats made the journey across. He swept his binoculars along both directions of the empty beach.

"Captain, a figure is in the surf, waving. It's one of our men."

"Yes, I see him. The boats are almost ashore. Lieutenant Reitsch will take control." The captain spoke confidently, but nothing could have been farther from the truth.

Lieutenant Reitsch leaped from the boat and urged the thirty-eight marines onto the beach. Two marines ran to meet Holtz as he staggered toward them. They half carried him over to the lieutenant.

"What happened?" Reitsch asked. The man's eyes held a look of manic terror. It took several minutes to calm him down. Then he stumbled through a report. At the end of it Reitsch was certain the enemy was not some "devil creature" but most likely soldiers recruited from a remote part of the British Empire. He prepared his men to move inland and recover the body of the fallen sailor.

Goramanshie watched the humans from behind the scrub bushes. He saw them fan out and slowly march up the beach in the gray, predawn light. He hissed orders to his own subordinates to deal with these humans directly.

When the marines were almost into the first dunes, strange figures rose from cover and ran at them, brandishing swords and halberds. The first volley of gunfire from the marines took twenty or more of the attackers, the next a dozen. Away down the line the lieutenant saw a marine fall. A second one followed, but these casualties were light compared with the slaughter of the enemy. He halted his troops at the dunes. Still the enemy swarmed at them. He blew his whistle, ordering his men to fall back on his position.

Goramanshie studied the humans. This magic of theirs was truly powerful. The olorc had never seen anything like it. The dark sorcery of the Warkrin was strong, stronger than this, but if each soldier of the enemy had such magic, their army could prove invincible. He told the olorcs to stop attacking. After all, his orders were to defend the portal and await reinforcements.

"They have broken off their attack," declared Reitsch. "We must go in and deal with them if we are to secure this beach."

The enemy appeared to be as seaman Holtz had described them: creatures the likes of which did not exist. They were also cruel and ruthless. He could only imagine the British government had found and trained these warriors, whatever they were. He had ordered the removal of one of the carcasses back to the *Ausburg*. Now they would deal with the others. "Prepare to move forward!"

"How about we just go in and ask them to arrange a new entertainment? After all, they liked the last one," Baranor said. They were all getting edgy. So far nobody had come up with a workable plan for initiating a talon grab competition.

"We need to persuade them to participate," Tempus said.

"Actually, that might be exactly what we should do." James outlined a plan, and the others readily agreed to it.

"You *can* teach an old dog—I mean, boy—new tricks," said Bartholomew respectfully.

"And speaking of which, I've never heard you talk so much as in the last days, Tempus. It's a pleasure to hear," added Solomon.

"We must be ready by noon. That's when the dragons are having their final meeting," James instructed.

Things were not going well for Goramanshie's troop. The enemy had pushed them back to the portal itself. Olorcs lay dead or dying everywhere. Perhaps a quarter of them remained. The magic struck his warriors even as they hid behind the archway, and yet they could not get close enough to bring their weapons to bear. He looked with loathing at the stone arch.

"Fall back into the portal. Flee this magic. Flee!" Goramanshie was the first to abandon their orders and take off through the arch.

"Cease fire!" The Germans stared, their weapons limp in their hands. Seconds before the black and oily creatures had cowered helplessly in the open as if attempting to hide behind some invisible object. Now the survivors were running to the same spot where the bodies had piled up under the withering rifle fire and then literally disappearing into thin air. The marines were left in possession of the beach.

Lieutenant Reitsch strode among the corpses. He kicked the sand at his feet, but there was no hidden bunker where the escaping creatures might have hidden. The faces of his men shared the same expressions of disbelief.

"Collect bodies for burial, Sergeant. No, make that cremation. It is better to rid the earth of them." The lieutenant also sent out a patrol to search the surrounding lands.

Corrick had recognized Harrington the instant he saw him. He had been too surprised to react, but Harrington had grinned and shaken his hand. Then his wife had shooed the children from the parlor. All the while Corrick remained stunned.

It took him a good hour to recount the events that had occurred more than a decade before. "When I got back I learned of the loss of the *Parsimony*. The only survivor listed was Captain . . ."

"Gilchrist," Sir Philip offered.

"He was forced to quit after that disaster," Corrick noted.

"I shared in the blame," Sir Philip said. "It happened on my watch." While this was news to Corrick, Philip was sure Harrington had known. "It seems your story is somehow linked to events now. And that is why we are here. Harrington, I have learned more about you through the chief inspector's story than from your own words. I think it's time you gave a full account of yourself."

"Yes, I agree," Harrington sighed. "I am . . . a spy, of sorts.

My true name is not important. It is enough for you to know that I am descended from a race of people who dwell beyond the portals.

"I came into this world long before man or history as you understand it. And I came with a host of others. Since that time our numbers have slowly declined until I believe I am now the last of my kind in the New World. I am older than any living thing of this world. I will continue to live unless I am killed—I am Elven." Then he told them of Eldaterra, and for the first time Corrick and Sir Philip could make some sense of the mysteries they'd encountered.

"My people came into this world to spy for the powers of Good, but cut off from magic, it has been a terrible loss." Harrington paused a moment, and the sounds of the children playing in the garden filtered into the room.

"We came to spy on the exiles, the dragons. They are the oldest of all living things made by Creation. The first were born in the birthpit, eons ago. And as the greatest of magical creatures, they proved the most susceptible to corruption. It was feared the exiles could use their power to break down the portals and seek vengeance on Eldaterra.

"But we and the dragons have both discovered that magic is the reflection of a world—its order and its beliefs—and in the New World, there is no knowledge of magic. It doesn't exist unless it is brought here. And the portals prevent that from happening."

He looked at the two men with a sad weariness. "Do you ever wonder why mankind has such tales of magic and superstition—four-leaf clovers, lucky rabbit's feet, and old wives' tales?

Your world cries out for magic. And you have replaced it with science. This will not change. It is the way of this world. We have our truths, you have yours. But now a new threat exists. The Warkrin are vile necromancers who have risen to power in the fifteen thousand years since the worlds were separated. They seek to overthrow the Old World with their olorc armies and recreate the evils of the past.

"I believe they were behind the experiments fifteen years ago, trying to pass magical creatures through the portals. But those with magic in this world came through in a time before the portals. Thus the female dragons, sent into exile without mates, have never reproduced again. The millennia have passed and they, like my people, have declined in strength and faded into lore. Those who rule in Eldaterra probably believed we were all long dead. But the dragons have somehow made contact with the Warkrin. And as we witnessed, Chief Inspector, their experiments succeeded. Dragon embryos were sent to this world."

"But we never found evidence of a dragon carried to full term," said Corrick. "It appeared the babies destroyed their surrogate mothers, whether by accident or intentionally. That is why they were implanting embryos into different types of creatures. Their first experiments were with females similar to humans—only the museum scientists made the distinction—so they had to find a carrier more compatible with the implantation process. And the olorcs' pregnancies lasted ten years, the scientists told me. I helped destroy their birthpit on that day fifteen years ago. So it would seem that we are safe from any future births?"

"That is my worry," Harrington replied. "In the years since, I have heard no more reports. Yes, you ended the work of the scientists, and perhaps neither magic nor science can succeed with this kind of unnatural creation. But I am not sure what is happening now, and that is what concerns me."

Sir Philip had been listening intently, hardly able to comprehend their words. Now he spoke, his voice quiet but firm: "I'd better tell you about my son."

"Ladies and dragons. Today will be remembered as a most glorious day." Komargoran Monarchmauler stood on her hind legs, wings outstretched, her long neck weaving from side to side as she held the audience's attention. In front of her the throng of dragons packed the room, ecstatic with the prospect of her words.

"For far too long we have been forced to slither like common serpents."

The restless dragons gave a roar of agreement, singeing the wallpaper and ceiling.

"We have lived secret, miserable lives under mountains and in caves, or forced to conceal ourselves in pathetic human form lest they hunt us down."

This brought a palpable wave of resentment from the crowd.

"We have been deprived of our rights and our status as the eldest of all Creation. We have endured the humiliation of exile. We have no power or position, no past and no future. None, unless we change it."

The room vibrated to the stomping of claws on the wooden ballroom floor. The dragons surged to be closer to their leader.

"But we can end this. Together we are strongest. We are Creation's chosen few!" she roared out, flames boiling from her mouth. The audience screamed for more.

"Today, dear sisters, we will receive a new destiny. From beyond the portal we shall receive a gift—a gift of offspring. I can announce that we have been working on something that will allow us to enjoy the thrill of motherhood once again." There was rapturous applause. "A new generation of dragons is coming that will aid us in overthrowing this puny world.

"I have sent Herr Dorpmuller to begin the invasion. When the portals open, an army will issue forth, sent by our allies. In this world the Kaiser awaits only proof of our army to commit his forces to the cause. Together we will create an unearthly alliance. Then in time the Kaiser will come to realize that he, too, shall be our servant. But first we must be united to change this world. Do you want to change it?"

"Yes!" they roared back. Two hundred dragons surged forward and smashed everything in their path.

"Do you really want to change it?"

"Yes!" they screamed, windows shattering.

Komargoran Monarchmauler's eyes lit up with a maniacal flash. Her silver and blue leathery wings beat the air and her taloned forelegs made wild slashing movements and her head writhed from side to side as she goaded them on. "Do you *really, really, really*?"

"YES!" Flames from the back of the room enveloped the dragons at the front.

And then one voice in the back said: "Actually, no. I quite like things the way they are."

A stunned silence fell over the gathering.

Monarchmauler's eyes scalded the room. She ignored the voice and screamed. "Yes, you do, I know you do, don't you?"

And the crowd roared back its approval. All except the solitary voice.

"No, I don't."

Dragons at the front now turned around to get a better look at the objector. Dragons at the back looked about, everyone trying to identify the culprit.

"Who is it that feels this way?" Their leader's voice was poison.

It was so quiet you could have heard a scale fall. No dragon breathed in case it was mistaken for an answer. Each one looked accusingly at her neighbors. A hiss from Komargoran Monarchmauler was the only sound, until the voice replied,

"Well, I know that's what Desmogorra Slaughterhouse thinks. She told me."

A space immediately opened up around Slaughterhouse, a particularly large dragon who was widely disliked for her bossy and sneering ways. Dragons on all sides of her bared their teeth and talons. The pack had turned on the bully, singling her out. But she was fierce and proud. Slowly turning around, she confronted her would-be assailants. Even with a roomful against her, Desmogorra Slaughterhouse was weighing her chances of winning a fight. She was so proud that she never once thought to deny the anonymous allegations.

But before the crowd could set to with tooth and talon, the

voice added, "And I know Ularinorra Slashmaster's been saying that Friedeswine Mountainscorcher never did catch that bear. It was just an old rug. She and Karliasa Stoneswallower rigged the whole thing." More gasps circled the crowd.

"And who got to maul a maiden from the local village? I hear she was found this morning. That wasn't part of the entertainment! Apparently it was the same someone who promised Mrs. Big-for-her-wings Chairdragon a weekend roasting bison on the plain, so we all know who *that* is." This last remark hit home. Maiden mauling was the single most sought-after nasty reward that a dragon could wish for.

With all the dragon-fever swirling in every bloodstream, it took only this final rumor to ignite the gathering. Instantly dragon set upon dragon. Talons and teeth, tails and necks, all flashed and thrashed. Dragon blood was shed in large volumes. The smell filled the nostrils, and the combatants fought with renewed frenzy. Injured dragons were collapsing on the floor and buried under the mass, whose hind legs instinctively raked and clawed those on the ground. The noise was like steam trains continuously colliding, and all about them the ballroom began to disintegrate under the brutal hammering of the dragons.

James, Tempus, and the two dwarves retreated through the servants' quarters and along the tunnel. Baranor joined them as they climbed the stairs to the top of the dam to enjoy a grandstand view of the talon grab.

Solomon slapped his brother's shoulder. "Good one about Mrs. Big-for-her-wings."

Bartholomew grinned back and said, "Well you started so strongly with Desmogorra that I just had to have a go. And I figured throwing two voices was better than one."

They watched for quite a while.

After the roof collapsed and the walls pushed outward onto the lawn, the dragons spread out, individuals dueling and debts paid back in full.

"Remember to stay very still," Solomon said. "Dragons can see movement but not much else when the bloodlust is on them."

The heat of the morning tired the surviving dragons. None were unscarred, and many were gravely injured. Baranor counted forty-two motionless on the ground.

"Look, there she is!" James pointed below. In the midst of the wreckage, Komargoran Monarchmauler stood bloodied but unbowed. A coating of plaster dust and dragon gore had dulled her brilliant colors. She held her left foreclaw protectively to her body and limped on a hind leg. At her feet lay a green-gray dragon, no doubt killed for some minor insult, real or imagined.

The fight had finally broken up entirely. Individuals took stock of their wounds and headed for home. Some flew directly off, heedless to the dangers of flight during daylight hours. Others crawled away to find somewhere to rest and use what magic they could summon to heal themselves. The cooler heads transformed back into their human forms, appearing the worse for wear, then beat a hasty exit. The dead and dying were ignored.

"That's as likely to stop their plans as anything," said Tempus, wagging his tail.

Sixty feet below, in the shell of the ballroom, Monarchmauler turned her head toward them.

"She's seen us," James whispered. "Nobody move."

The dragon continued to search. Tempus whispered back, "If we don't get out of here soon, she'll see us perfectly well when the bloodlust clears." Everyone fell silent as her gaze crawled over them, hunting for movement.

"Over here, bat wings!" a voice called in Monarchmauler's ear, and she spun away, looking for the new tormentor. The companions rolled over the lip of the dam and down the reverse slope out of sight.

A bellow of rage rose from the injured dragon.

"I will find you and tear your heart out, whoever you are!"

Sir Philip caught the next train north, accompanied by Harrington and Corrick. While waiting at the station, he telephoned his wife.

"Philip! I've been trying to reach you since dawn. Where are you?" Lady Jennifer gave a summary of events that morning.

"Are you sure it was rifle fire?" Sir Philip asked. She assured him she was, and he told her that he was catching a train that instant and rang off.

"I have to admit I'll be relieved when he gets here," said Amanda just as there was a knock on the door.

James opened *Talmaride's Answers to Questions*. He saw that the previous questions and answers had all been recorded on the pages. He considered the next question he wanted to ask.

"Are my father and mother all right?"

Your father is. Your mother is not.

"What do you mean? What is wrong with her?" James couldn't control his rising voice.

She has been taken by the enemy.

"No! Where is she?" he demanded.

In a house close to the Sea Arch.

James slammed the book shut and ran to the others, who were sitting under the trees. When he told them, Solomon looked especially concerned.

"After you went through the arch and the olorcs were defeated, Captain Dolmir returned to the Western Tower. There weren't enough men to leave a guarding force behind. The Warkrin must be sending more troops through the portal to aid the dragons. What we did here today won't stop the invasion if they're already through the archway."

"Let's not lose our heads just yet," said Bartholomew. "We've seen off the dragons with a good hiding. Now we have the chance to settle matters with the Warkrin, in this world where they have no magic. Perhaps"—he nudged Solomon in the ribs—"we'll get that glorious grand finale."

"A Pyrrhic victory?" asked his suddenly rejuvenated brother.

"Forget that!" yelled James. "My mother is in danger. We need to go after her now!"

They agreed that the dwarves should stay and watch the remaining dragons. The others would set out at once.

When they were alone Bartholomew turned to his brother. "Up on your Greek history, are you?"

In the ruin of the ballroom, Komargoran Monarchmauler dined on the liver and juiciest parts of a dead dragon, rare cuisine indeed. Now that the bloodlust had passed, she could take a more objective view on the day's events. She recalled her disquiet the other night after the hunt and later, in her room. *What is eluding me?* she asked herself, but Komargoran Monarchmauler was too wise to chase errant thoughts. She would let her memories come to her.

Her mind wandered back, to the times long ago when dragons were the rulers of the Old World. A time when only the Guild stood in their way. She had amassed a personal fortune, both stolen and won in battle. Not even a wizard dared question her rights then. And few dared to fight a dragon, even if it were to save their loved ones—whereas a dragon would fight to the death to protect a horde of treasure.

Mmm, treasure. A pile of dwarven gold, or elven jewels, or a mound of hunting trophies: skulls, bones, furs . . . And then it struck her. Her old memories came flooding back. That scent from the cellar door. Now she knew. The bearskin!

⌁ 17 ⌁

THE BATTLE OF BEADNELL BAY

· *1910* ·

Amanda opened the door to find a German military officer standing on the doorstep. He walked into the farmhouse followed by two soldiers. The housekeeper broke into floods of tears and sank onto a kitchen stool. Shock registered in Jennifer's face.

The officer's eyes alighted on the telephone and he signaled to one of the soldiers, who disappeared outside. The officer then spoke to Lady Jennifer.

"Good day to you, Fräulein." He clicked his heels with military precision, leaving little arcs of wet sand on the floor. "My name is Lieutenant Reitsch of His Majesty's Imperial Kregmarine. We are currently conducting exercises with troops of Your Majesty King George's army." He walked slowly around the room as if looking for something. "Perhaps you heard the gunfire? But of course you did and, being three women alone in a farmhouse on a remote stretch of the coastline, you would have been frightened and called for help, yes?"

None of the women spoke, Polly crying softly into her apron.

The officer stopped pacing. "I would leave you in peace now, under normal circumstances. But these are not normal circumstances, are they? Why, I ask myself, would three women in a farmhouse have a telephone when many wealthy people do not have such a device?"

The women remained silent. The soldier returned and reported to him.

"My man here informs me that this is British army field equipment. Very good equipment, not the sort your army lends to just anyone. Obviously you are the wife of someone important, yes? Are you alone in this house? Is this a trap to provoke a political incident? I would like answers," he commanded. "Now, if you please."

"When did you marry and have children?" Harrington asked.

Corrick turned from the window of the train. "Soon after I returned. After everything I witnessed in that other place, it made me realize . . . Those slave creatures had their lives taken away. They had no choice. It made me remember that life is precious and somehow I had to move beyond the death of my first family, and start again."

Harrington nodded in understanding.

"Do you have any idea what the purpose of the Sea Arch is?" Sir Philip asked him.

"I did not know of its existence until you spoke of it," Harrington admitted. "The few portals I have found, like the gateway in Essex that Corrick used, have all been in the south of England, plus the one in Belgium, but there are many more that remain hidden. In the beginning I believed they could not be opened by anyone, but that has proven otherwise. If your son has passed through a portal, it may be for a reason we cannot fully fathom."

Siganatoris Bloodboiler eased her wings back gently. The left wing was badly torn, and she could not fly until it mended. She didn't want to transfigure since it would leave her with a broken arm. She would have to rest and work some magic to repair herself first.

The silver and blue dragon walked up to her, her demeanor as imperious as ever. As Frau Feder, Siganatoris Bloodboiler was a humble servant, but in her true dragon-self she was disinclined to do the bidding of others.

"It was an excellent fight," Komargoran Monarchmauler began. "Superb entertainment. So very clever of you to have organized a talon grab for the final entertainment. It will go down in history, the final harvest of the weak before we stand victorious. Very clever."

Siganatoris Bloodboiler basked in the compliments, but it was Monarchmauler who was being clever.

"I must get to the portal and speak with our allies. By now Dorpmuller will have them pouring through the gateways. And Kaiser Wilhelm will make his move as soon as I speak with Captain Raeder. I must ask you, as my dearest friend and fellow liberator, to help one last time."

Siganatoris Bloodboiler was pleased with these platitudes, playing as they did to her ego. "Very well, I will talk with those dragons that remain to see if an alliance can be retrieved from the situation. Perhaps they too found my surprise talon grab entertaining."

"Indeed." At this Monarchmauler transformed back into her human form and, with her dress torn and her hair in considerable disorder, she took off for the coast in one of the functioning motorcars. As she drove away, she called out, "Be careful. We have enemies. The boy and that bear outsmarted Friedeswine Mountainscorcher, fool that she is. They still live. Watch for them!"

Anyone who saw a bear walking in the countryside would report the incident, so when they had to cross the main London-to-Edinburgh road, James had Baranor hide while Tempus ran off down the road to watch for people at the bend and James went north. A few minutes later Tempus ran back barking.

"Quick, out of sight. It's Frau Colbetz." James had no sooner thrown himself into the thickest bush he could find than Colbetz drove around the corner like a banshee. Seconds later she had disappeared in a wake of dust and exhaust fumes. James signaled to Baranor and, like a commando, he sprinted across to the other side.

"We're almost there," James said as the smell of the sea drifted toward them. Tempus ran ahead to scout the route. James climbed off Baranor's back, and they hunkered down behind a stone wall to await his return.

The hound was gone twenty minutes, enough time to learn of the soldiers on the beach, dead olorcs, and the arrival of Frau Colbetz.

"Lieutenant Reitsch, what has happened here?" Frau Colbetz's astonishment at the dozens of dead creatures on the funeral pyre was genuine.

The lieutenant spun around to see her struggling across the sand. He moved forward, his arms outstretched.

"Do not distress yourself with this scene. It is not for a woman of your delica—"

"Get your hands off me. I asked you a question. What has happened here?" Her voice matched the look she gave him and he hesitated. He took in her tattered dress and disheveled hair.

"Frau Colbetz, are you all right? You look as if you had trouble—"

She took a deep breath. "I am perfectly well, thank you. Now please, tell me what has been going on here."

"Madam, our shore party was attacked by these strange creatures that you see. We killed many of them along the beach before they disappeared. Now that you are here, we may return to the ship." He seemed hugely relieved.

"We are not going back to the ship," she said with a voice of iron will. "You will wait here until I give the order."

"Frau, my orders are those issued by my commanding officer. I suggest you have words with Captain Raeder, who you will find aboard the *Ausburg*." And with that Lieutenant Reitsch turned and stalked off.

❖　　❖　　❖

Farther up the beach, James, Baranor, and Tempus watched the boat as it made its way slowly through the surf toward the warship anchored in the bay. Something was not right. The white ensign flew at the ship's mast, but the marines on the beach were wearing the wrong uniform.

"Tempus, can you search for the house that the book mentioned and see if my mother is still there? It must be somewhere nearby. Then we can decide what to do." Before James could blink, Tempus sped off to do his friend's bidding.

Frau Colbetz was up the gangway before the boat was secured. Captain Raeder had watched her arrival through the binoculars. *This woman's power is unreal, unnatural,* he thought.

"Captain, I demand that you keep your ship here as arranged."

His back stiffened as he replied.

"Frau Colbetz, I cannot allow my ship to remain in these waters. This morning my lieutenant was obliged to defend himself against an unprovoked attack by the enemy. There was a great deal of gunfire that will have been reported to the authorities. We are inside British waters illegally. My men have effectively invaded a foreign country, and I expect the British to appear any moment. My ship flies the enemy's flag to confuse them. Meanwhile my lieutenant has also been forced to detain the wife of a government official who is staying in a house nearby, a coincidence I find hard to believe.

"I am here at the request of the Kaiser. I am not here to start a war." His voice rose as he brought the full weight of his anger to bear.

"You are wrong, Captain. That is precisely what you are here for—war!"

Tempus found the house and quickly returned to report his findings. "There are three women inside, guarded by a soldier and one outside the door."

"Baranor, can you go back with Tempus and deal with the soldiers?" James asked. "One of us needs to stay by the arch and keep watch."

"I'd be happier if there were more than two. It's an uneven contest. But I suppose it's necessary under the circumstances."

James warned his friends again about firearms so they would not make the same mistake as the olorcs.

The Bandamire brothers reached the foot of the stairwell to the underground passage just as Siganatoris Bloodboiler stopped at the lake to bathe her wounds. Only a hundred yards separated the dwarves from the dragon, and it would have taken a fully fit dragon a single wing beat to cover that distance. But her wounds slowed her, and the two dwarves scrambled to safety.

"What have we here? Two dwarves out for a stroll? I think not." Her voice echoed off the walls as the dragon poked her head down the tunnel.

Solomon and Bartholomew watched as her glowing eyes, light blue with yellow elliptical pupils, sought them out. They had ducked into a side room that contained all manner of equipment: buckets of sand, strange metal cylinders with hoses attached, ladders, and long canvas pipes on reels. Bartholomew studied the equipment while Solomon kept watch.

"I think I found something."

"Bartholomew," his brother whispered back, "we've got a great dirty dragon poking around at the end of the corridor! What did you find, exactly?"

"Something to kill her with, of course."

Tempus trotted around the corner of the house, his tail wagging, and made straight for the soldier as if they were already good friends. As the man reached out to scratch the dog behind the ear, the giant bear slipped behind him and brought a massive paw crashing down on his head. The soldier crumpled to the ground. Baranor dragged the body behind a bush.

Tempus jumped up, his front paws resting on the window ledge, and looked in.

"The other soldier's coming. He must have heard us. Careful, Baranor."

Lady Jennifer glanced at her niece. They had all heard it, a sort of shuffling noise at the door. They watched as the soldier unslung his rifle and went to investigate. He was perhaps a yard from the door when Amanda spotted a dog at the window. The soldier hesitated, looking to see what had surprised the young woman.

The door exploded inward, the wood shattering across the room in hundreds of splinters. An enormous furry creature leaped into sight, and in a flash of claws and bared teeth, the soldier fell wounded to the ground. The women screamed and the housekeeper fainted on the spot as the bear reared over the body.

Baranor roared once, looked around the room, and asked, "Excuse me, are you James's mother?"

"But they're all right?" James asked.

"They didn't seem up to much in the way of conversation, but no harm done. They're staying indoors," said Baranor.

"Then we've a more urgent problem." James pointed down at the beach. "Frau Colbetz has returned from the ship and she's walking this way."

"The olorcs must be the first part of the invasion army," said Baranor.

"Perhaps they were only a demonstration," said James. "And if I'm not mistaken, those men on the beach are wearing German uniforms. My father says trouble has been brewing for quite a while. Maybe Frau Colbetz really has persuaded the Kaiser to throw in his lot with her, like she said. That would start to make sense of it all."

"It seems that the enemy have been fighting among themselves," said Baranor.

"And that's why she is so angry," said James. "Her plan is coming undone. Without support in this world from the Kaiser, the olorcs and all the monsters they can summon won't be enough to beat a modern army.

"We need to find a way to reach my father," James said as they watched the dragon-lady stalk along the beach.

When the train stopped briefly in York, Sir Philip placed a call to his wife, but was informed the line was down. Calling his deputy next, he gave orders to mobilize troops.

Back aboard, Corrick asked how Philip had made the connection between himself, Harrington, and the *Parsimony*.

"The inscription on the Sea Arch had two clues that proved the hardest to unravel. The first led me to Harrington and the second to my past.

"When I was a junior officer in the Excise Department, my father was head of a rival department. He was interested in merging the two for efficiency. Then came the day the *Parsimony* was lost. My father had ordered the trip that you hitched a ride on. He was blamed for the disaster, and many said his disappearance was to avoid the shame. I was made the scapegoat instead. I accepted a transfer to the War Office, where I eventually took over the running of the Intelligence Service, and success gave me the power to erase my past. But then James's disappearance and the inscription on the arch forced me to relive it. Two particular lines caught my attention. 'Steady now your hand must act / And recall silence in your past.'

"'Steady now' I took as a nautical reference, and 'your hand must act' seemed an instruction to me. The 'silence,' well, I took it to mean that part of my life I preferred not to revisit. My wife assumed it referred to the crashing silence of my superiors at the time of the sinking. No one came to my father's defense or mine. The *Parsimony* was deliberately sabotaged on the orders of someone who stood to lose his job from my father's plans to reorganize.

"My line of inquiries brought me to the one man who can testify to the incident. He was there when you joined the

Parsimony that morning. He was the only one to know of my father's unofficial trip. He was behind the sabotage."

Harrington provided the last piece of the jigsaw. "The vessel was without suitable sea anchors that day. I never understood the significance. Someone had ordered their installation postponed. That means the person you speak of is—"

Corrick interrupted him. "The man I saw you talking to on the dock that morning we first sailed to Zeebrugge. I recognized his face in the newspaper recently, but couldn't recall where I'd seen him before. Now it comes back to me. It's the minister for war, Thomas Audrey!"

"It's a good plan," said Solomon.

"No, it's a great plan! Look at it this way, if we succeed and kill the dragon, we become heroes. If we succeed but die in the attempt, we become legends. If we fail and die in the attempt, we become heroic failures." Bartholomew whistled triumphantly.

Solomon was equally pleased at these prospects.

"And since it's my plan, you get to hold the hose," added his brother.

Down the corridor Siganatoris Bloodboiler was craning her neck into each of the storerooms. Every now and then she would send a blast of searing hot fire to make sure the dwarves weren't lurking in a corner or behind a pile of packing cases.

"We'd better get going then." Bartholomew waited for one of the blasts to clear, then sprinted off down the tunnel.

Solomon unwound the hose and laid it out in as straight a line as he could. He opened the valve fully, watched a pressure ridge race along the canvas hose, and grabbed the nozzle. They'd worked out how to use the fire-fighting equipment.

"Ready when you are," he yelled, throwing his voice into the other room.

The dragon whipped her head into the corridor.

It came from that doorway, she thought, and sent a jet of flames to cut off any retreat. The heat blistered the paint on the door. Solomon had left it open only slightly, but the intense heat sucked the air from the room, leaving him gasping.

The dragon stretched out her neck as far as she could, jamming her shoulders in the tunnel behind. Another roasting would do it, she decided, and opened her jaws to send a blast at the offending doorway. Her eye caught a movement at the door opposite and she angled her head to redirect the blast. That fraction of delay allowed Solomon to swing the door wide, release the lever valve in the nozzle, and send a powerful jet of water straight down the dragon's gullet, extinguishing her igniter in the process.

She choked and spluttered on the water that hammered into her throat. Clamping her jaws down sent the stream blasting into her eyes, and her head writhed from side to side in the narrow corridor as she tried to avoid it. The dragon even tried to bite the jet of water angering her.

Then out of the darkness a figure loomed, dressed all in white, running as fast as his legs would carry him. It was Bartholomew wearing a fireman's protective asbestos suit. He ran straight at the dragon, his sword held in both hands. "For the glory of the Bandamires!" His muffled cry could be heard from behind the helmet, and with that he disappeared down the dragon's throat.

As Frau Colbetz stumbled along the beach, her high heels sunk into the sand and her dress, already wet from the boat journey, became covered in sand as well. And the more irritated and angry she became, the more her human disguise slipped to reveal her true dragon self.

She arrived at the Sea Arch as a couple of marines were collecting the last olorc body. A new scent filled her nostrils. She turned, tracing the smell in the wind. *Bear!*

Frau Colbetz could no longer control herself. Starting at her toes, rage steadily grew in her, and as it took hold, her shoes disappeared and were replaced by long, scaly feet with white hooked talons at each toe. The dress changed into long silver-blue legs and a tail that uncoiled behind her. Her arms folded back and into wings, and another pair of smaller clawed arms sprouted from her chest. Great spines burst through her skin and shiny scales glinted in the sun. Her neck grew longer, like a swan's but thicker, with a ridge of spines along the back, leaving only the head of Frau Colbetz on top of this coiling and snaking dragon neck.

The German marines on the beach yelled in surprise and horror.

Bang! A bullet flew past the dragon, missing by inches. As Frau Colbetz's head stretched and formed into that of Komargoran Monarchmauler, she lunged across the sand and snapped her savage jaws down on the marine's head, removing it with one clean bite.

Down the beach the rest of the soldiers froze in astonishment and then, under orders from the lieutenant, began to fire.

Hidden in the dunes, James, Baranor, and Tempus watched as the battle unfolded.

The dragon was infuriated further by the wasplike stings that pricked her skin, and she turned on the new antagonists. In two beats of her enormous wings, she covered the distance and set upon them, her neck and tail flailing across the sand and tumbling soldiers like ninepins. She grabbed the officer in her foreclaws and tore at him. She pinned yet another soldier under her feet, pressing him deep into the sand until his struggling ceased. The remaining soldiers broke and ran, some to hide in the sand dunes, while others launched the boats into the surf and scrambled in.

On the ship's bridge Captain Raeder gaped at what he saw.

"Guns stand," he yelled down the voice pipe. "Engine room, prepare to make full steam." He snapped an order at his officers, who were still mesmerized by the events on the beach. "Clear for action!"

From their hiding place James saw the first gun fire from the ship. A puff of white smoke shot out of the barrel, and a fraction of a second later the *boom* of the gun rolled over the water and reached them. A geyser of mud and sand sprayed up only a few yards from where the dragon stood. Monarchmauler bellowed, and her attention switched to the new threat out in the bay. It was a terrifyingly magnificent sight to see the deadly creature wing her way effortlessly toward the long gray hull of the warship. The two adversaries closed. Guns roared from the deck, several striking the body of the beast. Tiny gaps showed where her wings were torn. Then she was on the ship.

The dragon crawled across the vessel, gouts of fire shooting from her mouth. Her tail pummeled the outer decks, tearing and twisting the railings and equipment. Her head smashed through doorways and roasted those trapped inside.

Captain Raeder stood with his men on the bridge. The armored shutters had gone up, and the watertight doors had been sealed. They were safe for now, but they could hear the terrible sounds and screams. Tearing metal and grinding steel mixed with the roar of the beast and the erratic blast of guns.

"It will tear this ship to pieces, Captain!" shouted a panicked junior officer.

They could hear the dragon getting closer.

"They won't be able to stop her," James said as they watched the gray warship being battered mercilessly. Tempus barked a warning, and they saw in the distance a long line of khaki figures climbing through the sand dunes.

"It's the British Army!" cried James, only to realize that the dragon would attack them next.

"We must warn them." But he knew that Baranor was in a very perilous position himself. "Tempus, go with Baranor back to the house and explain to my mother that she must hide him. We can't send you back through the gateway until we know for certain that the olorcs aren't waiting on the other side. I'll go to the army officers and warn them. We don't have much time."

Before anyone could disagree, James was off.

"Number One gun ready to fire, sir."

The foremost turret had swung around. If it fired a shell at such close range, everyone on the bridge would be permanently deafened by the explosion, but there were few options remaining. The *Ausburg* was fighting for her life.

James ran around the dune and slammed straight into a soldier.

"I must speak with your officer!"

The soldier picked himself up and brushed the sand off his uniform. "Now, now, this isn't a place for a young lad like you. We've got to clear this area."

"Listen to me, please!" James shouted. "I know what's going on, and it's very important that I tell your commanding officer. People will die; some already have." A blood-curdling scream cut the air. The roar of a large gun responded.

"Right, follow me." And the soldier doubled off with James running to keep up.

Tempus stood at the entrance to the house as the women hurried around the room cleaning up the broken wood that covered the floor. They had managed to get the housekeeper to bed. The marine lay where he had fallen.

"Excuse me, ladies," said the big dog, his tail wagging.

Both women studied the motionless body of the soldier.

"Did he say something?" Amanda whispered. They edged a bit closer to have a look.

"No, it was me," said Tempus.

Jennifer walked to the door and looked cautiously outside, distractedly patting Tempus on the head. "Is there anyone there?" she called in a low voice.

Behind her Amanda set down the kettle and picked up the poker.

"Yes, there is—me. We need your help."

Jennifer slowly raised her hand from the dog as she stared down at him in disbelief.

"You?"

"Yes. My name is Tempus. It was me you saw standing at the window a short while ago. And you also met Baranor. The one who doesn't use doors."

"The creature that attacked the soldiers?" asked Amanda.

"He's a bear, a very good one at that. And now we need somewhere to hide him. You see, we're friends of James. He sent me to ask for your help, since it seemed unlikely you'd accept this coming from a bear."

Baranor edged into the room and introduced himself to the stunned ladies. He offered to carry the unconscious soldier upstairs to one of the bedrooms. Then he went to Amanda's room, where he lay on the bed and dozed off. Tempus promised to return with help, leaving the women wondering what they were doing with a big black bear and a German soldier in the house.

"Father!" James called out as soon as he saw the familiar figure striding through the long grass toward the beach.

Sir Philip ran to meet him, throwing his arms around his son. "Where have you been? What's happening?" The sounds and smell of battle drifted over the dunes.

James looked at the entourage of men that accompanied his father and doubted they would believe him. But they *would* believe their own eyes and ears.

"Over the dunes, to the beach. Hurry!" James called. And he led them at a run back to where the British soldiers were just beginning to discover the horror of events.

Out to sea the *Ausburg* lay dead in the water, under siege. Black smoke rose from the triple stacks. On the beach the British soldiers were under strict orders not to fire on the enormous lizard that flashed blue and silver against the dull gray cruiser. They were busy rounding up the surviving German marines and tending to the wounded.

"Let's pray that thing doesn't lose interest in the ship before we're ready," Sir Philip said as he and James stood together among the dunes.

⤳ 18 ⤳

A FAREWELL TO ARMS

Bartholomew was in a vicious fight. Stumbling over the rows of fangs and teeth, he carried on, slashing in every direction with his sword. Siganatoris Bloodboiler had recoiled, attempting to spit the dwarf out. Her head snaked backward out of the tunnel, and her long neck convulsed in a frenzy of distortions as she tried to dislodge him.

The dwarf found himself tumbling down the dragon's gullet. His protective leather helmet flew off, and the white asbestos suit began to tear. He kept hacking around in the dark, both hands gripping the sword tightly as he thrust and lunged, ripping his way out of the stomach and into the vital organs.

The dragon screamed. It was as if a parasite was destroying her from within. She did not feel her legs and wings fail. Her tail still thrashed vehemently and her eyes, ears, and snout told her that the other dwarf at her side, attacking at her with an ax, was a mere distraction. But inside her, unreachable by talons or jaws, something was slowly carving her heart out.

She must act quickly, and with all her guile.

The ornamental lake glistened in the late sun, and the dragon saw that salvation lay there. She plunged in, holding her jaws open and letting water flood down her throat. She would drown the noxious creature inside her before she drowned herself.

Solomon waded in the water up to his waist, raining ax blows on the dragon that started high above his head and swung down trying to cleave the armor of the serpent. The dragon was oblivious to his efforts, and the wounds that he drew were shallow. But the dwarf knew that inside the enemy, his brother was depending on him. Solomon hacked on.

Bartholomew was squashed between two muscular ridges of flesh. His sword lay embedded in a sheath of tissue that rhythmically swelled and contracted. At his side the digestive stones rumbled together in the torn stomach. Blood and juices ran in his face and over his body. He had lost the protective headgear and kept his eyes firmly shut against the corrosive effects of the liquid. And then he was swimming, swimming and cartwheeling and twisting in a cascade of water.

He dragged at the hilt of his sword, which anchored him, but it would not budge. As he surged forward with a new torrent of water, his weight was thrown onto the blade and it sank into the dragon's tissue. Fixing his feet, the dwarf made one last effort. He gave a mighty shove on the sword hilt, pushing it deep into the flesh and striking at the dragon's soul.

And, at last, the great dragon known for eons as Siganatoris Bloodboiler, whose history stretched back to the very first moments of Creation, died. As the last spark of life left the creature, her tail lifted once more and then fell for the last time.

Solomon lay in the cold water with his back to the wall. White bone stuck through a tear in his trousers, and the whole of his leg was crusted in blood. His ax lay useless by his side.

The dragon's body lay by the lake, half submerged, her great wings splayed out on either side, drying and hardening in the late afternoon sun. Blood seeped from her mouth, turning the water in the shallows a sickly bile green.

Komargoran Monarchmauler had completely destroyed the *Ausburg*'s exterior, with deep rents in the chimney stacks and twisted metal everywhere until it no longer resembled a warship. The gun turrets and decks ran with blood.

The dragon stood and peered through the observation slit into the bridge. Her enormous eye blazed red and yellow, the pupil shifting from side to side as she held the humans in a trancelike state. She studied each of them, hunting for the man with the weakest spirit. She was looking for a soulslave—like Dorpmuller and the others before—who would open the door into the bridge so she could finish them off. Her eye settled on a terrified young officer. The other men on the bridge remained locked in her spell, unable to move.

Only rarely can the strongest will resist the power of a dragon. As Monarchmauler was about to make a new conquest, an old one found the will to resist. Captain Raeder pulled a pistol from under the navigation table. He shot a whole magazine of bullets into the dragon's eye.

She reared back, clawing desperately at her face to stop the pain. Captain Raeder had saved his ship, for now.

❖ ❖ ❖

Farther out to sea three destroyers accompanied the armored British cruiser *Cressy*. In the distance they could make out the silhouette of the wrecked German warship as it lay in the shelter of Beadnell Bay. The ships closed with the coastline, crews at action stations and guns trained on the *Ausburg*.

Standing astride the vessel, the dragon looked up with her one good eye to see more of the enemy sailing toward her. Screeching, she rose into the air to retreat.

"Look out!" Everyone focused on the great beast as it hurtled back over the water.

"Are we ready, Colonel?" Sir Philip asked. The beach was a swarm of activity. Soldiers took cover behind every dune while inland, six artillery pieces were being loaded.

"In just a few moments, sir." The colonel's voice was a good deal less sure.

"James, I don't suppose there's anywhere safer I can pack you off to. Your mother would be horrified to know what danger I've placed you in."

"Actually, I'm the one who has put us all in danger. That dragon is my problem. I don't think the army will stop it. Not with what they have here." Before his father could ask him more, a man screamed. . . .

"Get down!" They threw themselves on the ground as an enormous shadow passed over. James felt the downstroke of a wing beat. The dragon wheeled overhead, a khaki figure grasped in each hind foot.

Then she struck down, ripping a gun from its mounting and sending it flipping end over end before the barrel buried itself in the soft sand. Another artillery piece went careening into the next one in the line, and horses bolted as sporadic rifle fire gave way to sustained volleys that only served to goad the dragon.

"This is hopeless," Sir Philip called to the colonel who lay sprawled nearby. "We'll have a massacre on our hands before that creature is done."

James looked up the beach to where the Sea Arch stood unobserved and remembered what Sibelius had said about portals and magic.

"Maybe, just maybe . . ." He picked himself up off the ground and began to run.

"Aagh!" Bartholomew had placed his hand in more slime as he crawled over the ridges of the slippery esophagus. Extricating himself from the insides of the dragon wasn't easy. First he had to hack his way out of the body and into its throat. Once he reached the mouth cavity, he used his sword to lever the jaws enough to crawl over the teeth and escape, tearing his clothes until they hung in tatters. That was when he found Solomon.

"Brother" was all he could say as tears streamed down his face. He knelt next to Solomon, gently lifted his head and shoulders, and held him in his arms. Solomon lay limp, his body broken by the final fall of the dragon's tail. His eyes had a faraway look as if they were glimpsing a place no one else could see.

"Did you succeed? Did you kill your dragon?" Solomon asked, a catch in his breath.

"Yes, *we* did it . . . we got our dragon."

"And now we'll live on forever in legend, the . . ."

"Brothers Bandamire." Bartholomew choked back the sadness.

"Slayers of Siganatoris Bloodboiler and Deceivers of Dragons. That's us. We'll be famous, you and I."

And then Solomon was gone.

James ran as fast as his legs would carry him, over the last sand dune and down to the shore. He didn't hear the shouts and gunfire behind—only the sound of the sea and the beating of wings. He didn't look back, but he knew the dragon was closing in, swooping low to pluck him from the ground. He was almost at the Sea Arch.

Monarchmauler extended her hind claws, reaching down to grind the boy into mince. She stretched out her wings flat and wide, gliding in for the kill. Then she dropped out of the sky, one hundred feet, seventy-five feet. . . .

"Fire!" shouted the artillery officer, and the last working gun flung a shell straight at the dragon.

The solid shot tore a talon from her right hind foot and threw her sideways in the process. The dragon pulled in her legs and wheeled out of the way, overshooting the boy.

James felt the blast of the cannon shell overhead and was knocked down as something thumped into his back. He rolled over and saw the wicked talon claw sticking out of the sand. James grabbed it and got to his feet. Out of the corner of his eye, he saw the enraged dragon preparing to strike again. He was only steps away from the Sea Arch.

A gout of flame licked the sand, turning it to glass. James ducked behind the gateway. Just as the dragon spun around the top and shot toward him, James managed to push open the gate and scramble through.

"James is heading for the arch!" Sir Philip yelled to the others, but they didn't understand, and then the boy simply vanished into thin air.

"He has a plan," Harrington said.

Komargoran Monarchmauler saw James slip through the arch. The bloodlust surged, crashing through her brain and blinding her sight and reason. She arrowed straight at the ornamental gates, intending to knock them from their hinges and crush the boy for good.

"Spawn of the soulless! How dare you try to escape me, Queen of all Dragons!" she screamed, and flew through the gates after him.

James fell onto the long grass and looked back between the open gates. The great blue and silver beast hung there, trapped in the portal's magic, writhing like a worm caught on a hook. Her jaws snapped open and shut, her tail thrashed, and her wings beat furiously, but the only thing to pass through the Sea Arch was a terrifying noise that detonated like a hundred guns.

James watched as the portal's power overwhelmed the creature, draining her of her magic. And so too her soul drained away, until at last Komargoran Monarchmauler was gone.

On the beach there was as much pandemonium when the dragon disappeared as when they first laid eyes on the creature.

"What the devil happened?" Sir Philip asked. "Did they both go through the Sea Arch?"

Harrington shook his head. "I believe no magical creature may pass through a portal. But there's only one way to be sure."

"Corrick, you've been through before. You could go after him!"

Corrick shook his head also. "I'm sorry, Sir Philip. I am like the rest of the men here. I cannot see this gateway."

"Then *this* is why I can see the Sea Arch. I must go after James!" Sir Philip started down the sand.

James knew where he was, and with the gates shut on this side, he knew where he had to go. He had a while before the sun set.

A howl from up the valley was his only warning. His hand went to the hilt of his dagger. James briefly caught a glimpse of a big gray werewolf slinking into the glade. He turned and ran.

Philip was no more than fifty paces away from the Sea Arch when a great loping body raced out from the dunes. He didn't know what it was, but it was coming straight for him. He spotted a rifle discarded by one of the German marines and veered off to grab it. Lifting the stock to his shoulder, he tried to get a fix on the moving animal. Too late! The large silver-gray hound bounded up and brushed Sir Philip to one side, sending him to his knees.

"Stop! I'm a friend of James." The voice seemed to come from the dog. "He has gone back. We must help him!" The dog raced ahead through the open gates.

"Now what the hell has happened to Sir Philip?" The colonel stared at the spot where the man, the boy, and even the dog had vanished. The senior officers milled about, equally perplexed, while the junior officers attended to the wounded men. Harrington and Corrick watched silently.

Sir Philip stood in the glade.

"James was here, but he moved off down the valley. He's not the only one." The dog sniffed the air. "Werewolves. Maybe one, maybe a pack of them, I can't tell."

Tempus stood quivering from nose to tail. Sir Philip didn't know whether it was excitement or fear, but he knew why *he* was shaking, and it wasn't only the shock of having passed through the portal.

They set off down the path after James and whatever else might await them.

Sibelius gazed down at the pool of water in the center of the vallmaria. He had watched the water ripple once and then twice more. He had also seen a flash of brilliant light; it had registered something remarkable. He interpreted the three ripples as three individuals passing through the Sea Arch. The flash he could not explain. His skill at reading the vallmaria was limited. He would redouble his efforts to relearn the lost magic of the elders, but for now time pressed in on the old wizard. There was so much to do, so much to lose. . . . Or gain.

Sibelius noticed Lady Orlania standing at the top step leading to his observatory. "I was not aware of your passing through the dream generator."

"No, my good wizard," she said with a gentle smile, "I intended you not to know."

"I was thinking aloud. Forgive me," Sibelius said. He watched as the Elven princess strolled around his room, her fingers brushing objects. "I see that you still practice the art of resonant memory, my lady." Her hand withdrew behind her cloak. She was adept at the ancient power, learning of events simply by touching artifacts present at their occurrence. Lady Orlania could read the room as if it were a book, and the wizard was always cautious when she visited. He preferred to meet with other sorcerers and magi beyond the confines of his observatory and its secrets.

"One would think you were spying," the wizard said.

"I was. Your position as Master of the Shadows places greater knowledge and power in your hands than anyone else's in the world, yet you keep everything secret. These events affect us all, and we have a right to know." Her voice carried a hint of accusation. "James, for instance: what has become of him? You plot for the good of Eldaterra, I have no doubt. But still you plot in secret, a trait I do not fully appreciate in anyone, let alone a wizard."

"My knowledge of events is ever incomplete, and my labors often come to nothing." He walked toward his desk and picked up a small silver object that looked like three crowns, each sitting inside the other and all finely etched with delicate lettering. "I fashion pretty devices that are merely replicas of the tools used by the ancient sorcerers. I seek to unlock their secrets. Should I inform everyone of what I do, when I know not myself?" He replaced the object on his desk. "I know that James has passed again into Eldaterra. I do not know if he succeeded, or what his fate holds. If he survives long enough to reach the Western Tower, I will learn more. If he fails in any way, I will be required to renew my efforts, *plotting* to discover the enemy's intent."

"And will you not save James? He lies within Lauderley Forest, within your protection."

The wizard's eyes bore into the elf's. "With every use of my power, the enemy learns of our limitations. Of our weaknesses and our divisions. I cannot risk everything for one life."

Her eyes flared, but Sibelius caught a glimpse of pain and sadness.

"We all must walk the harder path," he said softly.

"I understand," she said, and departed.

James heard the crunch of twigs beneath the heavy paws. He lay in a cleft of roots that offered protection on three sides. Above him the pine tree swayed quietly. The branches were too high for him to climb, and he couldn't outrun the werewolf. He decided to face his attacker rather than be jumped from behind. He sat and waited, peering over the root and back up the path. It was only another few seconds before the werewolf broke cover.

The long, pointed head and rigid ears made it look like a giant wingless bat. A shaggy mane of gray fur sprouted unevenly along the spine. The legs and body were sinewy, and the limbs moved as if it required minimum effort. Its gait was relaxed, yet deceptively fast. The teeth and claws reminded James of the dragons.

The animal stopped a short way off, sniffing at the ground, as if it knew something was wrong. James had sprinted down the path before doubling back to where he lay hidden. Now it looked as if the creature's cunning had found him out. He tried to stop shaking as the werewolf scratched and mulled a while longer.

What was it waiting for?

Tempus leaped from behind a pine tree and gave a warning bark that caught the werewolf unawares. It moved toward Tempus and sized up the hound. The bearhound was indeed no match for a fully grown werewolf, and this one was enormous. But Tempus held his ground, challenging it to attack. The werewolf's hackles rose and its jaws fell open, spittle spilling from its mouth.

James jumped up to draw the werewolf's attention. The werewolf hesitated, confused that the hunted had turned on the hunter. Tempus barked again, and this time the wolf made its choice. It leaped at Tempus.

Crack! A bullet caught the animal in the chest and flung it to the ground. Sir Philip stepped out from behind a tree, the gun still at the ready. James and Tempus moved cautiously to the inert body—the creature was dead.

Captain Raeder left the smoldering hulk in the charge of Lieutenant Reitsch, clambered into a canvas dinghy, the only seaworthy boat to have survived the onslaught, and was rowed to the beach.

He gave a stiff salute to the senior British officer before him. "Captain Raeder of the Imperial Navy." The colonel eyed the German suspiciously.

"Colonel Smythe-Whitely of His Majesty King George V's Army, Royal Northumberland Fusiliers. It seems we've had quite a show today, one way or another." He slapped his walking cane against the top of his boot to accentuate the fact.

"These unfortunate events necessitated my bringing my ship within your territorial waters. We've been sorely damaged." It was clear the captain was searching for an explanation without having to describe it as a dragon attack.

"Captain Raeder." Harrington stepped forward and introduced himself. "I understand how you may have been obliged to seek the protection of this coast. Observing your ship one might imagine that it suffered from rather a bad crossing of the North Sea?"

The captain took the cue. "That is correct, Mr. Harrington. My ship was caught in a most savage storm. It resulted in the loss of a good many lives."

"And you put men ashore while repairs were carried out?"

"Exactly."

"Well then," Harrington said to the colonel. "The Foreign Office will be satisfied with this description of events if the War Office feels the same."

The colonel cautiously looked at both men and added, "Sadly this evacuation took place on a stretch of beach used for live ammunition practice. That can account for the dead and wounded on both sides . . . with a little bit of work."

~ 19 ~

The Truth About Everything

Tempus thrust his nose into the faint forest breeze. "This one was the lead beast. The pack follows, not far behind."

James and his father followed the hound down the path as quickly as they could, but they knew the pack would still be gaining.

"If we can make it to the hunting lodge, we can hide there for a while," James said. A terrible howling rent the forest. The werepack had discovered their fallen member.

"They'll be coming even faster now," Tempus said.

The three raced on and, in the distance, the lodge came into view, its windows, thankfully, shuttered. Behind them the pack burst onto the trail. There were perhaps twenty werewolves, all with long jaws and cruel eyes.

"Don't stop!" yelled Tempus, and fell behind to delay their attackers. James and his father pelted the last few yards through the broken door, throwing themselves into the gloom beyond.

Tempus growled a deep, dangerous warning. The pack slowed to a halt just yards away. They studied him with contempt. Clashing their teeth they paced slowly forward, moving in for the kill.

Crack. A large and fearsome werewolf sank howling to the ground, its rear legs useless. The other creatures faltered. Tempus fled, gaining a good lead. *Crack.* A second werewolf fell dead as Tempus reached the lodge door.

Much of the clearing up had been done by the time Amanda marched over the rough pasture to the beach.

"Excuse me, I am looking for my uncle, Sir Philip Kinghorn."

Harrington responded, "I'm sorry, he is . . . unavailable. My name is Harrington. I traveled with your uncle from London. Is there any way I can help?"

Amanda studied Harrington and decided she had no choice but to trust him.

"My aunt and I are staying in the farmhouse you can see in the distance. We have wounded guests." She glanced at the stretchers awaiting evacuation and quickly looked away. "If you would please accompany me back, we need your help."

Harrington immediately set off with her across the fields.

When they reached the farmhouse, he noted the fallen soldier outside. "I'm afraid he's too far gone" was all he said.

Once inside her eyes locked onto his. "Mr. Harrington, what exactly do you know of these events?"

"I know as much as your uncle, perhaps a good deal more. He is with James."

"We have a wounded German soldier upstairs. But there is one other guest. I'm not quite sure how to put this. . . ."

"Maybe I should take a look?"

Amanda pushed open the door. Baranor was sitting on the bed with his head in a bucket. Lady Jennifer sat next to him. She turned and smiled. "I made him some soup. He was hungry." The bear ignored them all and polished off his meal.

Dorpmuller continued to search desperately through the empty corridors and caverns but found nothing. The entire workings had been deserted. By chance he came across a doorway not indicated on the map and this led him upward, closer to the surface. In these levels he was appalled to see the vilest creatures one could imagine: great hulking monsters with thick arms and shoulders and heads like mastiff dogs with cropped ears. One of the creatures must have guessed the purpose of his visit and escorted him into a back chamber. There Dorpmuller was shocked to see a figure that resembled a human—an old, dark, oily-skinned human in decrepit armor with disfigured features and a grotesque body—but a human nonetheless. He was also surprised to see the cruel-looking olorcs treat the general with comparative gentleness, compassion even, setting a pitcher of black wine close to hand and trimming the torches that guttered in the wall brackets.

"I am most pleased to make your acquaintance . . . General

Balerust?" Dorpmuller said tentatively.

The general stared up at him with rheumy eyes. "I believe you must be Herr Dorpmuller? Freislung has told me all about you." He coughed, his breath wheezing in his chest.

"And he's told me of you, General, though I was led to believe—"

"Yes, you *were* led to believe. Did you think that a man whose services you bought could not be corrupted a second time? Freislung was as happy to collect payment from me as he was from you."

Dorpmuller's mind sped like a locomotive with no rails to grip. "You mean . . . there is no army assembling for the invasion of the New World?"

The general gave a little nod of his head.

The enormity of the situation came like a crash, and Dorpmuller collapsed into a chair. "After all these years . . . all Frau Colbetz's plans—"

"All those plans were merely wishful dreams. All I did was feed your servant the story you wanted to hear. Until the end, when he became unnecessary."

The general sat patiently while Dorpmuller absorbed the news. Outside the closed door, faint noises of activity could be heard.

"Some creatures have passed through the arch but that was a timely diversion that was not of my making. The Warkrin were hunting the traitor Freislung and someone who arrived through the Sea Arch. They dispatched the olorcs. I made sure they were told about the invasion. I fed them the same line I gave you, but there is *no* alliance, *no* invasion army." The general's voice trembled. "No one to lead them."

Dorpmuller's self-control snapped. "Traitor! You . . . you are not General Balerust!"

"Oh, I suppose after fifteen years I am. Certainly the olorcs believe I am." A look of satisfaction appeared on his weary face. "I have eaten the black substance they call shol and it has transformed me, as you can see, so that I've even come to resemble them."

Dorpmuller felt utter rage clamp over his heart and crush his chest. This pathetic fool had ruined the plans they had so carefully devised, a plan that would have changed his life, and the face of the world. He could have had everything, power, wealth, even an empire, but for this decrepit, meddlesome . . . Dorpmuller flew out of the chair. He seized the pistol at his side and pointed it at the imposter, who responded, "Tell your mistress she will never breed. And she will never rule. We destroyed the dragon birthpit long ago."

The old man nodded at the gun. "It will be a welcome release from fifteen years of servitude. Pull the trigger."

And Dorpmuller did just that.

James and his father barricaded the doorway with the upended table and backed it up with a large chest of drawers. Night had fallen, and the werewolves were growing bolder.

"They will break it down," Tempus said. "They are driven by the dark powers of the Warkrin. They must obey, or die trying. Don't let them get near you. A single bite can poison your blood and kill you."

Sir Philip checked the rifle. The magazine had only two bullets remaining. After that he'd have to wield it like a club. James still had his dagger. Together they set about building a fire in the hearth with the available wood.

When the yellow moon rose, the howling started up in earnest. They sat in front of the fire and waited.

All at once half a dozen bodies thudded against the barricade. Sir Philip raised the rifle but James called out, "No, not yet!" He leaped forward, dagger in his hand, and slashed at the first head pushing into the room. The creature gave a yelp, and the head disappeared. Blood ran along the blade. A second replaced it, the werewolf attempting to shoulder its way in. Sir Philip brought the stock of the gun down. The body sank, only for another werewolf to leap on it and scramble into the gap that was slowly widening.

"Keep the table steady, " James yelled, slashing again. Sir Philip thrust his full weight behind it. At the same time he brought the rifle level, stuck it in the throat of the werewolf snapping at James's blade, and pulled the trigger. The creature was blown out of the gap. James threw his weight behind his father's and the table eased back, closing up the hole. Outside the werewolves howled with rage and tore at the bodies of their fallen.

Sir Philip dragged more furniture from the far end of the lodge to reinforce the doorway. All the windows were still shuttered. James poked around in the kitchen and found a few meager morsels to take the edge off their hunger. They kept the fire stoked and eventually dozed off, leaving Tempus to guard them while they slept.

Baranor sniffed their new visitor.

"Elf," the bear said matter-of-factly. Jennifer and Amanda stared at both of them, not knowing which idea was stranger, the talking bear or the elf. Harrington smiled politely but said nothing.

Baranor waited in the locked bedroom while the British soldiers came and collected the wounded German and his dead comrade. Outside Harrington sent a request with them that a truck come back for the women's belongings. This ruse was necessary to transport Baranor. Since the dwarves had not caught up, it looked like they'd fallen into some sort of trouble. Baranor wanted to return to Cragside to see what could be done.

When the truck arrived, the driver was ordered to back up to the doorway, and while Amanda distracted the young man— an easy enough task—Baranor slipped out of the house and climbed aboard into the canvassed rear, the truck's suspension sagging under his weight. Harrington and Amanda got in the cab. She had offered to stay but her aunt urged her to go, saying Amanda might be able to help the dwarves if they were injured. Lady Jennifer would wait alone for the return of her husband and son.

They rolled onto the estate's gravel drive, and Harrington ordered the driver to wait there for them. He and Amanda opened the back and followed the bear as he slipped through the wrecked gardens.

Baranor could smell dragons down by the lake. The survivors

had fled, taking the magic-soaked carcasses of their brethren to dine on and thereby renew some of their own powers. When they reached the lake, Baranor padded over to where the two small bodies lay. He snuffled in the ear of Bartholomew, and the dwarf opened his bloodshot eyes.

Baranor helped Bartholomew lift his brother gently into the back of the truck. Harrington collected the fallen weapons and followed. Over on the far side of the park, Amanda shared a cigarette with the driver, his attention still diverted. Then they drove back to the coast, the headlights playing on the road ahead.

When they arrived at the house, the driver was sent to assist on the beach, Solomon's body was laid down in a bedroom, and the rest of the party stayed downstairs. Lady Jennifer had sent the housekeeper back to London. She was nervous enough herself, and the arrival of a dead warrior dwarf did not help.

Tempus's surprised yelp woke Sir Philip and James. The room was full of flying sparks and burning wood. In the hearth a werewolf fought to disentangle itself from the grate, the fire singeing its flesh and filling the air with a sickening odor. It leaped like a rabid animal, jaws snapping at the pain. James reached for his dagger, Sir Philip for the gun, but they were both too slow. The werewolf had already launched itself at James.

In the next instant Tempus sank his teeth into the neck of the werewolf, dragging it down. But the bearhound was no match for its enemy. The werewolf craned its neck to sink its own jaws into the dog. James lunged with the dagger, sending the needle-sharp point deep into the enemy's chest. With a final snap, the dying werewolf wrapped his teeth around James's arm.

As the beast collapsed, James felt the air grow warm and damp, and sank to the floor beside his attacker.

Dorpmuller fled back through the abandoned caverns below. It was many days before he found his way back to the gate. But he was greatly relieved to see the portcullis stood open, and he passed out of the Old World. Had he noticed the brass plaque, he would have seen this inscription:

Assassin cried the righteous dead
Who locked in fate here must lie
Leave this world by cautious tread
For in it none the fates defy
Walk the darkness of your world
Free to choose the cruelest road
And the banners yet unfurled
Lead to evil you have sowed

An endless time yet still to pass
When men shall harvest men
With the turning of the glass
Stirs the evil from its den
An angel of the wrongful kind
To stalk the worlds and deep

First a science they must find
And breach the walling of the keep

Your fate awaits you in the dark
And the magic fails before you
But as the hounds of war do bark
Recall who you come to bow to
For your second revolts anew
Marked it well as a subtle lie
For your third you finally threw
The crooked cross and live to die

There was a hammering on the barricade. James rolled his feverish head to the side and could just make out his father and Tempus defending the doorway before he drifted into delirium.

After hearing the officer's voice, Sir Philip pulled the barricade aside. The lodge was surrounded by horsemen, but their uniforms were none he knew. The officer explained that Sir Philip and the boy should ride with them immediately. His father lifted James from the blankets, and with Tempus by their side, they left the place.

When James next awoke it was dawn. For twenty-four hours he had been between life and death. Only the skills of Sibelius and Lady Orlania had saved him. He lay in the same bed he had woken up in almost three weeks ago, when he'd first arrived at the Western Tower. Lady Orlania stood next to him. "So our young warrior has returned," she said, and placed a hand on James's uninjured arm.

"Are my father and Tempus all right?"

She nodded as the door opened and Sir Philip walked in with Sibelius.

"Your four-legged friend returned through the Sea Arch to bring the others home. A detachment of cavalry stands awaiting their return," said Sibelius.

James's father sat on the bed and took his hand.

"Sibelius has told me what he knows of your undertaking, and with what I learned from Tempus, it is . . . Your mother and I could never have imagined . . . I am so proud. . . ." He could not go on. James felt his own eyes burn as his father lowered his head.

"I think, Lady Orlania, that we are expected elsewhere," said the wizard.

The return of the Bandamire brothers and Tempus was greeted with a mixture of excitement and remorse. Solomon was laid in the temple of rest, where Lady Orlania and her maids saw to his final ritual. Bartholomew and Tempus came to visit James, and together they mourned their brother and friend. James made a good recovery and was out of bed on the third day.

"We will stay for the funeral," Sir Philip said. "I asked Tempus to tell your mother that we'd remain here until you were all right."

"But will things ever be all right?" James asked.

His father sighed. "What I've learned from Sibelius is discouraging. The Old World is losing its magic. Then all this will be lost."

"Did Sibelius tell you about Grandfather?"

"Yes, what he knew." His voice faltered. "James, your grandfather came into this world and disappeared a second time. Sibelius has only now learned of his fate. He was killed recently . . . it is believed, by someone from our world."

"Dorpmuller!" James said. "He left on the warship bound for somewhere. Probably to meet the invasion army Frau Colbetz was expecting." James paused, thinking about his grandfather, whom he had never met and never would.

"Sibelius said your grandfather's fate was to remain in this world. He survived as a Shadow—a sort of spy—working indirectly for Sibelius. He took over the identity of an enemy general, and for years convinced the plotters he was overseeing the plans and preparations for an enormous invasion army to conquer our world. His fate was to protect both worlds. That is more than anyone could ever hope to achieve. He was a truly great man, and you possess the same traits."

"But what is my fate? Have I finished the task set for me?"

"I think maybe that's something only the portals can answer," his father said, looking at James with an uncertainty James had never seen before.

The little dinghy was inching up the Essex coast in the gentle morning breeze. Rawlings tacked the boat and ran it up the beach. Although his work was finished, something tugged at his subconscious. Instinctively he had come back to this stretch of coast that Gilchrist had mentioned to find something that linked the whole plot together, the *Parsimony*, Sir Philip, and Sir Neville. Something worth killing for. All he could see was flat beach and low-lying grass. He walked awhile, enjoying the sun on his face. Then he headed back to the boat. There was nothing here.

"Halt," a voice ordered. "Turn around, slowly."

Rawlings turned and faced a bedraggled gentleman pointing a gun at his chest.

"I need to get off this island. I will pay you." The man had more than a hint of desperation. His voice sounded foreign . . . German.

"I can take you to Shoeburyness. But the charge is five pounds."

"No, you misunderstand me. I need to get off this island of Great Britain."

"Then the price will be considerably more." Rawlings smiled.

Solomon Brunel Bandamire received his hero's send-off—the whole population of the Western Tower watched as the pyre burned into the night. A comet streaked across the midnight sky, and some called it an omen.

After the funeral James met with Sibelius. Among the many things they talked about, the wizard spoke of the Drezghul.

"I know little of this thing you faced, and it is of grave concern that such dark magic lies within the reach of the enemy. I fear that no amount of study will reveal all the secrets of the

Warkrin. Some of their darkest arts—like those we just encountered—we my know only when we face them."

"And what about my vision, Sibelius? The three princes and the boy in the shadows, the one I saw when I looked at the Drezghul?"

Sibelius frowned. "Twice you have seen a future, once in the eyes of the enemy and the other in the dream generator. I believe that was you standing by the king, not your father. The dream was your future. But the dream generator isn't an oracle. That knowledge came from you. With the Drezghul, was that also the future? I do not understand the meaning of the three princes, nor their horrible deaths. That is for time to reveal." He fell silent.

James handed over the velvet bag. "They are magical devices. They should stay in this world."

Sibelius placed the Antargo stone on the workbench and opened *Talmaride's Answers to Questions*. There he found the last question James had asked the book:

"What use is a dragon talon?"

A dragon talon is one of the rarest of all magical artifacts used by wizards and sorcerers. It possesses a range of magical properties that reside exclusively within the domains of dragon magic. Only on one previous occasion has a dragon talon been taken, and the talon was subsequently lost to the dark powers.

The exile of the dragons in 10,996 B.C. (local time) led to an Old World shortage of dragon talons that has never been corrected.

At the bottom of the bag lay the talon of Komargoran Monarchmauler.

But with every gain there is a loss. When Sibelius learned of the rifle that Sir Philip had inadvertently left at the upper lodge, he dispatched troops to retrieve it. It was gone.

∽ EPILOGUE ∾

OLD WORLD, NEW WORLD

Colonel Smythe-Whitely ordered the last of the wounded and fallen to be returned to the *Ausburg*. When every man had been accounted for, Captain Raeder ran the German Imperial Eagle flag up a makeshift masthead and the *Ausburg* steamed slowly back to Kiel under escort of *Cressy* and her attendant destroyers.

The *Ausburg* eased into harbor in the dying moments of the day, under strict security. Once the casualties and dead had been disembarked, the survivors were taken for debriefing. Captain Raeder was escorted directly to the Kaiserliche Marine Headquarters in Berlin, accompanied by the body taken from the beach that day. Some months later the *Ausburg* was quietly struck from the navy's list, and after a complete overhaul, the vessel was reborn as the *Bremen*.

Harrington made one final request of the army. Returning to Cragside with a squad of soldiers, he supervised the loading of a dragon carcass onto the truck, had it covered in tarpaulin, and dispatched to the local railway. Some weeks later the carcass arrived at its destination, the Natural History Museum in London, was accepted into storage, and promptly lost.

James and his father said their farewells to Sibelius and Lady Orlania, and then Bartholomew and Tempus escorted them to the Sea Arch. Baranor had already hugged his friends good-bye and disappeared back into the forest.

It was a strange good-bye, with the dwarf and hound standing together, drawn closer in their sadness, yet forever incomplete without Solomon.

"The wizard tells me we'll meet again." Bartholomew's hand gripped James's.

"Then I know we will. Good-bye, Bartholomew Shakespeare Bandamire! Good-bye, Tempus!"

James and his father passed between the stone pillars and wrought-iron gates, climbed the nearest dune, and watched as the Sea Arch began to fade. They stayed until it was gone.

At the farmhouse Lady Jennifer and Amanda were waiting for them. The four of them sat outside in the afternoon sun as James told his story from start to finish, with his father, mother, and Amanda interrupting to add their own parts.

They remained another day to pack up and then set off for home. On the way to London, Amanda told her aunt that she would not have missed these past weeks for anything.

"Now that James is back safely, I have to say I feel the same." Jennifer opened her purse. "That lovely bear gave me this. He lost it in the fight." She pulled out her gift. It was a magnificent two-inch carnasic tooth.

❖   ❖   ❖

James spent a week in London before returning to Drinkett College. There he discovered that his absence had been explained as a bout of whooping cough that had kept him confined in a boring sanatorium. He never told anyone of his adventure.

Sir Philip returned to the War Office. Three months later the secretary of state for war, Thomas Audrey, was voted out of office. He did not receive the customary knighthood.

Soon after Philip retired.

Chief Inspector Corrick enjoyed a quiet retirement with his family and on rare occasions took to walking the Essex coastline, keeping a professional eye on things.

News of the dragon talon traveled fast. The Guild requested that Sibelius deliver it into the hands of the central committee. He declined, saying that it was a personal gift from a friend. Others, too, coveted the talon. Its future lies in the balance. . . .

The Sea Arch is now invisible to all. The time and place of the next portal cannot be predicted.

The Natural History Museums in London and Oxford have never put any dragon specimens on display. All inquiries by interested parties have so far been ignored.

Cragside had to be largely rebuilt as a result of a fire. It exists today as a public museum. Some visitors have noticed strange markings on the fireplace, where the brickwork looks like something has clawed it. . . .